Unveiled

Book 2 Of

THE UNBREAKABLE SERIES

Zelly Jordan

Cover Design by Z.Jordan

Contents

What people are saying

Zelly Jordan is a master at story telling...the words literally jump out at you, so detailed as they take you into Kellan's world, it's as if you are right there with he and Charlotte, experiencing their chemistry or sharing his adrenalin as his beast prepares for battle.   - *Tony D.L. Bahamas*

The sequel to Fractured, a treat for lovers of destiny, sees the return of Kellan & Charlotte in Zelly Jordan's 2nd exciting romp through the streets of New York, as Kellan's memories are Unveiled. - *Julie C., Adelaide Australia*

This story promises to grab you at the beginning and refuses to let go until you feel the raw emotions felt by these two characters as they sort out their past and see if they have a future. - *Mary Lake, Florida, USA*

Zelly Jordan describes her characters so well visually that you are transported into the story, as if watching a movie. - *Claudia R., Bochum, Germany*

Zelly Jordan does it again. From the very first line of the first paragraph you won't want to put it down! - *K. Pace, California, USA*

Zelly Jordan's writing style is unique. She has this special gift of drawing you deep into the story, making you slip into the skin of her characters and won't let you go. Excitement, action and passion are guaranteed! - *Isolde N., Germany*

Zelly Jordan has created another wonderful story to take your breath away! It is so engrossing and hard to tear yourself away from as you want so much to know what will happen next! This is the second story in the Unbreakable series and it will grab you and keep you wanting more! Steamy, sexy and more! - *Ruthjc, San Diego, USA*

Zelly is a completely authentic writer. I love her detail to each aspect of her storylines and how she draws the reader in to want more. Zelly keeps the story current, interesting, heated and real. Zelly's astute writing leaves the reader feeling they are there and part of the story. I anxiously await the continued saga of Charlotte and Kellan! *Pamela Coordsen, N.C. USA*

Acknowledgements

They say it takes a village to raise a child. This book, just like its predecessor, Fractured, is definitely my "baby" and I was blessed to have a village to help me raise it.

It was never my intention to have this much time pass in between my first and second book but something happened after the release of Fractured........

Besides the all-new field of having to market and advertise my book and learning just exactly how to do that; besides quickly finding out how time-consuming and how creatively draining all of that was - I had a kind of..... crisis. And it went on for months.

You see, all of a sudden, I felt the incredibly heavy weight of expectation. (Cue the dramatic music). With my first book, no one really knew what kind of writer or story teller I was. Not even me in some ways. Many people didn't know I'd been writing at all and so I'd surprised a lot of folks. But with this second book, now people knew. Now they had expectations (or so I believed) and honestly, it messed with my mind.

A lot.

Thankfully, I'm blessed with some pretty awesome friends and loved ones who never let me give in; who encouraged me as I fought myself and the Dragon of Self-Doubt.

First and foremost, my darling son Rick whose name I proudly carry - you gave me the greatest honour when you chose me to be your Mum.

There is no higher calling and I treasure it forever. Thank you for your unwavering support and belief. Always remember to reach for your dreams and never settle for less. Love you endlessly.

To Jules and CC, thank you for holding my hand and calming my crazy.

To Kelly and Tony, thank you both for putting up with my fusspot ways and helping me with my awesome book cover. You both deserve the Medal of Valour in Trying Times - that's a thing, I'm sure of it.

To Issy and Kaz, thank you so much for your amazing tech and marketing help - you guys rock!

To my family and friends, thank you for your continued support and love and for tolerating my long absences.

There are so many more people in my "village" - a village that stretches around the world and the gratitude I feel for each of you is beyond expression. I can't mention every single name but every single one of you brightens my life.

Much love, as always,

Website. www.zellyjordan.com

Facebook: www.facebook.com/zelly309

Twitter: www.twitter.com/@zelly309

Goodreads: https://www.goodreads.com/ZellyJordan

Amazon: amazon.com/author/zellyjordan

Email: zellyjordan@gmail.com

Prologue

He lived just beneath my skin, embedded in the thickly corded muscle and sinew, in the raw bone that bent and flexed unnaturally.

He peered through my hazel eyes, breathed through my lungs; a part of me, yet seperate. His heartbeat was mine, thoughts and instincts his alone.

He was me - the beast within.

Human yet not, warped and mangled DNA flowed through my veins and tendons - a volatile mix of man, bear, wolf and jungle cat. And countless other animal species. I was not completely one but some of all, each animal contributing distinct abilities: the stealth and speed of a cheetah, the strength of a brown bear and eyesight of an eagle. I had the kill instinct of a wild dingo and tiger and the wolf's superior hunting skill. To name just a few.

Tethered within me by sheer will and fortitude, he lurked ever watchful, always ready to defend or attack, his basic instincts triggered by intense adrenalin.

The physical pain of transformation was burnt off with the speed and force of the mutation itself - lightening quick from man to beast and back. Sleek, lean muscle thickened and bulged, bones snapping and reshaping as my body became more animal than human, brute strength rippling through my chest and arms. My fingers curled into claws, blackened and sharp; teeth became putrid fangs and the hazel of my eyes disappeared as they glowed an unnatural wolf-gold.

Conscious humanity receded, overtaken by the base nature of the beast until I was the one peering out.

I liked to think I held the control when in my distorted state. But the truth was, it was a very tenuous grip at best.

Trained in the Armed Forces, skilled in combat and in martial arts, they were the traits that enabled me to keep him reined. Without them, without the discipline and rigorous self-restraint, the beast would have run rampant through my soul and psyche long ago.

Yet we were one.

And I couldn't remember a time he wasn't a part of me.

Chapter One

I sat on the cold step of the fire escape outside Charlotte's bedroom window, jacket tossed beside me, hands clasped around my head and elbows on knees as I stared blindly at a spot between my black dress-shoe'd feet; deep in thought as I absorbed the knock out one-two punch that the night had brought.

The cool temperature steadily dropped as the night wore on but was no bother to me. Exhaustion, born of a wretched mental fatigue, sat like a heavy blanket on my shoulders, tension cramping my stomach. The stench of smoke rose from my skin, grime and soot dusting all over the black of my suit pants and shirt. I needed a shower and a change of clothes. But I needed to talk to Charlotte more, so here I sat waiting for her to return. I'd figured it was better to wait here rather than outside her front door, considering the state I was in.

Shit, what a night it had been. Fire, flirting and fucking revelations.

My mind was chaotic, deeply disturbed by the unexpected memories tossed up from its murky depths.

That moment when the explosion had ripped its way through the Bellingworth Gallery, when Charlotte and I had crashed to the floor after I'd tackled her like a damn linebacker looped around my brain in slow motion, the shock and fear of that moment stinging like a hot poker jabbed without mercy into my belly. We'd survived the blast, my body shielding hers as the room exploded around us, deafeningly; deadly projectiles flying with vicious abandon on unsuspecting gallery guests.

Within seconds, Charlotte had snapped into cop-mode and I'd run towards the fire, an instinct I couldn't name urging me towards the smoke I could see belching from the corridor leading to the staff area.

Dragging in a deep breath, a trace of cold slid down my spine as if a ghostly finger had drawn a line coldly down the bone. And in a way, it had - the ghost of a barely remembered life slithering like a serpent in and out of my brain, taunting and prodding, shivering my mind as much as my skin.

Earlier That Night.......

"Damn it Kellan! Tell me the truth!" She growled, her hand on my foreman clutching tightly.

"Yes! Alright? Yes. I was searching for another....." I spat out in pure frustration, all my instincts screaming to get to the fire and contain it. To get Charlotte out of here before the whole building lit up.

"Another what?" Her nails were digging in through my jacket as my urgency tripped up my tongue.

"Charlotte, there's no time for this now!" I grabbed her shoulders again, eyes boring into her face intently. "I promise you I'll explain later, OK? Just get everyone out! Get to safety." And I slammed a hard kiss on her lips before tearing myself away and racing towards the fire.

I knew the risk I was taking, knew the dangers inherent to fighting fire and it didn't stop me. But I prayed hard and fast that Charlotte escaped quickly because the alternative didn't bear thinking about.

Pushing down the concern for her safety, I told myself to trust that she'd be okay; she'd get herself out of the building along with the gallery patrons that were scrambling brokenly through the doors. Chaos had erupted in the wake of the explosion; screams and frantic yelling filling the air as thickly as the dust and plasterboard debris.

I grabbed the fire extinguisher from the wall outside the large swing doors of the hotel kitchen, grateful that some quick-thinking soul had already broken the BGA just above it; its loud clanging alarm adding to the general shitfest of noise.

Shouldering my way through the swing doors, I ripped the nozzle off the extinguisher quickly and raced to the back of the kitchen where several small fires were gaining momentum along the cooktops. A large bin blazed in the east corner and long flickers greedily licked at the edges of the huge gaping hole the explosion had blasted through the wall behind it. I sprayed in wide sweeps, my moves instinctive and assured, working fast to ensure I covered everything before the tank emptied.

But I knew that the fire wasn't the danger.

Despite the overwhelming stench of mercaptan, the danger was in the structural damage to the building. And in the fact that explosions didn't just fucking happen.

The smell of garlic threaded through the putrid gas, further assaulting my highly attuned senses and my beast recoiled. I knew, without a doubt, that it wasn't a natural smell; not one caused by food, but the kind that came from acetylene.

This was no accident.

My hackles rose sharply; cold prickling along my neck and muscles clamping as I watched the dry powder smother the flames, a split second warning before my mind suddenly reeled and lurched with instability: thoughts and visions were clashing jarringly with the reality of what was in my view. Confusingly, I was no longer seeing what was in front of me but what was in my head - flashing through my mind at warp speed yet so clear and emphatic, it was almost tactile.

What the hell......??

Memories bombarded my brain with sledgehammer force. Memories of fighting fire.......other fires........scenes of burning buildings playing out like a movie through the fragmented departments of my mind, the sensory overload shockingly intense - I could smell and feel it all, I could hear it and see it - the coordinated shouts of the team as we worked to kill greedy flames; the loud hiss of the breathing apparatus as I sucked cool crisp air through my mask; fifty extra pounds of equipment strapped to my body; air tank and turnout gear a familiar weight; the fierce determination to win as you battle with straining,sweating muscles against the demonic bitch called Fire.

Elation and sheer adrenalin rushing through as you rescue trapped and frightened beings, whether two legged or four, satisfaction pumping like a wild drug through your veins knowing you'll be returning them to their loved ones that time.

And the crushing sorrow when you can't.

Every emotion, every remembered sensation pounded through my body and I gasped, my breath strangled. Sharp jabbing pain shot through my head and I cringed at its severity but it was over as suddenly as it began. Then, and as if someone were flicking pages in my head, I was suddenly flooded with different visions - a reliving of trauma in piercing flashes - even more intense and so clear it was as if I was right there: the rhythmic draw of my heavy breath through the BA mask as I made my way through thick black smoke, the walls and ceiling aflame all around me. Irons in hand to force open the heat expanded door as the cries of a young girl rose desperately. And then the disbelief as I discovered no frightened little body trapped by the flames but a recording device, an old style iPod sitting atop a steel box blaring out the sounds of a young voice crying out for help, over and over. In complete shock, the axe and Hooligan bar fell from my hands as I froze, unable to comprehend what I was seeing for a moment and then the sickening realisation that this fire was a cover for something far sinister. Screaming urgent instructions through the radio to the crew then the colossal BOOM! as the bomb detonated, the power so violent it blasted me off my feet and I flew through the blackened air, crashing against the splintered wood of the door I'd broken through not a minute before.

My breath caught now as muscle memory relived the agony that followed and my body seized in convulsive pain: the onslaught of searing heat, a wildfire burning from within, like liquid lava pouring through my veins, muscles and sinew ripping and shredding by some unseen force, screaming as bones snapped and scraped against each other, the blinding pain raging viciously through my entire being as I writhed against the floor, praying my death would be quick and merciful, my unheard screams turning guttural with horror as I watched in disbelief black talons breaking through my fingertips, nails disappearing as veins pulsed, protruding thick and blue, bones bending into claws. Desperately ripping off the headgear as my face distorted and twisted with the same hideous brutality.

What the fuck was happening to me?

My hands fumbled and almost dropped the extinguisher as I shook with the remembered terror. Only why was I feeling that terror? I was born a beast.

Then.........hiding like a beaten animal in the smouldering ruins as other firefighters - my crew - searched for me in vain; hunched and cowering as fear gripped my soul at the deep annihilating destruction of all that I was. As I became something.....other.

It didn't make sense. Holy Jesus, it didn't make sense!!

Another bolt of pain stabbed like a hot knife at my temple and I reflexively dropped the now empty extinguisher to the floor, one hand grabbing at my head as visions flashed with ever increasing speed - hiding endlessly in the ruins, all sense of time lost; soul shattered as the beast emerged, a terrifying monster that overwhelmed and overtook my entire being.

Running.......

Running as fast as I could when the beast retreated, from building to building, shadow to shadow, using the darkness as my shield, terrified he'd return and shit-scared I'd lost my mind.

Running till my lungs burst.

Running till I reached......where? Jesus Christ, where?

But, abruptly the memories changed tone, the sudden swing disconcerting and I dropped a hand onto one knee to steady myself. My breath heaving, I could now see Charlotte there.

Charlotte.....

Brief glimpses of her in skintight workout gear, fists raised in a boxer's stance, her hair pulled up in a high ponytail, looking fierce and determined.

Standing on the shore of what looked like a lake, fall coloured leaves rustling through the trees far behind her, smiling prettily, eyes sparkling as she hugged herself in some some hugely oversized sweater.

Laughing uncontrollably as she lay on a bed, shoulders bare as she clutched white sheets against her chest...... Oh God.......

My heart lurched, that weird thump returning to rattle against my ribs, beast growling at the barrage of remembered sensation.

Oh God, Oh God.......

My throat felt thick, clogged with rising emotion; sickness threatening to overwhelm me to the point of throwing up as the pain in my head sharpened to an excruciating level before suddenly exploding into nothingness. In the blink of an eye, the pain evaporated and I gasped in relief, both hands now on knees that didn't feel all that steady.

Holy fuck.

Stunned, shaken to the core, I dragged in deep breaths despite the foul air, willing myself to get my shit together. Whatever had just happened, I could process later. I could barely understand it, let alone deal with it just now - part of my brain reeled with the revelations while another screamed "receo" over and over, insistently demanding action.

A strange word if said that way.

But it wasn't a word. It was an acronym; one used for procedure by firefighters worldwide.

A shudder rolled down my back as I pushed aside the horrendous last couple of minutes and snapped into a mode that I barely had to think about, an instinct not of the beast kind taking over.

Assessing the scene, I was quickly assured the fires were out and no embers threatened. Without the mad noise of my fractured mind, I was able to focus, tuning my beast senses up high and spinning around at the faint heartbeat that suddenly invaded my awareness.

Having seen kitchen staff staggering bloodied and injured from the room when I'd raced towards the fire extinguisher earlier, there shouldn't be anyone left in here, I knew, but there was. There..... Across the long galley kitchen, down by the far wall, feet were sticking out from the walk-in refrigerator, the body laying trapped half in and half out.

Racing over, I grabbed the heavy steel door and pulled it away to reveal a pot-bellied middle aged man splayed on the steel floor, dressed in chefs' gear and head wound bleeding profusely. Quickly I took his pulse, eyes flashing gold briefly as I scanned him for further injury. Possible broken ribs, no doubt caused when the steel door slammed into his side. Looked like he'd been entering the walk-in when the blast happened and the return swing of the industrial size door had caught him. The head wound could have been caused by the door or from the fall but in either case, he needed help immediately.

For a brief moment I considered the damage I could do to his ribs if I dragged him to safety as instinct, as training, told me to do. Deciding it was the better option, I picked him up with an arm beneath his back and his knees, heading quickly to the gallery entrance, the man's dead weight not a bother to my beast's unnatural strength but well aware that I needed to at least make it appear as if I struggled.

Crowds of people spilled over the sidewalk and onto the street, victims, medicos and gawkers alike, the cops trying to marshal the curious lookers behind the barriers they were placing down. Sirens blazed as FDNY trucks came screaming into the street. Two ambulances were already pulled up, their lights flashing red and blue across the cool night air and bouncing off the surrounding buildings. I headed for the closest one even as I searched the chaos around me, spotting Charlotte immediately, my senses as always hyper aware of her. She stood with her back to me, talking to grey haired gallery guest who cradled one arm against his chest in pain, her silver dress catching the light and winking in its strobe beat. A breath I hadn't realised I was holding, escaped in relief.

She was okay.

Chapter Two

A paramedic rushed to meet me with a gurney and I carefully lay the wounded man on its bed, briefing the medic on how and where I'd found him, the possible broken ribs. Then, stepping back out of the way, I turned to head back into the building but paused to look Charlotte's way.

As if she sensed my eyes on her, she looked over her shoulder in my direction, our gazes locking across the distance. But then she swung her gaze to the fire trucks pulling up to the kerb and frowned, a look of concern......alarm?..... crossing her face. As the grey haired man pulled her attention back to him, she quickly schooled her features, glancing once more at me before turning back to Broken Wing Man.

I glanced back at the trucks myself, wondering what had caused that look and as I saw the crew swinging into action, that ghostly finger scraped against my nape again, just like it did when I stood watching Clements the other night.

When I watched another fire crew in action and had the same cold shiver run down my neck. And I hadn't understood why.

But I did now.

It didn't explain Charlotte's alarm but I didn't have time to sort that out - I had to get back into that building before the fire crew swarmed in. Turning, I made a quick run through the injured patrons, using the crowd to "disappear" as I switched to beast speed and charged through the doors, back into the kitchen to double check for other injured staff but there was no one.

The FD were fast and efficient but I was much faster than they could ever be - beast power and speed allowing me to search and rescue in mere minutes what would have taken much longer normally. I could have stood still and tightened my extra senses to tune into human scents and heartbeats on each floor - much easier and far less exerting - but with the number of security cameras placed all over the main gallery room, it was a safe bet there'd be many more elsewhere over the three levels. This way, once the cops viewed the footage, as they would no doubt, all they would see is an unexplainable blur, too fast for the human eye. Even slowed down, I'd be a ghost. The longer I stood still, the higher the chances were of being picked up by camera and I wasn't willing to waste time finding hiding spaces to avoid detection.

Ignoring the buzzing from my pocketed phone, I charged up the service stairs to the second level to find a large open area with several desks and work stations, file cabinets, printers, computers and other normal office stuff. All shut down for the night and empty of humans. But I still checked the two doors across the room and found only supply cupboards and a three cubicle bathroom.

The third floor revealed nothing but random art pieces: paintings and sculptures in various shapes, sizes and materials, many covered by cloths, others bare and casting strange shadows on the timber floor. High casement windows ran along the west wall just beneath the moulding, red and blue siren lights from the street flashing through the many panes to create crazy patterns on the ceiling, and adding an eerie feel to the dark room.

All clear, I made my way back to the service stairs and managed to get to ground level just as the fire-crew were dispersing in various directions for their own search and rescue, several men heading for the stairwell I'd just left, others through the destroyed kitchen and gallery. I sped through undetected, once more using the swarm of people outside to slow and return to human speed.

Charlotte was now talking to a uniform cop, the broken-arm guy gone, no doubt on his way to the hospital; several more ambulances parked haphazardly over the kerb in whatever space they could find around the fire trucks.

Needing a moment to regroup, I stood to the back of the crowd with fists jammed in pockets and head low, just watching.

The jittery sensation in my gut was disturbing, my equilibrium shaken and I took slow and steady breaths. I dug deep for every bit of control I could drag up from within, stoically and methodically locking down my emotions as those last minutes in the gallery kitchen threatened to overwhelm me with the force of a tsunami.

Not here. Not now.

My beast was highly agitated, growling and straining at his tethers, his instincts screaming to lash out in defence: protective of me and pissed at the stunning assault on my mind. I held tightly to control, almost grateful for the distraction of him and pushed him back ruthlessly.

Goddammit! Not here. Not now.

Scanning the crowd, I saw no sign of Lewinski or Ridley - my targets for tonight's mission.

It was possible one or the other had been injured and was already on their way to the hospital. Or neither man had shown up to the fundraiser at all, as I suspected. During my surveillance earlier that night, there'd been no sign of either man and even with Charlotte's arrival at the gallery causing a major distraction for me, I wouldn't have, couldn't have missed the scent of beast.

Assuming there was in fact a beast. The Commander didn't have clear intel on which one was the mutated human. Maybe both. Maybe neither. Confirm and eliminate had been my directive - a task that I had been in the middle of when Detective Alistair had arrived and chaos had soon followed.

I avoided looking directly at any of the firemen; something in my gut telling me to not go there. However, my gaze got caught instead on one of the trucks' bumper, the number 4 boldly painted in gold against the red metal. Tensing up and jaw clenching, I felt the wash of cold slide beneath my skin.

Shit.

I didn't know if this particular ladder truck was significant or not but my heart was thudding so hard and a deep uneasiness swirled in my belly.

The red and gold paint seemed to leap out at me, glaring hugely as if alive and I quickly looked away only to get snagged on the 34 emblazoned on the second truck.

Fuck.....

No.

Enough. Enough. !

The word echoed in my head as I lurched back a couple of steps, a quagmire of fractured memories and emotions looming too large in front of me and I knew I was dangerously close to snapping. Both man and beast.

Get out of here, I told myself. Just go.

But.........

My gaze swung back to Charlotte, reluctant to leave her. Which was damn stupid - she was a cop. She knew how to look after herself. Yet, despite the logic of that, I couldn't stop the twinge of protectiveness. Didn't matter though - she was surrounded by other cops, firefighters and medics. She was plenty safe right now.

Staring at her elegant profile as she stood talking to a black dude in a tux, I traced the smooth line of her jaw, her cheekbone high and shadowed in the night light, willing her to look my way. Moments later, as if I'd reached out and drawn a finger down the enticing nape of her neck, she swung her head and unerringly found my gaze. The distance between us took away nothing of the intensity; green-gold locked into hazel, silently conveying her concern as I took a couple of slow steps back, hands in pockets and turning to walk away knowing she'd get the message - that I was leaving, not disappearing.

I swear I felt the change the moment her gaze left me.

With an outward calm I didn't feel, I walked away from the sights and smells of an emergency scene that was new yet familiar. The urgency of the Search and Rescue dissipated and a numb kind of shock settled in its place, leaving my skin ice cold and my mind a chaotic jumble of disconnected thoughts.

I concentrated on putting one foot in front of the other, no destination in mind and letting the rhythmic sound of my scuffed up shoes on the sidewalk soothe my senses: each step through the darkened streets of Manhattan easing bit by tiny bit the clenched ball of tension in my gut. No one looked twice in my direction: typical New Yorkers unfazed by the oddity of a man walking down the street in a grimy, dusty designer tux. They'd seen it all.

I lost track of time, aware only of the gradual sense of returning equilibrium and by the time it occurred to me to pay attention to my surroundings, I found myself one building away from Charlotte's apartment.

I stopped, looked up at the eighth level where her place was, taken aback by where my subconscious had led me.

But, should I be?

With the events of the last few days and the memories that had crashed through tonight, it shouldn't surprise me that this was where I'd been drawn.

I breathed out a shaky sigh. Even knowing she wouldn't be home for hours, I turned towards the fire escape running along the dark brick of her building. I had so much to think through so the time didn't bother me.

And I needed to talk to her.

It was just as I sat down on the fire escape step that I remembered the Commander. I'd been too busy with search and rescue earlier to pick up his call, his timing really unfortunate.

I sighed heavily, not in any kind of mood to deal with his mysterious ass but considering he may have Intel on my targets and their whereabouts, duty forced me to push that aside and get on with it.

Taking my phone from my pocket and firing it out of sleep mode, I was startled to see that the text message icon was brightly lit against the dark screen. I frowned - what was this?

The Commander hadn't ever sent a written message to me so it couldn't be him. Unless it was Charlotte...? Quickly I punched the icon, pulse skipping a bit at all the possibilities. I liked the idea that she would reach out this way.....

Like brakes squealing when stomped suddenly, my thoughts abruptly halted as I read the text: possible target spotted heading into gallery food services.

Blinking uncomprehendingly, I frowned. What the hell? I read it again. Then again. And the hackles on my neck shivered with instinctive unease.

A fine tremor shook my hand as I stared down at the text, seeing that this wasn't a message from Charlotte. In fact, there was no number at all - the sender declared as "unknown".

Who the fuck had sent this?

And then I noticed the time stamp on it. My pulse tripped and sped as I realised this text had come through no more than five minutes before the blast happened.

Possibly even less.

My beast began to strain with agitation, a growl vibrating in his throat as my fingers tightened around the phone, rage mounting as the implications sunk in; my vision hazed over with a furious red before I managed to pull myself back from crushing the cell into a thousand pieces.

Holy shit.........if I'd heard the buzz of a message coming through, if the music hadn't drowned out the sound.........if I hadn't been dancing with Charlotte, I would have been in the gallery kitchen when the blast went off.

Right at ground zero.

That ghostly finger of apprehension now trailed down my spine, senses alarmed at the close call.

Only two people had this number - Charlotte and the Commander.

And it wasn't Charlotte.

Taking a deep breath, I gathered every ounce of control, locking down both the beast's and my own agitation so I could think clearly.

Goddammit. What the fuck was going on?

For the Commander to send that message meant he'd had eyes on the targets, which was expected given the clandestine nature of this mission. But it also meant that someone didn't want me getting to Lewinski and Ridley if they were prepared to blow me up to protect them. Or it meant that either man had in fact been the intended victim and I would simply have been collateral damage.

But for that to be true, it meant the Commander's message and the explosion were two separate events and their close timing was one giant fucked up concidence.

And I didn't believe in coincidence.

No. It had to be that someone knew why I was there tonight. Had Lewinski or Ridley somehow discovered the plan? Or someone else? Someone who had unknown reasons to want to stop me from completing the task?

Looking back down at the cell phone still in my hand, darkened back into sleep mode now, I realised hackers might have infiltrated the Commander's communication system, gaining access to his conversations with me. Or the damn thing was bugged.

My lip curling in a snarl, I quickly turned off the cell before I ripped it open and inspected every inch of it, inside and out, but there was nothing visible. Of course not, I decided. When the hell could someone have bugged it? It was always with me, always pocketed.

Hackers. It had to be hackers. And who knows how long they'd been listening.

Shit.

Reassembling the phone, I hesitated to turn it back on but there really wasn't a choice.

Better to make it seem that all was normal. Besides.....the Commander would be calling again and I needed to figure out a way to alert him if he didn't already know about the breach. If he did know, that could be the reason he hadn't tried calling again after that earlier missed call.

I slipped the phone back into my pocket with a weary sigh, deciding to give it time and see how it played out before I made my next move.

I had more than enough to deal with tonight as it was.

Running one hand through my short dark hair in a rare show of tension, I leaned my elbows on my knees and let my mind return to the memories that had surfaced earlier, a sharp twinge stabbing in my chest at the vivid yet elusive pictures. Concentrating, I lingered on each memory, no matter how painful, willing myself to remember more; remember the context of them but it was like trying to grab onto smoke.

However....of one thing, there was no question.

I was a firefighter.

A dead one.

At least as far as the world was concerned.

Because if I wasn't presumed dead then why wasn't I still working for the FD? And why was I, in that one particular memory, so traumatised by a beast transformation that I had hidden while they searched for me? Why did that mutation feel so soul destroying when I was born a monster? Why had I run so hard and fast? To where?

And if I was a dead firefighter, then why was I working for an unseen someone as a soldier?

Fucking hell.

I'd finally gotten some quick glimpses of a different life and now all I had was a million more questions.

And Charlotte....

Those tiny fragments of memory played on repeat and brought with it a confusing sense of knowing, of some deep emotion unconnected and adrift of anything else. And that knowing wasn't nearly enough. It felt fragile - like whisper-thin fog, elusive and translucent. The more I tried to identify my feelings, to grab onto them and connect to more memories, the more they slipped through my fingers. My body pulsated with clamouring emotion that withheld any sort of traction.

Jesus H. Christ. I wanted to howl in frustration. Why the fuck couldn't I hold on? Why could I see the memory of Charlotte yet know there was something just out of reach, just out of my recognition? Each memory had a feeling - a longing, fascination and an adrenalin rush yet I instinctively knew there was more.

Much more.

Goddammit.

My beast suddenly came to attention, distracted from his agitation by the scent of Charlotte somewhere near by. My head swung towards the closed window, realising she was home.

Finally.

Chapter Three

My sensitive ears picked up the sound of her front door unlocking, keys being dropped onto a hard surface and the click of her heels on the timber floor.

My heartbeat accelerated in anticipation.

The window was locked but the blinds only halfway down and within seconds, lights came on somewhere inside her apartment and cast shadows into the darkness of her bedroom.

I watched as she entered the room, turned on the side-table lamp and threw her evening wrap onto the bed. The muted light shone softly on the silver of her dress, highlighting her tiny waist and slim arms, her long glossy hair still miraculously pinned in its elegant style but only just - long chunks of it were falling loosely every which way, dust and grime was splattered all over her.

So beautiful.

She startled as she turned and saw me sitting there on her fire escape but recovered quickly, a look of concern crossing her face as our eyes met through the glass.

Hesitating for only a moment, she walked towards the window and pulled the blind up fully, unlocking and sliding the glass open to the night air. And to me.

Our eyes clung, hazel into green-gold.

The wariness in her eyes pierced sharply and I had to swallow the thickness that suddenly clogged my throat.

"Are you okay?" she asked, quiet dignity shading her voice.

My heart squeezed, inner beast quivering as she asked about my welfare before anything else despite her uncertainty.

"Yeah. Are you?" I asked quietly, senses attuned for any signs of injury yet unable to drag my eyes from her face. She nodded wordlessly. Need coursed through my veins - the need to touch her, hold her, explain everything so she'd understand. But what could I explain when so much was unclear? When so much of it was like fragmented shards of broken glass, shiny and jagged, impossible to piece together again? But I could start with what I did know.

"When I was running towards the fire, Charlotte, I realised that......" I had to pause as my stomach twisted. "I realised that I was more concerned for your safety than I was about the fire itself."

She tried real hard not to show any reaction to that, but I saw the flicker in her eyes, the slight widening of her pupils.

"I didn't understand why just then but later......I had flashes, Charlie....." Her eyes widened further and she seemed to hold her breath. "Memories.... Of fighting other fires. They were so clear, it was like I was right there. I remembered an explosion, getting knocked out and .....and.....beasting out.....only I was terrified of myself. Shit-scared. I thought I was dying. I remembered running and... running...." Charlotte's mouth dropped open, lips trembling and I clung to the wide look of hope in her eyes as an anchor to my spinning emotions. "I'm a firefighter, aren't I?" I said in a non-question.

"Yes," she whispered in a choked voice, a sheen of moisture glittering her eyes, one small hand reaching up to press trembling fingertips to lips.

"And.....they think I'm dead, don't they?" I continued, recalling the concern on her face when the fire trucks had begun arriving earlier. It hadn't made sense in that moment as I hadn't yet put two and two together - she'd been concerned that the firemen would see and recognise me, or vice versa.

Not knowing I'd had some memory flashes by then, she'd been rightly worried about what might happen should I recognise anyone.

Or vice versa.

"Yes," she whispered in a thick voice, eyes hooked steadily into mine, keeping me anchored despite the constant tumult. I hadn't wanted my presumed death to be true despite knowing it was and still somehow Charlotte's quiet confirmation had the weight of a lead balloon. Christ.....what the hell had happened to me?

But I pushed that aside, eager to reveal the other significant memories.

"I saw you, Charlotte" I said in a scratchy voice, "I saw you.......you were dressed in work out gear, throwing punches......at me, I think......your hair was in a ponytail."

Her heartbeat spiked sharply as she gasped. Despite her best efforts to remain impassive and composed, I saw each small nuance; I watched her that closely.

"And somewhere like a lake or river, I'm not sure, you were standing there, just at the water's edge and the sun was setting," I continued. "Charlotte, I know they were just flashes and they weren't as long as the firefighting ones I had but......they.......... they gotta be memories too, don't they?" I asked, feeling more vulnerable than I can ever recall being. "I saw you, laughing, you were in a bed, but it wasn't that one there or the one at my place. You were on some white pillow, I think."

Raising my ass off the step, I instead leaned my knees against the window sill, sitting on my haunches as I got closer to her, determined to convey how intensely honest I was being.

"Charlotte, I don't know why I haven't gotten more memories of you yet but I'm getting something. Maybe I'll get more, maybe not but I...... It's a start isn't it?"

Silence stretched out between as I waited for her. The vulnerability was palpable but I couldn't be sure if it was hers or my own and I hated how unsteady I felt. Like a tiny rowboat wildly pitching in a stormy sea - off balance and nauseated with the lurching waves.

"Yeah, it is. Kellan, I.......uhh...... I shouldn't have........" She licked her lips nervously and trailed off.

"You shouldn't have.....?" I repeated with a lift of my brow. What was she nervous about?

She took a deep breath, as if for courage and said: "I shouldn't have expected so much from you. You're back but you're not the same and I was expecting you to just automatically snap back into the same relationship that we had before. But I'm a stranger to you."

"Charlotte," I began, surprised at her words. It didn't feel right for her to apologise. And she wasn't a stranger. Not anymore.

"Just like in many ways you're a stranger to me. Your personality is different. You're keeping secrets from me and Finn and you would never do that before."

She ran one hand over her nape, seeming to be thinking aloud. "But since you don't remember him either, then why wouldn't you?" She muttered in an undertone, staring at the floor. "I did this all wrong."

"Did what wrong?" I frowned and she looked back up at me, her gaze steady and serious now.

"I was wrong to expect anything from you when don't remember me," she said clearly.

Well, yeah but...... wouldn't anyone in her position have reacted the same? Maybe even me?

"But you were wrong to lie when I'd made it clear I was trying to help you," she continued, cats' eyes glinting in the shadowed light of the lampshade, conviction in her tone. "You knew at Finn's place that we were telling the truth, the day we found you. You had the proof right there."

"Yeah, of Finn. But not........." I trailed off, kicking myself mentally.

"But not of me," she finished. Her face tightened as she seemed to brace herself.

"No," I admitted quietly, reluctantly. But dammit....it was the truth. I'd seen pictures of Finn and myself but none of Charlotte.

"I didn't believe either of you, despite the yearbook Finn showed me, Charlie. You know I didn't."

It suddenly occurred to me that I'd called her that - Charlie - twice now. I blinked at the natural way it just rolled off my tongue, without thought.

"Yet you had the nerve to ask me to trust you," she said with bitter irony. "While you kept lying to me. Even after we slept together." Her eyes darkened with harsh accusation, the green-gold stormy. "You lied to me tonight. You purposely led me to believe you were only there to protect me, which by the way, I don't need. But you were there under orders."

She became all-cop but I caught the flash of hurt in her eyes before she managed to lock it down. She crossed her arms, raising her chin as she demanded: "Whose orders, Kellan? What were you searching for?"

I sighed heavily, hesitant to reveal anything even though I'd blurted earlier that night that I'd explain everything to her. But what could I explain? How many people would I be endangering if I did? There were valid reasons for the secrecy and I shouldn't even be contemplating it for a second. But I needed to explain some part of it - I'd said I would. My mind was scrambling, debating which way to approach this and what I could safely say.

But she misread my hesitation.

"Yeah, I thought so," she smirked sarcastically, taking a step back.

"No, it's not like that," I said, madly searching for the right words to get through to her. "I don't have clearance to discuss the mission with anyone, Charlotte. You know what that means. You're a cop."

"Kellan, that relationship we had, the one you almost remember......we never lied to each other. We trusted each other. But now......... You don't trust me but want me to trust you. That's not how this works, though. That's not how WE work. Or at least the "we" that we used to be," she sighed huskily, her disheartened eyes reaching into my chest and squeezing so hard my breath hitched.

"I don't know what we are now," she continued. "But I'm not willing to blindly give all when you won't concede anything yourself." I could see her gathering a protective shell around herself, closing off defensively. But she didn't need to do that.

I wouldn't let her do that.

"I'm conceding myself," I told her huskily, laying it all out there. "I'm saying that even though until tonight I didn't have any memories of you, I still wanted you. I ...ahhh......don't seem to be able to prevent that. And now that I do have some flashes - that just makes me want you more."

If my words couldn't convince her of the truth, surely my eyes would - everything I was feeling was there for her to see, I'm sure of it; the connection we shared powerful and undeniable.

"I'm saying that even though I'm trying to do my job as a soldier and I'm not meant to be getting involved with anyone, I'm breaking that rule. I've already broken it." She had to see that. "That I now know I was a firefighter and I'm supposedly dead which means there's a damn hell of a lot more going on here than I originally thought. Even though I'm so damn confused about everything, about who I am, I still wanna work through this.......especially with you."

Our eyes held for long, endless moments as she took in my words and I thought I could see the tiniest softening in her gaze.

But she shut it down.

"I can't live with the lies. And the distrust. It's too hard," she said, stubborn resolve in her voice. "This is too hard."

She began to step back again and in desperation I grabbed her face, cupping my hands around her jaw as I laid my mouth on hers, kissing her hard, the sweetness of her lips sending my beast into a ecstatic shudder.

She stiffened in surprise but didn't push me away.

Without letting go of her, I blurred my way through the window to stand properly, pulling her closer and sliding my lips against the smooth, soft fullness of hers.

Her heartbeat picked up speed just as mine did, her hands coming up to clutch my biceps. God, she tasted so good.

But then she broke away, looking up at me with luminous uncertain eyes and I held my breath, desire pulsing through every nerve ending as I waited for her next move.

Suddenly her hands came up, gripping my shoulders to pull me towards her but I didn't need help. Our mouths crashed together as I snatched her up against me tightly, lips devouring, both of us moaning. My beast growled low as long scratches of lust ripped down my spine.

Yes. Hell yes.

Fire raced across my skin as my tongue slid across hers, muscles quivering as her hands slid into my hair, tugging and clutching and spiking up my temperature. Kissing her wildly, I swear I would have swallowed her whole if I could have.

My hands raced down her back and hips restlessly, wanting to touch her everywhere at once, the silk of her dress cool and slippery against my palms. Sliding one hand down to her ass, I pressed her hard against my throbbing cock, kneading her sexy curves and she shivered in reaction, moaning into my mouth.

She felt so damn amazing in my arms, so responsive, the physical chemistry intense and incendiary.

Desperate for a breath, I reluctantly released her mouth and slid my lips over her jawline to her ear, tracing over the cute little shell before biting her lobe, causing her to throw back her head, moaning and giving me access to the sweet scented skin of her neck. My beast wanted to take a giant swipe so I did - my tongue scraping slowly, thoroughly.

I shook with hunger.

My hands clutched her tighter, hers digging into my shoulders, our bodies straining and burning with heat.

I walked her backwards as our mouths returned to each other, sliding wet, open and desperate for more. Tongues swirling, lips biting, groaning.

Oh God, yes.

And then she ripped her mouth from mine, dragging in ragged breaths and halting our backwards trip. So I zeroed in on her neck, nibbling and kissing the tender skin there as she tilted her head back and smoothed one hand through my hair, clutching my nape.

"Kellan," she moaned in a low voice. "Wait. Kellan, wait," she pleaded.

Whatever she wanted, she had it.

"No, stop. Please," she said, her words in complete contradiction to her clutching hands, her pressing body.

Huh??

But I stopped.

I froze in fact, too damn scared to make the slightest move as the agony of stopping sent a keen knife's edge of pain through my muscles. My beast almost howled and I had to grip the tethers tighter.

"Charlotte ......," I moaned her name, my breath hot against the hollow of her throat.

"No," she said breathily. "No. This isn't gonna happen, Kellan". She didn't sound like she believed herself.

"Why?" I asked, daring to lay some nibbling little kisses across her collarbone. She shook in my arms.

"I want you, Charlotte. I know you can feel how much I want you." And I pressed my hard-on into her belly in a hard slow thrust. She moaned huskily and convulsively gripped my hair.

"And I know that you want me too. You can't deny it cause I'd know you're lying - I can smell how wet you are," I said with a deep groan. And that knowledge was twisting my stomach in painful, ruthless knots.

Lifting my head, our eyes met as her cheeks flamed and I smirked at the completely flustered look on her face. She wasn't gonna let that faze her though as she said insistently: "That's irrelevant. I'm not falling into bed with you again, like the other night."

Dammit.

"Charlotte, I'm not gonna push you into bed," I told her, although I wished I could. There was one right over there.

Jesus, don't look at it.

I shivered as I reigned in my need for her.

"But I'm not gonna let you push me away either," I told her adamantly. "I want a chance to follow through on that date, on getting to know you. And me. The me you talk about."

I stared intently into her eyes, determined for her to see and feel my sincerity. The fire was banked a little but still burned hot; hands still wrapped tight around her back and waist, wanting. Wanting so much. Her cheeks were flushed with heat, lips wet from my mouth. So beautiful.

I worked hard to stay in control.

"I know there's things I have to figure out about my work and I've gotta figure out my past - with you and with everyone else too. There's so much I don't know about myself and I don't have anyone to ask about it, except you. And McGregor, I suppose, but that's not the same thing. You know everything about our relationship and I don't."

I raised one hand to her hair, tucking an escaped tendril behind her ear and rubbing my thumb over her soft cheek, her skin like satin.

"And I want to, Charlotte. I want to know everything about you and me, that trust you said we had. But that's gonna take time. I wanna take that time."

I could see the indecision, the wariness. But there was longing there too.

"I...... " she began then blinked, swallowed nervously and took a deep breath, like she was preparing to step out on a ledge.

And in a sense, she did.

"I need time, Kellan. You can't expect me to accept all your secrets and to not have trust issues with you. You're different now. You're not the man you were."

"Maybe I'm not, I don't know - I don't remember that man. But we can figure it all out, I know we can, just as long as you don't shut me out."

She blinked up at me, green gold eyes shimmering in the muted light.

"Charlotte.....you want time, you have it. As much time as you need." I swear I'd be patient, no matter how long it took. "I promise you that."

Her eyes searched mine, measuring my sincerity and after a long moment, she pulled out of my arms, stepping back and leaving my body craving her warmth.

"You need to go now," she said in a clear, strong voice, "It's been a long day and I've had enough. Close the window on your way out."

And with that, she turned and left the room. Left me standing there in her bedroom, alone, with a million emotions coursing through me. I sighed heavily, wanting so badly to follow her but I knew I'd pushed the situation as far as I could tonight.

So I turned and climbed out her window, back onto the fire escape. I grabbed my jacket off the step and put it on, feeling a slight chill now as I came down from the physical high of being near her. Beastie-boy whined like a lost puppy.

With one last look around her room, avoiding the bed as much as possible, I left.

But I did shut the window.

Chapter Four

I shut the laptop with a sharp snap.

Nothing.

Not a single message from the Commander. Encrypted or otherwise.

Sitting back in my chair, I grabbed my glass of scotch and took a mouthful as I contemplated my next step. I'd arrived back at the apartment just a few minutes ago and after tossing my jacket onto the sofa, I'd ripped my tie and shirt collar open, glad to be able to breathe freely again. I'd grabbed the scotch, a glass and the laptop, sat at the dining table and gave the computer a complete going-over. But even with beast vision, I hadn't seen anything that indicated tampering of any kind; no suspicious markings, nothing that could be a bug, no matter how tiny.

It was as I expected - the laptop hadn't been touched by anyone but me. And if someone had broken into the apartment to tamper with my stuff, I would have sensed it - my extra sensory ability able to pick up residual scent. And there'd been none. Just the sweet aroma of Charlotte, lingering from our sexcapades of the other day, faded and faint now but still potent. So that meant any possible hacking had to have been from a remote source. Or maybe my phone was the only device affected?

Dammit.

I needed the commander to call A-SAP; needed him to confirm or deny a security breach. He should have gotten news of the explosion by now - surely he'd be wanting to verify his operatives' safety?

I smirked to myself - yeah right, O'Ryan.

However, I couldn't just sit on my ass twiddling my thumbs and wait till he called. I didn't have the patience for that and although I was damn tired from all the upheaval tonight, I knew I wasn't ready for sleep either. I couldn't switch off mentally, not yet; not until I knew what I was dealing with now.

Drumming my fingers on the table, legs sprawled, I stared thoughtfully at the phone sitting there between the scotch bottle and the silver laptop, eyes boring into it, willing it to make a sound. But I got nothing.

Fuck it.

Snatching it up, I decided I wasn't gonna wait any more. Besides - if there'd been a security breach, then the damage was already done. I'd just have to make sure no specifics were spoken of. Punching the code onto the screen keypad, I waited an unusual length of time for him to "pick up" and grimaced impatiently. Jesus, the one time he's slow to respond, he chooses it to be now.......I growled under my breath. There was never a dial tone or ringing to be heard on my end - just silence then a metallic click that indicated connection. And there it was finally..........

Click.

I was about to speak when something held me back - instead of his distorted, digitalised voice coming down the line, there was complete silence. Dead air.

But every hackle on my neck stood up.

He was there - I knew he was. I could feel his dark and murky presence. Why the fuck didn't he speak?

"Sir?" I prodded.

A faint indrawn breath, then..... "O'Ry.......O'Ryan?!" The explosive shout was full of shock.

Yeah, okay, he wasn't happy I'd called on a compromised line. I didn't give a damn. "Yes Sir," I confirmed, fully prepared for the ranting reprimand he was no doubt gonna bombard my ears with.

Still didn't give a damn. I just hoped he made it a quick one so we could get to business.

But it didn't come. Instead, silence stretched out again. A silence that increasingly felt dark and loaded with fury. Even his harsh breathing gave off an aura of menace, his anger disproportionate to the situation and I wanted to just tell him to calm the fuck down. Seriously.

"Sir, I know I shouldn't......." I began impatiently but he interrupted, his voice barely under control.

"Goddammit O'Ryan!! ......what.......where the hell are you?" He barked.

"Uh..." I barely had the chance to open my mouth before he cut me off again.

"Never mind, soldier. Report in," he demanded, his voice blisteringly cold.

The sudden piercing pain in my temple, as if a knife had stabbed hotly into my brain, had my free hand coming up to press against my eyelids, eyes closing tight against the harsh flashes of light that blinded me momentarily. Jesus, no..... Not now......but as quickly as it had begun, it stopped and my breath shuddered in relief.

"But, the text......then the......err..... "incident" ...." I scrambled to get my thoughts straight and not refer to any specifics but my mind felt scattered; disorientated in a weird way. I got up out of my chair to pace a little, hoping to shake off the strange sensation.

"Text?" The commander asked and I stopped in my tracks with a frown. A whisper of tension slid into my gut unexpectedly and I stayed silent.

"Right, right, the text," he said, a odd tone creeping through the mechanical voice, almost......contemplative? Distracted? I couldn't quite put my finger on it. But then: "that's taken care of," he added dismissively.

"So, this line is secure, Sir?" I wanted confirmation before I gave any damn report.

"Didn't I just say so?!"

He roared explosively, the fury almost hot enough to singe my damn ear. Well, what was up his ass then?

I scowled into the phone, pissed at his psycho mood swings and holding tight to my own temper. Had my call come at a bad time - is that why the shithouse manner? Maybe he was in the middle of screwing some woman when my call came though. Or some guy? Who the hell knew. He could have been screwing another digital robo-voice for all I cared and it still didn't warrant his assholeness.

My beast was snarling, equally on edge and I shoved a curled fist into my pants pocket, a fine quiver racing through my muscles as I forced back the urge to punch something.

"Report in, soldier," he snapped, his animosity almost palpable.

"No sign of either Lewinski or Ridley in the building at all," I returned in an clipped rasp. "Verification of mutated DNA therefore incomplete. It's possible one or both were taken to hospital but I wasn't able to pick up any trace of beast anywhere on site. However, that could be because of chemical override. Whoever set up that explosion used an excessive amount of acetylene. There's no question it was arson."

Again, thick silence.

"Sir," I tacked on in a voice dripping with false deference. I didn't give a shit if he took exception to my tone.

"Not good enough, soldier. You're meant to be the best tracker but that's not what I'm seeing," he sneered condescendingly, another pause stretching out as he waited for a response. But I stayed silent, seething at his insult and determined to stay in control.

He huffed, a weird stupid sound when filtered through a voice modulator. Why did he need one anyway? Plenty of secret ops were successfully run without the robo-crap.

"I'll set up another avenue of verification, but be warned O'Ryan, I won't tolerate a second failure." And with that, the line disconnected abruptly.

Pulling the phone away from my ear, I stabbed a finger at the call end button and wished like hell that it was an old fashioned phone with actual buttons you could press, like the kind we'd had growing up. It didn't have the same satisfying feel of slamming a phone down when you just have to tap a screen.

I did, however, slam the cell down on the dining table, which helped a little. Then I stalked over to my gym and threw several hard smacking fists into the punching bag, grunting as I released some of the repressed anger curdling in my blood.

Fucking asshole. No thankyou, no appreciation for the shit I'd dealt with tonight. He hadn't asked a damn thing about the explosion. Offered no explanation about the breach in security so I still didn't fucking know what the hell had happened! A hard right cross sent the bag swinging wildly.

And why wasn't he more concerned about the breach? Why so dismissive, like it was nothing? Sure, maybe it was because I'm not meant to know certain aspects of the mission but considering it was my ass on the line, he could offer up something better than "that's taken care of", couldn't he? He pissed me off at the best of times but tonight I had zero tolerance for him. I couldn't even dredge up the smallest amount of deferential respect for his seniority and I figured that had everything to do with tonight's revelations.

One last pounding punch into the leather had my knuckles singing with the impact and I snarled loudly then stepped back, the edge taken off the rage that still simmered inside, hands propped on hips as I calmed my breathing. But then, like a wrecking ball to my chest, I remembered what I'd thought just a moment ago and gasped, my breath stalling and gut clenching in shock: "like the kind we'd had growing up."

Holy shit.

A tremor slid over my suddenly cold skin and with a couple of shaky steps to the nearest chair, I sat heavily on the charcoal leather, every ounce of energy draining away.

Christ.... Was I losing my damn mind?

How could I have that thought yet have no mental picture to go with it?

I somehow just knew we'd had that kind of phone, but I couldn't see it, couldn't attach any memory to it. It didn't make sence. And who was "we"?

Elbows on knees, I scrubbed my hands over my face, dejected. My belly did a slow flip, queasy with the sensation of yet again having the rug pulled out from under me.

Was this what it was gonna be like every time memories resurfaced? Nausea, disorientation? Or that stabbing head pain? Maybe.......

Probably.

My lip curled in distaste. God, I really hoped not - it was damn exhausting.

I sat quietly for a few minutes, focusing on that phrase : "like the kind we'd had growing up", willing my brain to tell me more but nothing came no matter how hard I tried, not a single vision and I had to admit eventually that it was futile.

So I stood, grabbed my half full scotch glass from the table and downed it in one gulp before heading for the stairs, switching off the lights as I went. Upstairs, I stripped naked, leaving the dusty designer suit where it fell on the floor, shoes, shirt, socks and boxers tossed aside carelessly. With a weariness that seemed to saturate my bones, I fell face forward onto the unmade bed and lay unmoving awhile. I'd had the vague thought earlier to do some research into the explosion and fire I'd remembered but I couldn't find the energy anymore - I'd dealt with enough shit tonight.

With a sigh, I rolled to my back and pulled the crumbled grey bedcover over my hips, reaching for the lamp switch and plunging the room into darkness. But it wasn't as easy to switch my mind off and I spent a long time staring up at the ceiling, arms crossed under my head as I waited impatiently to fall asleep, an almost impossible task given the multitude of new questions I now had.

Nothing made sense and despite the new memories, I was as much in the dark as before.

I woke up the next morning tired, confused, pissed, frustrated and horny. As HELL.

It had taken hours to fall asleep and when I did, my dreams had been filled with all kinds of disjointed, random stuff. I couldn't tell if they were actual memories or simply the result of an overworked mind.

There were vague and misty visions of sitting on the bank of a huge lake, Charlotte tucked up in between my legs as my arms encircled her, just watching the water together; another of slow dancing with her, both of us in jeans and tee, her hair loose and curled as she rested her head on my chest - that dream was soft and sweet: innocent in some indefinable way. Another one featured myself, a chessboard and Finn's disgruntled face as he lost the game of chess we were playing. Of all things - chess? Really?

But then the dreams turned dark and disturbing: running through a tunnel chased by an unseen force breathing malignantly down my neck; locked in a steel cage that sat centred in a completely empty, white room - white walls, white floor and one solitary white door. No windows. A stark and coldly sterile room that had a thousand eyes. Then, another cage, only this time it was pitch black, the floor unsteady beneath my prone body, sickness and pain washing in waves relentlessly as my sight flickered from thick inky grey to blinding white, like strobe lights punching thorough my eye sockets. Menace, both verbal and physical, taunted in gleeful circles: wildly mocking jeers echoing hollowly in a cavernous space that stunk of malicious intent; stinging jabs poking at my skin with white hot sharpness, my chest crushing in a vise grip of horrified fear.

I woke violently in a cold sweat, my breath strangling in my throat and heart pounding like a jackhammer. An overwhelmingly frantic sense of foreboding beat through my entire body, the unconscious threat agitating even my beast. He strained mightily against his tethers and I yanked at them hard to control him.

Christ Almighty.

Scrubbing a hand over my face, I shuddered. What the hell was this? Since when did BeastieBoy freak out over a nightmare? Since when did I even have nightmares? But then again........I don't fucking remember, do I? So who the hell knows how my beast reacts to them.

I scowled at the dark ceiling in frustration before rolling to my side and reshaping the pillow with a couple of good whacks. If I pounded it a little harder than necessary, well, that was just too damn bad.

Unless it wasn't a nightmare?

The words crept into my brain quietly and kept me tossing and turning for hours until I once again fell into an exhausted sleep. This time, however, as if in atonement for the earlier nastiness, my dreams consisted of only Charlotte and I: the two of us sitting at a small timber table, papers and maps strewn all over its smoothly glossed surface, laughingly arguing over something; standing on a rooftop with her, the New York skyline a snowy backdrop to our serious conversation, her cheeks red from the biting wind; kissing her while she had some sort of black stuff painted around her eyes like a mask, all exotic and mysterious and so beautiful that even in my dream state, my body filled with aching desire.

But the dream changed tone. Desire deepened to a gut-wrenching lust, carnal and raw as she lay spread out before me, her skin a feast of decadent lushness. Shadows flickered on the darkened walls from the flare of brightly lit fat candles and painted her soft flesh with intriguing patterns. Naked and sweaty, our moans echoed around the room, her body straining against the handcuffs that shackled her to the timber slats above her head - holy shit - and my heartbeat raced. When I tried to hold those images in my mind longer, they slipped away, switching to something else only to return again and again. I could feel everything so clearly - the burning heat of her, the smooth velvet of her legs as I trailed my tongue up over her thigh higher and higher, reaching for her breasts and cupping them as she thrust them into my hands, back arching and groaning her pleasure breathlessly.

Holy Mother of God.......

So the morning found me disoriented, panting and disturbed with a cock that was ready to bat for the New York Yankees. Goddamn, that was a hell of a dream.

I sat up, rested my elbows on drawn up knees, shaky with the depth of want that coursed through my veins over this woman. Had she been here with me right this minute, I'd have pounced on her. No doubt about that. But the thing is.........

Were they memories or just weird dreams based on all the confusing shit I'd been dealing with lately? Not just the Charlotte parts, but all of it? I wasn't sure at all. And that was frustrating.

Maybe I should go see McGregor today and see if he could clarify a few of them? He might know something about the nightmare stuff.....possibly. And I figured he'd know about the chess thing, for sure. But he wouldn't, couldn't know about the handcuffs.

Hell no.

I wasn't asking him about that, I smirked. That was reserved for a conversation with Charlotte and I almost laughed aloud imaging how that would go down; the reaction on her face something to look forward to.

Jesus, I hoped that part was real. But if it was just wishful thinking on my part........well, damn - I had a really clear imagination. As the dream images flashed through my mind again, my dick throbbed to remind me of its' neglected, lonely state.

There was no way my erection was going anywhere without some help, so I got up out of bed and headed for the shower. Sleeping naked like I normally do meant that I could simply walk straight into the glass enclosure and get the water going nice and hot, the steam billowing around me as I wrapped a hand around my steel-hard length. The sensitive skin was hot and tight as I ran my thumb over the engorged crown, spreading the slickness already pearled there and letting every moment of the sexy dream replay in my head - in slow motion over and over - the all too brief vision of squeezing her tight nipples as I traced wet circles on her inner thigh with the point of my tongue; the beautiful arch of her body as she pulled against the handcuffs, silently demanding more. My breath accelerated, my hand pumping harder, stroking longer and imagination taking me further as I visualised her here in the shower with me - all wet hair and naked dewy skin, her hand squeezing tight instead of mine. Or better yet..... her full lips wrapped around my pulsing length, tongue swirling and licking as she took me in deep and slow, cheeks hollowing as she sucked hard. Oh God, yes.......... Heat and desire burning in the wanton eyes she would flick up at me, the green-gold scorchingly intense as she watched me take the pleasure.

Painful need twisted tighter and tighter, my belly quivering and blood rioting through my veins.....faster....harder.........until my body clenched and with a strangled moan I came hard, neck arching back as I spilled over, the release shivering over my hot skin.......damn.....so good....

Long moments later, however, as I came down from the blissful high, I felt an odd sense of....... emptiness? .....creep in - an indefinable sensation that curled in the pit of my gut like an oily snake. Unsettling and unwelcome. The memory of having her in my bed just a couple of days ago, real and connected, mixed with the vague images I'd had yesterday and with last nights' dream - all of it converging and melding into a giant ball of need and hollow want that had nothing to do with physical desire.

I wanted to say that the dreams were memories, but I couldn't be sure - I mean, dammit, I was sleeping! How the fuck would I know if they were memories or not? Growling impatiently, I went about the job of actually showering, all remnants of satiation completely obliterated.

That done, I dried off quickly, got dressed then picked up the clothes and underwear I'd left laying around the floor last night, tossing it all onto the still unmade bed to deal with later. Downstairs, I got the coffee going and grabbed some cereal, not patient enough to make anything more complicated than that.

I was restless as shit now. Edgy and moody, I wanted to go see Charlotte straight away, but fuck, I needed to give her SOME space. I thought of going to see Finn McGregor but it was still relatively early and I didn't know if he'd be at work or home or somewhere else. I mean, did he work? I didn't know anything at all about him or his routine.

Crap. I swirled the coffee in my mug, watching the black liquid and debating what to do.

I wasn't quite ready to face whatever I might find in researching the explosion I'd remembered - pretty sure that reading about my own supposed death would be quite confronting - but I needed to burn off this energy and without an official task to occupy my mind, there was nothing else that could really distract me from Charlotte.

So, after breakfast and cleaning up the kitchen, I got into my workout gear and began a rigorous couple hours of boxing, rowing, weights and free style martial arts, working my muscles hard until they shook from the strain and sweat was pouring in long rivers down my skin, soaking my black tank.

The physical exertion took the edge off my shitty mood and cleared the sluggishness from my mind enough so that as I cooled down afterwards with some bottled water, I decided it was time to get back to the research I'd begun yesterday.

And then........my "death".

Chapter Five

I sat back in my chair heavily, heart pounding wildly as every sinew and muscle I owned quivered, the shock reverberating to all extremities.

Jesus Christ.

Blinking slowly at the screen, my gut rolled over and cold washed over my body, a chill that dug deep into my marrow with icy claws and pebbled my skin. A part of me refused to take in the info I'd read twice already. Didn't want to take it in.

But it was there in black and white with a headline that screamed : 3 FDNY dead in TriBeCa Fire.

With a shaking hand, I reached out and scrolled back to the start of the article to read it a third time but that didn't make it any easier to comprehend. Scrubbing my hands over my face then reaching for the water bottle to quench a suddenly parch-dry throat, I stared at the laptop. I don't know why the impact of seeing my "death" reported in print was as great as it was - I'd known of it already. I'd recalled it in clear and painful detail. Yet somehow, it shook me still.

Maybe a part of me hadn't quite accepted it despite the memories? Hadn't absorbed the implications. Because.......shit, it was only last night I'd remembered and last night was packed full of distracting events so......yeah...... hadn't had the time to take it all in yet. That had to be the reason I now felt like I'd been kicked in the guts. Or maybe it was as simple as most people would freak the fuck out reading about their own death so why would I react any differently?

The New York Post report was dated mid April, just over five years ago, and described the scene of a huge fire and explosion that had engulfed a White Street residential complex resulting in hundreds of thousands of dollars worth of damage to the decades old building and the deaths of seven people including three firefighters - Firefighters Paul J. Adams and Mario Gonzales, 3rd and 2nd Class fighters respectively.

And Lieutenant Kellan O'Ryan - missing and presumed dead - his last known location right at the epicentre of an explosion that gutted the third floor.

I shuddered reflexively.

The other four victims were all believed to be residents - their identities not yet released to the public. Arson was highly probable according to the reporter who was full of praise for the fire department's prevention of an even greater disaster. I scowled at that - seven dead was a disaster.

Even when it was six.

My beast snarled, alert and defensive. But there was nothing to defend.

The article also contained a few graphic shots of the blaze; the Renaissance-Revival style condo so common to the TriBeCa area belching huge thick plumes of black smoke through its shattered windows, a massive orange-red inferno engulfing three of the five levels, long trails of flame shooting towards the grey sky. I enlarged the biggest picture to get a closer look, nausea returning as the visual evidence merged with my memory and amplified it's devastating impact. I wanted to hurl as the fake little girl's voice echoed through my mind, her cries for help a deadly mockery. The shock of discovery and the bomb's powerful detonation replayed in a loop and my hands balled into fists. Beast eyes flashed gold at the screen for a moment, my control dipping as I realised that I had full recall of my fire training. All of it. Every piece of equipment. Every tactic and skill. Acronyms, drills and muscle memory flooded my brain - the knowledge, the experience just suddenly....... there.

Shit.....

My pulse spiked high, jaw clenching tight as my composure was severely shaken.

Christ....My breath shook in a long exhale. I now knew that it was a damn miracle I'd survived that blast, knew all the technical reasons - the firefighter's reasons - why I shouldn't have. Two of my crew hadn't yet as my eyes traced over their names - Paul J. Adams and Mario Gonzales - nothing of them came to mind. No faces or voices. No memories of any kind and in a fit of pained temper, I shoved the laptop away from me and launched out of my chair to pace away, shaking and straining to hold back the beast who roared in fury. The laptop nearly slid right off the smooth surface of the table but stopped just in time.

Pacing like a caged animal, I muttered their names through clenched teeth over and over, desperate to push any tiny morsel of them out of my broken memory. But nothing shook loose and I felt sick at the thought that two guys who I'd presumably been friends with as well as work colleagues; two guys I'd trained with, shared a laugh with, a meal or a beer no doubt, men whose families I might even have known, who'd been under my command - died on duty and I couldn't even fucking remember their faces now. Not one thing about them, not any kind of grief or sorrow over their deaths - just nothing.

And that wasn't right.

Turning sharply, I stalked across to the east wall and slammed my fist hard into the exposed brick, beast strength smashing through the rustic uneven mortar and sending debris flying, the pulverised cement raining down on the hardwood floor. The pain that shot from my abused knuckles and up my arm was welcome - I wanted to feel it. Wanted it to hurt because goddamn, I should feel some sort of pain for their demise.

For a fleeting moment I relished in the agonising throb of cracked bones and swelling tendons but all too soon the beast DNA that warped my body began healing the shredded skin and knitting the bone back together, repairing easily the damage I'd inflicted.

Within moments, my hand was completely back to normal and I was beyond pissed - I should be writhing in fifteen levels of agony as penance for not remembering them. I was a monster, I knew .... but this was fucked up.

The guilt I felt over two faceless names sat like acid in my belly and I let go of the tethers with a snap, setting my beast free to roar loud and long in desperate release.

Head thrown back, my shoulders and arms clenched violently as veins protruded thick and blue; visible power quivering through the corded muscle as I let the fury and frustration scream forth in deep guttural howls until my throat was scraped raw.

It wasn't enough and a part of me wondered if anything ever would be.

Although it took major effort to rein the beast back in, I managed to do it before he trashed the place completely. As it was, I had to spend some time straightening tossed and flipped furniture and sweeping up the debris from a second dent in the wall, three inches up and over from the first, this one twice as big and wrecked.

I stood staring darkly at the ruined brickwork with my hands on my hips, annoyed and resigned to the fact that I'd have to get that fixed.

Someday.

Right now, I was in no mood.

Only a few days ago my sole purpose and focus had been on the mission -nothing and no one else. No distractions. No questions about who and what I was. Now, with the destructive force of a lightening strike, every thing I'd known was obliterated into dust and I had nothing but questions, the biggest being: what the hell had happened to me? How did I go from "dying" five years ago to working covert military missions? And despite the deeply instinctive and carnal attraction I felt for Charlotte, how did I really know that any of the visions I'd had of her, of our alleged relationship, were real? The dreams I'd had could easily be explained as the subconscious drooling of a man with a supreme hard-on for a beautiful woman. What if it was all a giant mind-fuck game she and Finn were playing? With props like the yearbook he'd shown me? He was a biochemist, for fuck's sake. Was I being mislead by them as well as by my own rampant hormones? I raked my fingers through my short hair, wanting to tear at it in frustration - it was like trying to put together a jigsaw when you only had half the pieces.

Beastie-boy gave a loud, annoyed snarl just then; a prodding reminder of his presence that seemed to say "snap out of it - I'm here."

Yeah right - as if I was ever likely to forget that, I thought with a sneer.

However, it was enough to pull me back from another spin-out.

He was right to be peeved at me - my beast instincts were infallible. I knew that. Should never have forgotten it. But I had - the Colossal Unknown that was my life messing up my cognitive reasoning processes, along with everything else.

I just needed to remember, to focus on the fact that no matter how wildly confusing this situation was or was likely to get, I had him to rely on - I could trust my inner animal. He wouldn't let me lose my mind.

I hope.

Much later, I sat with another black coffee, scanning through a couple of online articles on cases involving the 75th precinct; interesting enough but having nothing to do with my situation so I was able to calm down somewhat.

I'd read through as many articles on the TriBeCa fire as I could find, scavenging for every bit of information available and while it was reported that arson was to blame, no details of any suspects were given. Many interviews with survivors, witnesses and officials of all kinds, including statements from the Mayor, the Commissioner and the Fire Chief. The victims names were released and there'd been notifications of their funerals along with those of the fallen firemen. But no funeral notice for me. A memorial instead to honour my memory.

A weird sensation panged in my chest as I read those words - "memorial to honour the memory of Lieutenant Kellan D. O'Ryan" - not just because I was very much alive but how damn ironic that they honoured my memory when I had none.

The lame attempt at some levity had failed miserably and soured me from reading any further. I couldn't stomach any more and I'd switched to researching Charlotte again, purely for the distraction that thinking of her provided - and soon enough, the tension in my body eased and I breathed a little easier.

I don't know why or how she had the ability to ease my pressure but I'd take it - the morning's emotional revelations taking a heavy toll on my system that somehow she managed to relieve. A damn neat trick considering how much she also wound me up.

Unfortunately there had been nothing I hadn't already discovered in yesterday's research so after I'd lingered over the measly few pictures posted on social media accounts, I'd switched again, this time to police articles, looking for anything that might connect back to the TriBeCa fire and in particular, any mention of Ladder Co #22.

Engine Company No. 77, Ladder Company No. 22.

My firehouse.

The news reports had very kindly divulged that bit of info and although it would be easy to hunt up pictures of the fire station online, I'd held back. Later, I told myself, not quite ready to deal with another emotional slam.

The cell phone started to buzz, it's little blue light flashing and I looked over at it in surprise, not expecting to hear from the Commander this soon after last night's weirdness. I was tempted to just ignore it, really tempted but then the thought that it might be Detective Sex-Dream had me reconsidering and I quickly picked it up. However, her number wasn't showing and I scowled down at the screen.

Dammit.

I hesitated, not in the best state of mind to deal with his mysterious ass. Although........ if he had an assignment, that would be great because I was definitely in the mood to kick some ass so with a hard jab of my finger, I connected through to his cold digital voice.

"Yeah," I answered abruptly, not bothering with fake deference.

"O'Ryan" he said just as snappily. "What do you know about the police investigation into Tanaka's disappearance?"

Okay, that struck me as random - why would he think that I would know anything about their investigation? Unless he knew I'd been in contact with Charlotte?

Or suspected it and was just fishing? Then again, what exactly did the Commander know of her? A prickle of unease at the back of my neck had me tensing - something didn't feel right.

"Nothing," I answered in a casual tone.

"Should I know something?" I threw the question out there just to see if he'd pick it up.

Shouldn't he be the one to know about any police investigation, given he was higher up the authority chain than me? With contacts in other law enforcement fields, no doubt? And why describe Tanaka's situation as a "disappearance" when he knew well and good it was an assassination. Perpetrated on his orders. Why bother with the innocent phrasing?

Yeah, something was off.

"No," his voice was cool and detached, despite the distortion. "But when and if you do, you are to report it to me immediately." A beat of silence then, with condescension dripping heavily from each word: "do you understand?"

"Yes......Sir," I said, tacking on the salutation with blatant disdain and mentally adding Prick.

He was questioning my duty as a soldier to follow through on orders which was highly insulting yet...... A couple of days back, my obedience would have been absolute but now - not so much. Because that was exactly what I was planning, wasn't I ? To disobey orders and not give him any information about any investigation?

Yes, I was.

If it involved Charlotte, every instinct I had told me to stay quiet.

Pacing around the living area, I decided to push him a little, see where this led. "You're saying then that there's been a report that he's gone missing?" A direct question that he could only answer with a yes or no.

He did neither. "Unsubstantiated. There's no......."

"Do you know who's instigated the investigation? Which precinct is in charge?" I interrupted impatiently.

There was no reason to think it would be the 75th....logic said it would be a cop-shop closer to the crime scene or Tanaka's home.

As I'd expected, my insubordinate rudeness pushed him to lose his cool, but only for a moment as he barked down the line:

"You will watch your tone with me, Soldier!" His breathing went all Darth Vader-ish as he seethed and I could almost visualise him trying to pull back his fury. Could have if I'd known what his face looked like, I thought with a sneer.

I didn't answer, distracted as I was by a sudden wave of disorientation, a brief but intense sensation that brought me to a halt, mid pace. It raced through my system from head to toe - an odd feeling sort of like when an elevator stops roughly under your feet and shakes your balance. It went away as quickly as it had begun and I frowned at the weirdness of it all. What was that?

I had no time to linger on it though as the Commander's barely controlled voice pulled my attention back to him just then.

"You will be told when you need to be told and not any sooner," he said in scathing tones, the digital disguise doing nothing to cover his anger.

I didn't say a word. Interesting that up until last night the most I'd heard through the fake voice was icy arrogance or impatience but now he was easily triggered. Why? I didn't believe it was simple frustration that the mission hadn't gone as planned. Covert work usually involved some sort of adjustment and replanning so this anger was disproportionate to the situation. As was his over the top assholeness.

"The mess you made with Lewinski and Ridley has to be cleaned up now," he said and my brows snapped up high. Say what?? That I made? My beast growled at the accusation and I quit pacing again, lip curling in fury at the insulting inaccuracy. Where the hell did he get off trying to put that load on me? My blood sparked, eyes flashing gold as my hands clenched into fists.

"And that will take time," he continued. "Time that this mission can not afford to be wasting! Do you even realise the money and resources it takes to put together a mission such as this?" The abrasive tone was pitching louder with each gritted word.

What, now he thinks I'm an idiot?

My knuckles turned white with the effort of holding back my temper and I grabbed the beast's tethers as he began snarling.

"Of course you don't. But I do and I won't tolerate your incompetence, you hear? You are costing me a fortune! Remain on standby until your next assignment," he snapped and abruptly hung up.

I disconnected my phone and very carefully put it back on the dining table before I crushed it; the rage running through my body white hot. Incompetence?

Fuck you, asshole.

Fists against the charcoal table top, I leaned in with stiff arms, taking several deep breaths to calm down before I lost it yet again. That sonofabitch, I growled under my breath - the failure of last night's task was entirely the result of two absent targets and an arsonist. Lewinski and Ridley hadn't been verified as possible beasts because a goddamn bomb had gone off. It had absolutely nothing on me or my competence.

It took awhile before I cooled down enough to not be in danger of beasting out again but I couldn't contain the energy that burned like a live-wire through my blood. Feeling very much like a tiger in a cage, I stalked over to my boxing bag, punching hard a couple of times before settling into a fast but steady rhythm.

Over an hour later, my muscles trembled with strain and sweat poured off me as I started to wind it down finally - the unplanned second workout had provided much relief from the emotional upheaval of the morning. But now, as tendons and ligaments sang with exertion, I was exhausted physically and mentally. Even my beast was done in.

So, after a quick cool down and another bottle of water, I trudged upstairs for my second shower of the day, tossing my sweaty clothes in the corner to deal with later and walking naked through to the spacious shower. The hot water beating down on my overworked muscles was pure heaven.

Well.........almost.

Afterwards, I hitched a towel around my hips, shaved, brushed my teeth and then sat on my bed as an aching tiredness slammed into me. The lack of sleep last night collided heavily with over three hours of hard exercise and a long hot shower to totally wipe me out.

With a deep sigh I lay back on my unmade bed, intending to rest for ten minutes.

Maybe twenty.

Half an hour max.

I was out like a light in two seconds.

Chapter Six

I woke up slowly and blinked up at the high ceiling, feeling rested and relaxed but cold. Yawning, I realised that I still wore only a slightly damp towel and no covers which explained the chill. Stretching lazily, I noticed the time on the digital clock sitting on my side drawer - just after 1 pm and I was grateful the two hour snooze hadn't been plagued with nightmares. In fact, I could only recall one or two things: a vision of myself sitting fully clothed, winter jacket and all, on Charlotte's bedroom window sill, holding a cup of coffee in one hand while I watched her sleep in her bed. Which felt vaguely stalkerish and odd - why wasn't I in that bed with her?

The other one was more a collection of feelings and impressions than a dream vision - wind rushing at me, brisk and fresh, streets flashing by in seas of colour, red, blue and neon, my eyesight dark, then blank empty roads, white stripes flickering monotonously on the ground as I leaned into my flight, freedom and joy bursting through my chest as warmth and softness rested at my back. I flew everywhere but arrived nowhere.

I couldn't make much sense of that one but it left lingering traces of .... comfort? peace?...... I didn't know what exactly, only that it felt damn good and I wanted more of it.

But that first vision, I mused - watching her sleep seemed like a probable memory; something I'd surely have done with a girlfriend, right? Would have made more sense if I wasn't fully dressed but nevertheless, chances were high that is was another returned memory. Pity I hadn't dreamt some more of that handcuffed scene/possible memory of last night.

My mouth watered at the thought of what else might have occurred with those cuffs. I smirked up at the ceiling - yeah but I could live off the small recollection for quite a while. My beast growled in agreement as I licked my lips.

Hell yes, we could.

As the familiar tightening began in my groin, I knew I'd soon be taking care of another hard-on if I didn't quit this so I dragged my mind away from the delicious lady-cop and sat up.

It also occurred to me that I'd killed enough time indoors and needed to get out of here for awhile. Getting dressed in dark jeans, black v-necked tee and leather jacket, I headed downstairs to grab a quick lunch - turkey and avocado on rye - and made plans in my head. First I'd go past McGregor's place, see if he was home and maybe we could talk over a beer or something. He claimed to be my best friend so surely we'd done stuff like that? It was hard to imagine that the pretty boy geek and I had much in common at all - we seemed nothing alike - but he'd said we'd been friends forever, so there must be.

Time to find out something about that.

Afterwards, I'd go check on Charlotte; make sure she was alright. I'd have to find her, of course but I'd start with the precinct and if she wasn't there, well, I'd ....I'd call her. Just to check on her.

That's all, I told myself.

Yeah, right.

Despite having been there only once, I made my way to McGregor's easily enough but the warehouse apartment showed no signs of life when I got there. Knocking loudly had no response and when I tuned in my beast senses to pick up his scent or heartbeat, there was nothing. He wasn't here.

Dammit.

I scowled at the darkly panelled door, mighty peeved at this turn of events.

The closer I'd gotten to the building, the more I'd begun to anticipate this talk with McGregor - Finn - keen to get as much information as I could and quite prepared to interrogate him if need be. But he had to be here for any talk or interrogation to happen.

Moodily, I gave the front door one last thump before turning my back to its annoying barrier. Shoving my hands into my front pockets, I stood on the entrance step for a moment, watching the street and revising my plans. For a moment I was hugely tempted to break in and see what I could find, because dammit - I didn't owe McGregor any loyalty or respect for his premises. However, I couldn't shake the instinct that said it was wrong - it was one thing to break into a target's premises while on a mission, it was another thing entirely to wilfully invade the privacy of someone - like a common criminal.

I couldn't help but sneer at the word "common" and a middle-aged passerby gave me a wary double take as she walked past, hastening her steps a little.

Yeah, I was no common criminal but full humans still sensed the unexplainable menace in me and shield away. At least the smart ones did. So what did that say about Charlotte and Finn, I mused. That they weren't smart enough to be afraid of me?

Or that they had reason not to be?

My heart seemed to skip a beat at that thought; a feeling too close to hope slipping into my chest and squeezing and I rolled my shoulders uncomfortably, frowning at the ridiculous idea.

Hope?

Hope for what exactly? That there were some redeeming qualities lurking in my murderous beast/human DNA? Yeah right, I dismissed with scorn - that was complete foolishness. And I'd be a prize fool to think anything different.

Shaking off the lingering twinge in my chest, I stepped out of the arched entrance and turned east. With no idea of Finn's whereabouts, his habits or routine and with no patience to track him, I headed downtown to the 75th instead, telling myself it wouldn't take long to check on Charlotte. Just a quick minute, make sure she was okay and then I'd leave, give her that space I'd said I would.

Yeah, easy plan.

However, as I got within a block, I felt the beginnings of that pull; a gradual awareness that slid into my veins smoothly, telling me she was near. And the closer I came to her building, the stronger it got - distinct, beguiling and inevitable. The lure of her scent had my beast sniffing the air, inhaling her perfume like the drug that it was and getting high on its tantalising richness. I smirked at him - he was hopeless.

Directly opposite the precinct stood a tall sandstone building housing several different businesses that had a nice open lobby with lots of people coming and going.

Perfect. No better place to disappear than in a crowd.

Stepping through its gilded glass front doors, I walked oh so casually through the entrance to the service stairwell, then blurred up to the rooftop six levels above. An overcast day with a sharp bite to the breeze, it was much cooler up here than on the street but the chill didn't bother me as I went to the edge and leaned on the safety wall, resting my palms on the cold concrete and looking down directly into the offices of the 75th precinct. A four story, multi windowed dark brick building, the lower height gave me a great angle and although I couldn't sight her anywhere yet, I knew her general whereabouts, her heartbeat and scent pinpointing her to the second floor. Settling in to wait, I scanned through the entire building, taking note of all that was visible through the encased windows and paying particular attention to the human activity - cops and perps alike spread throughout the four floors, locked in the holding cells or cuffed to desks as they were questioned. Uniformed and plain clothed detectives milling around looking busy doing God knows what. Good guys and bad guys - an age old battle and one where it wasn't always obvious which was which.

A good half hour later Charlotte finally came into view and I almost smiled. Ignoring the sudden jolt in my pulse, I watched as she walked and talked with the tall female cop I'd seen her with at the gallery; her partner J.C - another person I'm meant to know but like so many other things right now, a mystery to me.

They crossed a large open area and sat down at desks facing each other, continuing their conversation as Charlotte picked up a file and rifled through it.

I wondered what case she was working on. Although I could tune in with beast senses and listen to them if I wanted to, I was content for the moment to just watch over her. She seemed to be perfectly okay: no visible side effects from yesterday's explosive drama. That didn't really surprise me though - you don't get to be a detective with New York's finest unless you were tough, smart and resilient.

I was suddenly struck by a surge of déjà vu - a huge wave of it flooding my senses uncomfortably and my shoulders twitched in reaction.

What the hell?

Straightening up, I stuck my hands into my jacket pockets, brows drawn fiercely together and damn disturbed by the unsettling sensation. How can I have déjà vu when I barely have memories? That made no sense at all.

Yet that's exactly what I was feeling right now - a sense of familiarity so strong and intense that a heated shiver prickled between my shoulder blades. My eyes flashed golden for a moment as I focused intently on Charlotte across the road. I must have stood on this rooftop before, I decided. Or one exactly like it somewhere else. And if it was this particular rooftop, it didn't take a genius to figure out the reason why. Question was - had I been stalking her or protecting her?

Another little mystery to add to the growing pile of them, I thought with a sarcastic twist to my mouth. Just what I needed.

With a disgruntled sigh, I refocused on the here and now, noting that Charlotte was now staring with great seriousness at something on her computer screen, her booted foot tapping the air over her crossed legs.
She was okay. Perfectly fine, in fact. And now that I had done what I came here for, I could leave.

Yeah.

I could.

I really should.

I took out my cell phone instead, punching in her number and watching as a hundred and twenty feet away, across the other side of the street, she reached for her own phone, sitting there by the keyboard.

Intent as she was on her screen, she answered without looking at the caller ID so when her voice came through the line with a distracted "Alistair" and I replied with a simple "hi" I was able to catch every nuance of her unguarded reaction.

Her eyes widened, her pupils dilated and her heart rate jumped excitedly, the screen completely forgotten as she sat up a little straighter.

I smiled.

"Kellan," she said, surprise and a breathy huskiness to her voice.

"Yeah" I said, enjoying the frazzled beat of her pulse. I gotta admit - I liked this reaction from her. A lot.

"Is everything ok? Are you ok?" she asked, switching gears and startling me with her concern. Just like at her window last night, this was the first thing she asked about - whether I'm okay?

Amazing.

My heart did its weird thumping thing, practically knocking on my ribs.

"Everything's okay," I told her in a raspy voice. "I just wanted to make sure that you were okay, after what happened yesterday?" This was true. She just didn't need to know that I was over the road, literally watching.

"I'm fine" she said softly, a little smile tugging at her lips. She seemed pleased about something.

"Good. Listen, uh......." I searched for the right words. "Charlotte, can we talk? We really need to......."

"Kellan," she cut in and I saw the frown that furrowed her smooth brow.

"......just talk, Charlotte," I said.

"Kellan, I don't want to get into another heavy discussion like we did yesterday," she said. "Especially while I'm at work."

"Not now. I mean, over a coffee or something,"

Yes, great idea, man. "A beer, wine, whatever you want."

I hesitated a moment before blurting out truthfully: "Yesterday was pretty intense and I......I'd really like to just sit and talk. Nothing heavy, I promise."

Silence on her end. Bated breath on mine.

"Charlotte ....it's coffee. A beer. Casual stuff - just hanging out, nothing more," I said quietly, willing her to say yes.

Indecision obvious in her nervous fidgeting, she ran one hand through her long hair, bit her lip, leaned forward, picked up a pen only to put it back down, then sighed as she leaned back again.

"Okay, fine. Just drinks," she said in a rush, like she had to get the words out before she changed her mind.

My beast wanted to howl in victory. Or maybe that was me.

"Great. How about I pick you up around...." I started to say but she interrupted abruptly.

"No! I'll meet you. Casual, remember? Just hanging out. No picking me up at my door." She was adamant.

Dammit. Why was that such a bad thing?

"Okay, then...." I said, thinking quickly. "How about this - there's this little coffee place about a block from your apartment that I noticed the other day......"

"Murphy's?"

"Yeah, that one. I'll meet you. 8 o'clock okay with you?" I asked, taking a guess that she'd be off duty by then. If not, then whatever time she wanted.

"Sure, I'll see you there. Bye," she said hurriedly and disconnected before I could reply. Startled at her hastiness I watched as she stuck her elbows on the desk and dropped her face into her hands for a moment.

Her partner J.C, sitting at her own desk taking a call on the station phone, covered the mouthpiece and whisper-yelled "what?" but Charlotte just shook her head and mouthed "later." Then, sweeping her hair back from her forehead, she sighed and turned back to her screen with a determined twist to the set of her lips, her heartbeat still fluttering madly.

Fascinating.

I snorted smugly - seems that I'd rattled Detective Alistair's composure.

I liked that too.

A lot.

Pocketing my cell with a small smile, I lingered for a moment longer but just as her pulse settled and I turned to leave, it suddenly skyrocketed and I swung back to see a tall guy in a charcoal grey suit stopped by Charlotte's desk. Possibly Latino, he was dark skinned with slicked back black hair and he stood with his hands in his pockets, hip cocked and an aura of arrogant darkness around him.

Immediately my hackles rose, beast snapping to attention as my senses sharpened, eyes flashing golden again before I could reign it in.

Shit. What was this? Who was this guy?

I quickly zeroed in to their conversation and something about his tone, his words grated on my nerves. Although simply discussing the progress of a burglary case, he spoke with contemptuous superiority; self importance dripping from every smarmy pore. He stood too close to Charlotte, crowding her personal space and I wanted to rip his throat out.

Charlotte's heart was pounding, her tension palpable. She was keeping her professional demeanour, cool and outwardly calm but I could feel the recoil in her. Her defences were up and if she'd had hackles, I swear I would have seen them rising, just like a she-wolf. She didn't like this guy. Neither did I - everything about him had my animal on edge, keenly alert.

He smelled wrong.

The instinctive need to protect her had me working hard to keep my beast at bay. Hands clenched into tight fists, my nostrils flared and a low snarl rumbled in my chest as I resisted the urge to charge into the building and rip his chest open. That wouldn't be a smart move in a room full of cops and I'm pretty sure Charlotte would be very pissed at me.

And then it hit me - the reason my senses were haywire.

He smelled wrong because he smelled of predator. Not the animal kind however - he wasn't a beast like me but he was a predator nonetheless. He stank of it.

Did Charlotte know this or did she just sense it about him? The partner - she too had a wary vibe as she watched them carefully from across the two desks. My jaw clenched with the effort of staying calm.

Just who the hell was this prick? The boss Charlotte didn't like? What was his name.....Sanchez? Santos?

No.

Suarez. That was it. That was the name I'd heard at Finn's apartment the other day - it had to be him. Which meant that Charlotte worked with and for a guy that instinct and beast told me was as much of a hunter as I was. But a hunter of what? You can bet your ass it was something more than bad guys.

I needed to find out what and........deal with him.

He walked away just then and I focused on tracking his movements through the building for a long while. I watched and I waited till I saw him exit the front entrance and get into a chauffeured town car parked at the kerb, a late model navy blue Lincoln Continental that I quickly memorised the license plate of.

With a final check of Charlotte's whereabouts - she was in an small room that held a single table and four chairs, going over some files - I left the rooftop and made my way through the crowded streets back to the studio.

I had more research to do.

Chapter Seven

At 7.50pm that night, I sat on a tall timber bar stool, sipping a beer and patiently waiting for Charlotte . I'd decided to sit here in the back where the pool table was, rather than in the front coffee/dining area as there were less people and therefore less noise. I wasn't worried about not seeing her walk in - between my beast and I, we'd know when she was here, sight unseen.

I'd spent the rest of the afternoon hunting down information on the Suarez. Seems that he was Peruvian born, orphaned and adopted to American parents when just a little kid. Normal life growing up, school, college etc, nothing unusual. He'd worked in the DC area before transferring to the New York offices about eight months ago.

I'd dug up some articles about his previous work in various cases, both here and in DC and although they hadn't revealed anything sketchy, I hadn't expected them to - anything worth knowing wasn't likely to be glaringly obvious and splashed across newspapers. No. It would take a lot more digging than this and I was quite prepared to spend whatever time was needed to figure out who and what this dude was. Especially once I'd come across a close-up picture of him, one that showed him facing forward and I'd looked at his eyes. Something cold and calculating lurked there - hidden but not well enough. I'd wondered if part of the reason I'd reacted with so much instant animosity was more than simply my beast instinct; maybe I already knew why I hated this guy, somewhere in my damaged memory? Seemed feasible.

I'd also thought about going past Finn's again before meeting up with Charlotte, on the chance that he'd be there this time. But I'd gotten so caught up researching Suarez that I'd run out of time.

After showering and changing into fresh clothes, I'd headed out, deciding to walk the distance and clear my head a little. There'd been no further contact as yet from the Commander and I hoped it stayed that way. At least for a few more hours of peace.

So now here I was, waiting for the delectable detective to arrive and feeling a little nervous about it.

Why, I don't really know.

Maybe it was because she seemed to have so much power over my beast - he responded to her so viscerally; like a wolf to its' mate. Or maybe it was just that she turned me on so hard - blazing inferno level hard. Me - the man.

Or maybe it was both?

I shifted uncomfortably at that thought: the idea that both sides of my being could be equally vulnerable to her allure was very unsettling. But......I must have somehow dealt with that issue to have been in a relationship with her, right?

Just then, a tingle slithered over my skin; a deep awareness that was innate and instinctual coming over me just before the sweet and spicy scent that was Charlotte's personal aroma assaulted my senses. My beast shivered in delight.

I got up and walked through the bar - she was smoothly weaving her way between the crowded tables of the cafe area and we met halfway, under the arch that seperated the two rooms. She'd changed her clothes; now wearing different jeans and a skintight dark grey top with a rounded neckline underneath a maroon leather jacket. Her top hugged her curves like a race car on a winding track - close and dangerously tight. Long hair flowed down her back, shiny and thick and her face tilted up to meet my eyes as we stopped within a foot of each other, her green gold eyes sparkling exotically at me, lips slicked with something shiny that I immediately wanted to lick off.

Very slowly.

If she was going for a 'casual just hanging out' look - she'd misjudged badly because she looked sexy as hell to me.

God only knows what would happen when she tried for a seductive look. I'd probably combust. As it was, my inner animal was salivating. Down, boy.

"Hey," I said with a scratchy voice.

"Hi," she replied and we stood there for a silent moment just staring at each other, the magnetic pull between us palpable.

"So, uh, do you wanna sit in the cafe or back here in the games area?" I asked her.

"The games area is fine," she answered and I turned and indicated for her to lead the way. She did and I had to snap my tethers tight as she passed by me, her proximity sending waves of delirium over my beast.

Man, I needed more control around this woman - much more. But my eyes immediately fell to her ass and Jesus, those jeans had no respect for my sanity, cupping her cheeks with loving attention and snickering at my helpless lust. It was worse now that I knew exactly what that ass looked like, FELT like. My beast growled in want, palms itching to touch while I followed her gently swaying hips to wherever she lead.

She stopped at a small round table and I snapped back to myself and pulled a chair out for her. Then, after asking for her preference, I took myself off to the bar for whisky and wine, using the time away to calm my heart rate. Hers was also thudding heavily and something about the beat was incredibly intoxicating to me. I realised that I would have to deaden my senses to her if I wanted to survive the night. So with gritty determination, I shut it down and shut it off before taking the drinks the bartender guy handed to me with a wide smile and returning to Charlotte. Placing her wine in front of her, I took my seat opposite her.

"Thanks," she said, picking up her drink and giving me a small smile.

"You're welcome" I replied, doing the same and we both drank, watching each other over the rims of our glasses.

The silence was thick, but somehow not awkward. More like......hesitant.

"So, how was your day?" I asked, looking for a way to start the conversation.

This seemed safe - generic small talk between two normal people, even if one of us wasn't.

"It was busy," she answered, a little laugh sparking in her eyes at the lameness of my question.

"Working on anything in particular?"

"Ahhh....." She hesitated, uncomfortable.

"No specifics, Charlotte. Just regular chat like any other two people," I reassured her quietly.

Her eyes searched mine as she considered my words.

"An arson case, possibly a serial offender," she said eventually.

"Uh huh," I muttered, wanting to ask more about it but not willing to push her too far. I was actually genuinely interested in her work despite it being a touchy subject for us.

"Can I ask how your day was? Or is that encroaching into the no-go zone?" She asked, her voice tinged with mild sarcasm and playful challenge as she tilted her head, the overhead lights catching on her dark hair. I wanted to run my fingers through its thick lushness.

"Considering I didn't work today, it's all good," I told her with a smirk and she saw the humour in that, her dimple flashing as her lips twisted in a half-smile. Funny that we both had dimples, I mused, wondering if mine charmed her the way hers did me.

"Charlotte," I switched back to a serious tone. "You can ask me anything you want and I'll answer what I can. If I can." Eyes hooked into hers, I willed her to see my sincerity.

"And that would be a very one-sided conversation since you can't tell me much of anything."

"Not necessarily," I denied. It wouldn't be an easy conversation but it wouldn't be one sided either, I was sure. She quirked a silky eyebrow at me, however; disbelieving. "Besides," I continued. "We don't have to talk about work stuff at all.

We can talk about plenty of other things."

"Like.......?" She took a sip of her wine, lips pouted against the rim and I wanted to be that glass.

"Like favourite football teams, favourite food ....and any other favourites you wanna mention," I said in a cool voice while inside my mind I was thinking: favourite places to be touched....favourite ways to be kissed......favourite positions.... the list was endless.

Good thing she couldn't read minds, I thought, suppressing a smirk but then immediately wondering what her reaction would be if she could - angry or turned on?

Either way, my blood heated another degree.

Silence stretched out between us as she considered my statement. I watched as she shifted restlessly in her seat before leaning forward and wrapping her hands around her glass.

"This is weird," she said quietly, looking down at her hands for a moment then back up, pretty green gold eyes glinting under long black lashes. She was unsettled and edgy in a way I'd never seen her.

"What is?"

"This," she repeated, as if I should already know. "Sitting here, out in public, in a bar....."

"Why is that weird?"

"We.......Uhhh.....never went out in public," she said after a pause. "At least, not in the usual way."

Huh?

"Never? That can't be right." I frowned darkly at her. And what did she mean by "the usual way"?

"It's right."

"Restaurants? Dinner? Movies?" Something, surely?

"No," she insisted.

"You're telling me that I was a such a loser boyfriend that I didn't take you anywhere?" I challenged her. What about that lake?

"No, it wasn't like that. There were a couple of places we could go but not things like the movies or restaurants. Not locally," she explained with a slight shrug of one shoulder. "You would have but you couldn't."

And that still made no sense to me

"Couldn't?" Why not? I was doing it right now, wasn't I ?

"Yes. Because of.......you know......what you are." She said this in a near whisper, mindful of the other bar folk. "You would never have taken that risk before." The barest hint of censure slid through her tone and that too made no sense. What risk? Of not being able to hold back the beast?

"So you're saying I hibernated out of fear of losing control? Yet I'm somehow perfectly fine being in public now." There was no mistaking the scepticism in my voice. I mean, really? Scared of losing control? That didn't sound like me at all. BeastieBoy might be a tough sonofabitch to hold back sometimes but I had a good grip on him.

"Are you?" Her head tilted questioningly. "We don't know that. Not for sure. You have no memory and I don't know what your triggers are anymore. What might make you....." She rolled her hand in a kind of "you know" gesture. I did know but I wanted her to say it.

"Make me what?" I was beginning to sound like a damn parrot, repeating everything she said.

"Lose it," she said in a fierce whisper. "Look, can we not talk about this here, around all these people?"

The direct way she met my eyes said this was clearly a rhetorical question - we weren't discussing this here and that's that. My mouth quirked in appreciation.

"You're right," I agreed. "Not here and now. And we did say no heavy stuff."

The smallest sliver of whiskey-brown rimmed her pupils before bursting into a golden yellow and mixing with the green of her fascinating cats eyes; barely noticeable unless you were really looking.

And I was.

She tilted her glass at me in a little salute before taking a sip, watching me watch her.

"So," I began, "how long did you put up with my crap boyfriend skills?" A part of me wanted to think that she wouldn't have tolerated what sounded like truly lame behaviour from me for long because, hell.......why should she? But another part of me wanted to believe that she'd stuck by me despite that. "How long were we together?"

A soft smile hovered around her lips and she reached up to tuck her hair behind one ear before answering. "We met just under a year ago now, through a case I was working on at the time that lead me to you and Finn."

Okay, that was interesting - something I'd definitely have to get back to later. But right now I really wanted to know about "us." I'd apparently been gone for three months out of that year so........

"And in a relationship?" My eyes held hers, entranced as always with the secrets lingering there. Didn't someone once say that the eyes were the windows to the soul? If that was true, her soul was hidden behind a sheer curtain - tangible but indistinct. A self protective measure I could fully understand.

I took a drink of my scotch and nearly spat it back out on a choke as she said:

"We...uhhhh....got together about five, six months later."

What?

It took me six months to get her in my bed?? What the hell was wrong with me?

"Was there something wrong with me?" I had to know.

She laughed, a rich husky sound that rolled over my skin smoothly, obviously amused at the dumbfounded look on my face. But seriously - six months? What took so long? And if it wasn't for her dimples flashing at me, I'm sure I would've been offended by her laughter. As it was, my beast was really starting to fall for her dimples.

"No, nothing wrong with you," she said with a smile. "Just a million complications and reasons why we shouldn't get involved."

Ahhhh, okay.

That was acceptable. And probably quite normal given what I was. Still...... six months seemed a hell of a long time to wait when the attraction was this intense. And I had no doubt it would have been as hot then as it is now.

I sat forward, resting my elbows on the table and wrapping my hands loosely around my glass, a mirror image to her. My beast shivered at the closeness of her heady aroma, fingers tingling with the need to touch her, just for a moment.

"Yeah, okay, that may be so," I acknowledged with a nod, "but obviously we didn't let that stop us."

"No, we didn't but only after you'd tried everything you could to prevent it," she replied with a wry twist to her lips.

"What?" Did I hear that right?

"You kept trying to push me away."

Which means I was an idiot as well as slow. "I'm not sure if I like the sound of this," I grumbled with a scowl, not impressed with myself.

The corners of her mouth twitched as she held back a grin, green gold eyes dancing disarmingly.

"We have a complicated history, Kellan," she said, ruefully. "One that isn't easy to explain. Believe me, I've tried and it comes off sounding like some ridiculous fairytale turned nightmare."

I quirked one eyebrow at her, surprised at the fanciful description.

"Trying to explain it to you when you can't remember it is too.....uhh...." She frowned at the table as she searched for the right words, the frustration visible in her pressed lips. "It's like a minefield."

I waited patiently till her eyes returned to mine.

"I wanna remember you, Charlotte" I told her, deeply serious. "I do. More than anything."

Chapter Eight

My words hung heavy in the air as she weighed them, searching my face and blinking up at me slowly.

"I believe you," she said in a soft voice after some moments, lips lifting in a gentle smile.

My heart knocked hard at my rib cage in relief before turning over in a roll. I could only imagine how intense my feelings for this woman must have been when I could remember her - if this is how it was when I couldn't.

And that just about blew my mind.

"Those memories I had of you yesterday? I think they set off some kind of reaction," I said, taking another swallow of my scotch.

"How do you mean?" She asked, head tilted in curiosity.

"Last night I dreamt a bunch of stuff, weird random stuff, " I began, so glad that we could talk about this. "Only........ I don't really know if they were just random or if they were......more memories, you know? You were in some of them and there was one with McGregor so........"

"Finn?" She exclaimed, eyes widening a little in excitement.

"Yeah, Finn......." Which reminded me.........."By the way, does he work?"

"Yes. Why?"

"I went by his house before I called you and he wasn't there. So I wondered if he was at work or something. I was gonna see if he could explain some of the things I dreamt."

For some reason, this statement made her eyes smile; the pretty green gold sparkling softly, luminously; a look of pleasure and approval twinkling in their depths. Warmth spread through my chest even as it did it's weird thumping thing again. I don't know why it made her look at me that way but, damn - it felt nice.

"Try me," she offered. "What did you dream? Maybe I can explain some of it."

My pulse jumped sky high as I imagined her trying to explain the more scandalous parts of my dreams - either she'd destroy my hopes that we'd fooled around with handcuffs or she'd completely kill me with the confirmation that we had.

Hot damn......

I couldn't decide which would be worse.

My beast was practically drooling now and I gulped some more scotch hastily, bringing to mind the visions I'd had of Finn and that doused most of the flame. No offence to him.

"Nothing much really......" I stopped to clear the gravel from my throat. "Just that we were playing chess and I won. He looked annoyed." I couldn't help smirking a little.

Charlotte gave a little gasp, her soft lips falling apart, eyes wide.

"And we weren't at his joint or mine but in some other place; I think it was another apartment but I'm not sure."

"Kellan," she said on an exhale, "that's not some random image. You and Finn used to play chess a lot."

My heart thudded.

"We did?"

"Yes, you did!"

She smiled at me with so much warmth, it was like I'd stepped into the sun.

"And that other place," she continued excitedly, "must be your place. Where you lived, not that studio you took me to."

Wait - the other day, when I'd had her in my bed, she'd mentioned that she'd never been there before and I'd been so distracted with her and my suspicions that it hadn't occurred to me to ask her where she thought I lived. Was this what I'd seen in the dream? My actual home?

I felt cautious hope curling through my gut and I tried to rein it in but...... if I was seeing stuff like this in my dreams - that meant progress, right? It also meant chances were very high that everything I dreamt was true. Or at least a good portion. Subconscious memories manifesting as dreams? Yeah, absolutely feasible.

I needed to see this apartment.

"Where is this place?" I asked her.

"At Finn's," she said, her answer a complete surprise. Finn's? Really? "You live in the basement level. Lived," she corrected, her slim fingers clutching her drink like an anchor and I understood the need to hold tight to something.

Eyes locked to hers, I willed myself to stay calm and cool. But my heart pounded heavily, echoing dully through my entire body with every beat.

"So you think that was a memory?" My voice was smooth as sandpaper.

"Yes!" She exclaimed. "It has to be. You also said something at my window last night about a river....a lake that you saw in a vision? We'd sometimes go upstate to this cabin......maybe that's what you're remembering?" Intense gentleness in every facet of her expression, she held my gaze steadily, my own personal anchor.

I blew out a pent up breath, body vibrating with nervous tension. Okay, that too was feasible - cabins usually sat on lakes.

"What else did you dream?" she asked eagerly.

"Ahhh......well......" I hesitated, unsure for a moment how much to reveal of my nightmare but then deciding that there wasn't much point in holding back. "There was this huge white room that was totally empty except for a steel cage in the middle and I was locked in that cage. All white, no windows, one door. And it felt like I was being watched."

She didn't say anything, her only reaction a widening of her eyes but I could feel the concern emanating from her. And so I told her more.

"There was another one where it was pitch black dark; I think it was some sort of cage too, I'm not entirely sure, but it felt like I was trapped and the ground kept moving under me. I was sort of fading in and out of consciousness, like I was sick or something," I said, purposely watering down the disturbing dread of that dream. "Then, I was being chased through some tunnel only I couldn't see who was doing the chasing. But, I figure everyone has those types of dreams so they probably don't mean anything."

Being chased, falling, drowning......all common bad dream scenarios so...... yeah, just subconscious ramblings.

At least, I hoped they were.

Charlotte's bottom lip trembled and she blinked dazedly at me, still silent.   A little fearful of how overwhelmed she looked right now, I hurried to distract her.

"Did you ever have some weird stuff painted around your eyes?" I asked and her lashes fluttered in confusion at the sudden question.

"Painted?"

"Yeah, it looked sorta like a mask but I couldn't tell for sure. It was all black and swirly and you were wearing some fancy dress, I think. A black one," I said and a look of amazement crossed her face.

"Midnight blue," she said in a shaky whisper.

"What?" Now I was confused.

"It was a midnight blue gown. Not black," she explained and something twisted painfully in my chest as the air between us filled with overwhelming emotion - hope, cautious excitement and despair at the realisation that this too was a memory. Christ........were all of them true?

Her beautiful eyes welled up, glistening brightly and I wanted to kick myself for upsetting her.

"Don't cry, Charlotte," I said in a rough voice, her tears clogging up my throat.

"I'm not," she denied even as she blinked rapidly in an effort to prevent them falling. "I'm just a little emotional - you seem to be getting more and more memories. And that's wonderful." Her smile was tremulous and soft.

"Yes and no," I said. "I'm getting flashes. But....... I have no way of knowing how long it'll take before it's all back. Or....if I even get it all back." And that was a very real possibility - what if these snatches of memory were all I ever got? If my mind remained this disjointed? As much as that thought was horrifying, the thing that really curdled my gut was this - every vision or dream confirmed as a memory meant that my current reality was falling to pieces, bit by bit.

What happened when there were no more pieces?

I shuddered.

How did I then explain my existence? What I'd become - and how I'd become - a trained assassin for the government?

Pressure squeezed like a vice across my chest, bruising and pinching, my mouth grimacing in discomfort. No, not dwelling on that tonight, I told myself, gritting my teeth against the rising sense of disconnect. I shoved it aside ruthlessly. Tonight, goddammit, I just wanted to enjoy my time with the beautiful woman in front of me; connect with her and maybe even relax awhile, for once.

"So I'll take what I can get for now and hope for more," I said and she nodded in understanding; acceptance in the curl of her lip.

I tipped my glass at her in a small salute before taking a drink, the scotch easing a little of the tension that had been rebuilding in my shoulders. If God was in a good mood, then maybe all the jagged pieces would slide into place and every memory would steamroll through my head, completing the picture of who I am.

But I wouldn't bet on it.

My gaze turned speculative as a thought occurred and I leaned back in my chair, legs sprawled, hand wrapped around my glass and head tilted slightly. "If we never went anywhere, then how am I remembering this fancy dress occasion?"

Vague whispers of suspicion were floating on the edges of my mind but they had no depth or traction, unable to grip effectively. Something had definitely shifted, I realised - the inconsistencies weren't an automatic alarm bell in my mind anymore. Instead, they were simply new jigsaw puzzle pieces that needed placement.

"That was a masquerade fundraiser," she explained with a little huff of amusement. "A political shindig for the Governor. You used to help me with my cases sometimes and I was there tracking a suspect. So you decided that with a mask of your own it was safe to be there with me, all decked out in our finery."

I quirked a brow at her in surprise. "I was working a case with you?"

"Yes."

Huh.

"Did we solve it?" I asked.

"Yes, we caught the bad guy." Her smile was wide and I blinked at its bright warmth.

So, in my previous life, I helped the good guys but now I'm killing on order? The two were so completely opposite to each other, I may as well have been Jekyll and Hyde. Come to think of it, given my internal beast - I wasn't far from that. But shit - how did any of this fit with the memories I was just beginning to scavenge? I frowned down at my scotch as my gut rolled over slowly.

I wasn't the same guy that Charlotte described - a firefighter boyfriend who sometimes helped her solve cases. Fuck - what the hell happened to that guy? I was as far removed from the good side as could be.

Flicking my eyes back to meet her soft gaze, I took a calming breath and raised my glass in a salute. "Well, good for us." She reciprocated and we each took a drink, the scotch burning welcomingly down my throat.

"Maybe it won't take long for all your memories to come back, now that some of them are surfacing," she said as hope sat heavily between us, overwhelmingly fragile.

Needing a moment, I noticed that her drink was running low so I caught the bartender's eye and raised my hand to him, signalling for two more and with a nod, he went about filling the order.

Turning back to Charlotte, I could see she was regrouping, resettling herself much like I was trying to do.

"You know, it seems to me that when we were dancing at the Bellingworth Gallery, something about that brought on those first memories of you," I said in a thoughtful tone. She looked at me with curiosity, unsure where I was heading with this. "Just like holding the fire extinguisher triggered memories of working with the fire department. And then later on when I kissed you at your window, I had more memories come through that night."

The waitress interrupted at that moment with our drinks, and I paid her quickly, telling her to keep the change so she'd leave that much faster.
As soon as she did, I looked at Charlotte, a little smirk escaping as I told her: "Seems I've figured out the way to get my full memory back."

"Really?" She frowned. "How?"

Lost in her fascinating eyes as usual, I said in all sincerity: "I have to keep touching you."

After all, it did seem to work like magic, didn't it? Made sense to me.

Giving me a coolly amused look, she quipped: "If that were true, then you should have had all your memories come back when we slept together."

Dammit - she was right about that.

"Yeah, okay......that's true," I acknowledged. "We did a helluva lot of touching then. And there was no sleep involved." I couldn't help teasing her a little with that line and she raised one brow snappily, in a kind of "touché". Nevertheless, she returned my amused smirk with one of her own, her softly slicked lips tilted enticingly. With her long lashes casting shadows on her high cheekbones, dark hair flowing loose and cats eyes gleaming that unique stunning colour, she held my beast enthralled and I wasn't much better.

"No, seriously," I went on. "I don't know why they didn't come back then. But it seems that once the crack was made with the firefighter memories, then the others started to slip through. And each one was after I touched you in some way." The gravel in my voice worsened with that last sentence.

She didn't say anything to that, just looked at me impassively but her elevated heart rate was loud and clear. Her body heat rose, heightening her aroma and my beast groaned. She'd never be able to hide her physical reaction to me, no matter how much she might deny or dismiss it verbally. Or ignore it, like she was doing now.

I'd always know.

"Casual, remember?" Her words were insistent but the underlying tremor in her tone betrayed how off balance she felt.

"You want me to casually touch you?" Okay.

Reaching over to the hand that rested palm down on the timber table, I ran one fingertip very gently, very lightly from the top of her wrist down slowly over her ring finger and sliding off the smooth shiny nail, watching the shivers race over her soft skin. Her hands were so delicate looking; small and feminine, yet she handled guns, bad guys and kickboxed....such a contrast.

Looking back up at her from under my lashes, I caught the flush that infused her cheeks, the nervous swallow as she tried to control her reaction to my touch.

"Like this?" I asked, holding her gaze intently.

Not giving her a chance to answer, I then reached out and slid my fingers over her cheek, her flushed skin burning against mine, tracing her jawline with my fingertips while my thumb slid to her bottom lip. "Or like this?"

Heat flared in her eyes, her heart rate colliding with mine and internally, he growled long and low in want. Hazel into green gold - clinging. Throbbing. Intense.

"Stop it," she demanded huskily in complete contradiction with what her eyes said.

"Something tells me things could never be casual with you and me, ever........" I told her in a dark rumble. This I knew unequivocally - the feelings she inspired in me were too raw, too extreme to ever be mistaken for casual.

I watched my thumb take a slow swipe, collecting a tiny bit of the sticky gloss before bringing it to my own mouth and wiping the taste of her onto my lip, keeping her there. She followed the movement closely, pupils dilating, darkening and I heard her heart thump hard as her pulse skyrocketed. My beast began snarling and straining as my blood heated, pressure building in my groin.

Damn.....I shouldn't have done that.

Hunger simmered and with great control, I held back from licking the spot, anchoring myself on the dazed look across her face. A look that should have made things worse but somehow didn't.

She broke eye contract first; glancing away with fluttery lashes to regroup while I took my own calming breath.

"You're right," she finally said. "They never were before and they won't be now."

I had no doubt.

"They aren't now," she added quietly. The words went unspoken but I understood her - let go of the subject and give us some breathing space from the overwhelming intensity.

She was right - we needed to lighten this up.

"And we did say just hanging out, didn't we?" I gave her a mild look as an idea snuck into my brain. "Okay, let's play pool."

"Pool?" She repeated, taken aback.

"Yeah, pool. You know........billiards," I said, indicating with a nod of my head the pool table over behind her left shoulder. "Didn't we ever play it before?"

"Well, actually no........we didn't," she said in a bemused tone.

"Then we're overdue," I tossed down another swallow of my drink before I challenged her with: "You do know how, don't you?"

And just as I knew she would, she frowned at me and said in a slightly miffed tone; "Of course, I do."

Grabbing her drink, she got up and walked towards the pool table; a dark, mahogany beauty with a deep red felt top, leaving me to do the same behind her and with a smug smile, I did just that.

Chapter Nine

There were probably about a dozen or so people here, most of them sitting at the bar or at one of the corner tables over by the windows. We chose our cue sticks and I set up the table, smiling in amusement at the look of determination on her face. Maybe she'd played before, maybe she hadn't. Either way - this should be fun.

"Ladies first," I said and she walked around the table to line up her shot.

She broke the balls and sunk a solid into the far right pocket. I quirked a brow at her as she looked up at me from across the table. Wordlessly she walked to her left side and took her next shot, nearly sinking the red 3 but missing by millimetres as it rolled to a stop just in front of the side pocket. Okay, pretty good so far.

She turned to me and said "Your turn," in a sweet as cotton candy voice.

Hmmm.

Picking up my cue stick, I scanned the table, figured out my best moves and then walked over to the opposite end to line up. With a loud smack, I sent the colourful balls racing around the table top, sinking two stripes and pushing her solid red 3 out of the danger zone, screwing up her next plan, no doubt. I looked up in time to see her disgruntled frown and I wanted to laugh.

Oh yeah - fun.

Seems Detective Curvalicious was a tad competitive.

I purposely missed my next shot, not wanting the game over too fast. In between sips of scotch I watched as she lined up her cue and took aim -she had a really good eye which came as no surprise at all given that she'd be well practised with a gun. And sure enough, she smoothly sunk another solid, grimacing a little when she missed the next.

Leaning over and positioning my cue, I saw that she watched my every move avidly, so I deliberately missed again just to see how she'd react. Although she quickly tried to cover it, a definite smug look came to her face and damn, she was fricken cute.

Did I say a tad competitive? Ha!

For the next few shots, it was an even game as we sunk balls one by one into the pockets, circling the table slowly and eyeing each other from opposite ends. Fake groans of commiseration at the other's misses or congratulatory "good shots" when a ball aimed true. And with each go around the table, the challenge between us seemed to climb a notch, taking my temperature with it.

Deciding to yank her chain for the pure hell of it, when there were just a couple of solids and two of my stripes left, I picked up my stick and rounded the table to the far side. She stood directly opposite, hip cocked, drink in hand and scanning the angles of play, long hair shining under the pendant lighting. After a quick swallow of whiskey, I set my glass down on the timber edge, lined up my shot and let my beast vision take over for the briefest of moments. The cue ball went flying over the red, smacking a stripe hard into a side pocket then one of her solids into the far left corner before it bounced off the cushion and crashed into the last two remaining colours, scattering them into the front two pockets and side-swiping the black. I watched with satisfaction as the eight-ball rolled smoothly towards the side, slowing down a little before edging over and falling neatly into the waiting pouch.

I looked up just in time to see Charlotte's jaw drop, her eyes wide as she stood there gaping at the cleared table. I nearly burst out laughing and yeah, okay, maybe that was a little mean but it was so worth it to see that face.

Her eyes flew up to mine and she glared accusingly.

I stood there, one hand holding the stick to the floor, the other stuck in a pocket, thumb out, giving her a pseudo-innocent look and she stalked over, got right into my personal space and hissed angrily: "Did you just use your beast vision?"

"No," I fibbed and her brows scrunched down fiercely, lips pressing together as sparks shot out of her eyes in blatant disbelief at my lie.

"Okay," I fessed up with a laugh, unable to hold back. "I did. But just once. I promise."

She gave a snort of disapproval, looking at me like I was some naughty school kid and I grinned at her, highly entertained. My beast was delighted with her play, charmed with the spitting mad kitty-cat demeanour.

Remember to never say that out loud, Kellan, I told myself, pretty certain it wouldn't go down well with her.

She stepped back out of my personal space sadly, cool calculation glinting in her eye and raised a sassy eyebrow at me. "Another game?"

"Sure," I replied. Damn, this woman was endlessly fascinating.

"NO beast vision," she insisted, keeping her voice low.

"Alright, but you gotta admit that was fun," I said with another laugh.

She ignored that and gave me a mild withering look. I smirked.

She turned and walked towards the bar unexpectedly and I watched in curiosity as she spoke to the bartender briefly before she slid her leather jacket off her shoulders and handed it to him. I froze as I took in the fact that she now wore only that skin tight top with tiny tiny shoelace straps and her rounded shapely ass was no longer partially hidden under the jacket, but was on full delicious display. My beast's jaw dropped when she turned and walked towards me, jeans clinging tight and low to her hips, grey shirt lovingly cupping small but full breasts, cut low to show a hint of lush cleavage and with her shoulders and arms almost completely bare, her softly tanned skin glowed flawlessly in the muted light. She was bra-less.

She had to be - there was nowhere to hide any straps and no lines were visible anywhere.

Holy..........

Swallowing hard, I stood there immobile, pulse racing as my blood pressure shot sky high. She noticed my intense stare and shrugged, giving me a sweet smile.

"It's getting hot in here," she said.

No fucking kidding.

Picking up my beasts' jaw, I exhaled shakily and dug deep to reign us both in, determined to keep my cool.

Racking the balls for a new game, it started off harmlessly. Once again, she went first while I stood as far away as I could in an effort to keep calm but all that did was give me an unimpeded view of her every move as she leaned over the felt to take her shot; long smooth arms stretched out and hair swinging down over her bare shoulder, her posture displaying tantalising cleavage that teased my senses cruelly.

And she knew it.

Goddamn. This woman......

My heart beat erratically, skin heating as my blood simmered. She flashed me a innocent look as she straightened up, The fire in my eyes should have scorched her where she stood but she just quirked her brow at me cheekily. I growled beneath my breath.

Right.

Game on, baby.

I stoically ignored her sexy self as I took my shot, sinking a couple solids and missing the next. Not too bad considering how hot and distracted I was.

Speaking of hot....

I really wanted to remove my own jacket but couldn't; it didn't camouflage much but it was better than nothing - and it was becoming increasingly necessary.

But then she started to ramp it up - taking a slow stroll around the table and drawing my eyes to her gently swaying hips as she came closer and closer. She took her next shot by placing herself directly in front of me and bending over as she lined up her cue stick. My eyes fell to her denim encased ass and my breath caught at her provocative stance.

Jesus Christ.

My mouth watered, inner animal straining at my tethers.

She paused, looked over her shoulder at me as I snapped my eyes back to her face, and said mildly: "Excuse me," as if in apology for crowding my space. Then, turning back to her shot, she shifted her position slightly, causing her butt to move oh so temptingly.

I think my eyes crossed.

Fuckin' hell, she was determined to torture me......

Torn between drooling and laughing, I couldn't help but admire her playful boldness. But I could play this game too.

Gathering my control tightly, I took my turn at the table, first grabbing the chalk and dusting up my stick while I casually asked her: "By the way, what was that black painted stuff around your eyes?"

She tilted her head slightly, obviously surprised by my random question.

"It wasn't paint," she explained, green gold eyes glinting just like a cats' in the low light. "It was a henna mask, sort of like a regular mask but softer so it sticks to the skin. Why?"

"Huh. No wonder," I said mysteriously and waited for her to take the bait.

"No wonder what?" A little furrowed line appeared between her brows; curiosity tweaked and bait taken.

Strolling slowly around the table towards her, I assessed the layout of the balls as I said off-handedly: "No wonder it didn't melt."

She watched me closely, uncertain of my intentions as I looked up, latched my gaze to hers and advanced on her with a measured stalking gait. Her heart rate picked up speed with each step closer and I refused to let her look away, pinning her in place with the heat I bared to her.

"What with that kiss and all...... You see, I remembered holding your face...." Her pupils dilated, wide and wary as I came within centimetres of her, invading her personal space, still walking as I leaned in close to her ear and said: "kissing you........."

Then sliding around her back to say, "long and deep and wet......" against her nape in a voice as dry as sandpaper before I continued on along the table, leaving her standing there, cheeks flushed, her breathing shallow and heartbeat pounding.

Lust slithered through my blood, her aroma twisting and taunting my senses and I scrambled for control of both myself and the beast. It might be fun to enact a little revenge for her teasing but....Jesus......I was killing myself here.

With a nonchalance I didn't feel, I played my next shot, needing the momentary breather before I was steady enough to face her again. She looked as if she was doing a little scrambling herself.

"You.....err........" she stopped to clear her throat, then tried again. "You remember that too?"

"Yeah." And so much more.

We stared at each other for a long heat-filled moment, until I said pointedly; "Your turn" and she dragged herself out of her daze and began assessing the table play with an excessive amount of concentration but her act didn't fool me - she was as distracted as I was.

I grabbed my drink and finished it off, hoping the alcohol would put out some of the fire in my system. My beast was trembling with need and I was finding it hard to breathe normally. Maybe starting this game wasn't such a great idea, after all.

Especially, when I turned back to watch as she went about her turn: the Torturer had decided to ramp up the tension even further. She didn't even try to pretend she wasn't getting back at me as she deliberately stretched her body across the felt, hips pressed tight against the timber edge, aiming for her shots from the most ridiculous and difficult spots, all in an effort to bring me to my knees.

She wasn't far from succeeding, I had to admit to myself as I completely screwed up my next shot. But dammit, how the fuck could I concentrate on the game when all I could think about each time she leaned over the table, all smooth bare skin, peeping cleavage and tight rounded ass, was picking her up, plonking that ass on the red felt and taking a big healthy bite out of her? Or better still, laying her out entirely and climbing up over her......

Lost in that fantasy, I only just managed to catch the smug little look on her face as she sunk her ball smoothly into the left side pocket. Smiling at me, she strolled over to her next target, lined up her stick then grabbed her hair and smoothed it over one shoulder, ostensibly to give her a better line of sight but her quick glance my way told me differently. She knew my gaze would zero in on her exposed neck.

And it did. Dammit, I could see clearly the flutter of her pulse under the delicate flesh. I wanted to reach out and touch it, smooth my thumb over the erratic beat and feel its echo against my skin. I could smell her heat, that incredible scent and I hurt ....

Dangerously on edge and digging deep, I held myself brutally in check - we were in public, for Gods sake and even though no one paid any attention to us, it still wouldn't be a good idea to blur-jump over the table and toss her over my shoulder. No matter how wild and animalistic she made me feel.

But........her torture-games deserved some payback, so like a masochistic dumbass, I upped the teasing, unable to resist.

"Do you know what else I dreamt? Which I now know to be as true as the other dreams....?" My voice was rusted over with deep carnal need as I rested my cue stick against the table and wandered over to her, holding her gaze prisoner.

She watched me warily, yet didn't back away one bit.

I could see the resolve in her face. God, I loved the fact that she would take it as much as she dished it out.

"What?" She asked, a hint of challenge in her tone.

I didn't answer immediately, waiting till I was once again behind her, only this time I stretched my arms out against the pool table on her sides, effectively trapping her. Leaning close to her ear, I said: "I remembered you spread out naked in bed...." Her heart skipped a beat then raced in a mad tempo.

My breath blew gently across the skin of her nape as I continued. "You were handcuffed to the headboard, a dark timber one, strong and very sturdy........"

A deep shiver racked through her, the arousal rolling off her in waves at the provocative words and my beast quivered. I clenched every muscle tight, the dream playback in my mind scraping rawly at my belly. Damn......maybe I was a masochist?

"And I was drawing little circles on your inner thigh.........with my tongue." She gave a pained little moan that I felt in every sinew of my body. "Seems to me, Detective Alistair, that your police-issued cuffs weren't meant to be used quite like that."

Putting my lips against her ear, I whispered: "but I won't tell."

She spun around in the close confines of my outstretched arms, eyes blazing with green gold fire and heart thudding heavily in tandem with my own. Hands clenching into fists on the table's timber edge, I fought the urge to yank her against me and devour her. Pebbled nipples stood out in mouthwatering detail against her sexy tight tank, the scent rising from her cleavage weakening my knees.

Oh Jesus.

He must have heard my prayer because right at that moment a loud argument broke out behind me followed by smashing glass and both Charlotte and I snapped around to find two guys screaming obscenities and getting in each others faces. Their buddies were trying to calm them down; a female pushing hard against the chest of one guy, pleading with him to stop but he was having none of it.

He threw a punch at the other, connecting solidly with the guy's jaw and then it was all hell breaking loose, fists flying as the two fighters jumped at each other while others either cheered them on or tried to stop them.

Immediately Charlotte swung into police mode, shouting: "Police, break it up!" and wading into the middle of the chaos. I grabbed the closest fighter hard by his arms and yanked him back, but he kept at it, struggling to escape and hurling vile threats at his opponent. As jacked up as I was on adrenalin, I was tempted to use beast strength to knock the punk out but resisted, simply holding on to him while Charlotte grabbed the other idiot, ordering him to back off or she'd arrest him. But he was so wild with anger and booze and possibly other shit, that he didn't pay attention and instead took a swing at her, closed fist and all.

Every instinct I had screamed at me to let go of the brawler still fighting my hold, to protect her but in the split second I was about to do exactly that, Charlotte blocked the asshole's fist with an hard uppercut to his jaw that staggered him back a step or two, dispersing the crowd like a wildly thrown bowling ball. Dazed and shocked, he shook his head and then - obviously having no fucking brains whatsoever - he roared like a wounded bull and charged at her.

She snapped out a fast side-kick that pounded into his rib cage, momentarily slowing him down but again, with alcohol-infused rage, he lunged for her and this time, she grabbed his arms, yanked him off balance, slammed her elbow hard into his gut and flipped him over her back to smack heavily onto the floor, where he groaned and shuddered once then lay still.

By this time, the bartender and two bouncers were taking over crowd control, with the bar guy yelling: "Are you okay, Officer?"

As she stood there, catching her breath, she turned and caught my eye for a brief moment and every single molecule in my body seized up in agonised lust, my beast screaming and snarling in pain. My hands clutched hard at the no-longer struggling brawler, clenching so tight he'd no doubt have fantastic bruises and as he yelped in pain, I hurriedly shoved him hard towards a burly bouncer and slid my hands shakily into my jacket pockets, frantically holding onto control.

Seeing her fight in my beast vision was one thing - seeing her fight in reality was like a stick of dynamite thrown onto a burning fire.

Her petite compact body, though highly feminine, was graced with a warrior-princess strength and agility, an innate protector and fearless defender, and her very essence called out to my beast like a siren.

She was the sexiest thing I've ever seen, standing there victorious, powerful and in charge. I felt my eyes change to gold and my claws unsheath.

Fuck, fuck, fuck.

Hold it together, dude. Muscles trembled and sweat clamoured across my brow as I held myself very very still, not daring to move an inch.

I watched, head lowered to hide my eyes as Charlotte gave instructions to the bartender and bouncers. Several staff members were fussing over the "officer" - obviously they knew what she was, despite her not wearing a badge or gun - did she want to press charges? Should they call her precinct? Was she hurt?

She reassured them repeatedly - no, she didn't want to press charges against her attacker, he hadn't touched her; yes, she was sure; no - there was no need to call her precinct; no, she wasn't hurt, just get them out of here and so the brawlers were dragged off by the linebacker-sized bouncers to be thrown out, together with their buddies.

Once they were finally satisfied that everything was under control and she was fine, they left to clean up the broken glass and spilled drinks. She sighed and turned to face me, standing there - anything but fine.

Immediately she recognised that something was wrong; ultra nervous tension vibrated visibly off my body and she quickly came over, concern all over her face as she reached me. "What is it, Kellan?"

Then, as I looked up from under my lashes, showing her my gold eyes, she gasped and said, "Please. Not here," - obviously fearful that I would beast out here in the bar, in full view of the public.

But she had it all wrong.

"Charlotte, it's not bloodlust I'm feeling."

My voice growled from the pit of my gut, raw desire throbbing through every word, the heat sizzling like a live wire at her nearness.

Her beautiful eyes flared wide as my meaning became clear.

Chapter Ten

Moments that felt like hours passed as Charlotte's eyes, wide with trepidation, stared into mine. I trembled on a dangerously fine edge, a whisper away from losing it.

I needed her.

And she knew it. I could see it in her eyes: the full awareness of just how precarious and potentially disastrous this situation was. If I couldn't rein it in...........

She suddenly grabbed my hand and turned to walk hurriedly to the bartender guy she'd given her jacket to earlier; needing to drag me dumbfounded and resistant once I realised where she was headed.

What the hell was she doing???

Horrified, I wanted to yell at her, scream that she was crazy to risk me being anywhere near him or anyone else. We needed to get outta here. Right now!! Somewhere safe - didn't she understand that? How the hell could she not understand that? Oh fuck....this wasn't good......

My hand shook within hers, clutching tight to her in panicked fear. Charlie, for Gods sake.....

But then.....

"Derek, you have a private space I could talk to my.....partner?" she called out to the guy, her small fingers squeezing my hand.

He looked up from his work, took note of our clasped hands, a brief look of curiosity and an odd disappointment crossing his face and then, seeing the intense seriousness on Charlotte's face, he immediately dug into one of his front pockets.

"Sure thing, Officer," he said in a thick midwestern accent. "My office. Down that hallway there. You'll need the key," and he nodded in the direction of a small corridor that ran down the right-hand side of the bar. I could have howled like a mad wolf right then and there, overwhelming relief shaking my knees.

Thank God.........

Tossing the keys to her, she caught them one-handed without breaking stride while I made a mental note to find out later why she knew him by name. Because I sure as hell couldn't focus on that at the moment; could barely focus on a single damn thing. A thick fog of lust blurred my vision and hearing - all of my senses acutely attuned to her and only her, everything else an indistinct grey.

We headed down the short hallway side by side - no dragging needed now - towards a blue door marked "Office" at the end of the dimly lit area.

Hurry. Hurry.

The words pounded through my blood, keeping time with my racing pulse. She had to let go of my hand to use the key, unlocking the door with trembling fingers as I crowded in against her back, leaning down to her neck and growling as I breathed her in, shudders of ecstasy winding down my spine. Goddamn.....that scent.....

At the click of the door unlatching, I put one clawed hand on the curve of her waist, the other flat on the door and rushed her through into the dark room, wasting no time to just get the hell in there, NOW!

She quickly found the light switch while I slammed the door and turned the lock. The room flooded with light, revealing the usual office paraphernalia: big desk, filing cabinets and other crap I couldn't give a shit about as I stood there shaking, breathing heavily, hands fisted tightly down by my sides and eyes locked on Charlotte, hardly daring to move for fear of losing the savage grip I had on my control.

Charlotte - all beautiful, exotic eyes, trembling herself as she took in my predatory stance and the fire in my gold eyes. "Kellan ...." she whispered brokenly.

Reaching out towards my face, she cupped my cheek with a shaking hand as she'd done once before; running her slim fingers gently over my stubbly skin, soothing, calming.......

At the touch of her soft skin against mine, my eyes closed in pleasure and I tilted into the caress like a cat being stroked, a fine tremor racing over my whole body. Tension pulsated thickly between us as I opened my eyes, still glinting gold and found her watching me closely - lips quivering, black pupils obliterating her irises with a searing desire as fierce as mine. Everything within me seemed to hold its breath, the very air around us exploding when she suddenly muttered "dammit" and launched herself at my chest. I snatched her hard against me, mouth crashing into hers as she wrapped her arms around my neck.

Ferocious in our hunger, we devoured each other, bodies pushing desperately, straining to get closer. My claws sheathed themselves as my hands raced roughly over her; squeezing, moulding, cupping anything I could reach and moaning at the blazing heat, the carnal want that sizzled like a live wire over us. Her hands clutched at my hair, my shoulders, clinging tightly as she plastered herself against me.

With mouths open and tongues duelling, she bit my lower lip and I snarled, my beast delirious for his mate, wanting nothing more than to lay her down somewhere, anywhere, and bury himself, myself, inside her wet heat and take her hard, until she screamed and screamed with her release. God, Charlotte.........

Her hands frantically pushed my jacket from my shoulders and I let it fall to the floor forgotten as I picked her up, hands full of her luscious ass and carried her to the desk, her legs hitching themselves around my waist.

I sat her down on the edge and ran my hands all over that sexy grey tank, moulding themselves to her breasts as my mouth raced down her neck, licking and kissing the soft skin until I reached her cleavage, groaning at the scent emanating from that glorious spot.

Fuck, she smelled so good.....

I could barely keep myself in check as her aroma drowned my senses, every sinew and pore flooded with her lush fragrance.

Groaning, I reached under her tank and pushed up, revealing a white smooth strapless bra that I quickly shoved out of the way, latching my mouth to her tight nipple. Sweet Jesus, yes..........

She gasped breathlessly and pushed a hand under my shirt to dig her nails against my back, sending hard quivers of painful desire racing through my system, the scratches only fuelling the wild need between us. Sucking her nipple hard as my tongue flicked the trembling flesh, I ground my cock against the seam of her jeans, hitting her in just the right spot to make her moan loudly. "Oh God....."

My belly clenched with twisting, scorching need, cock throbbing so damn hard I was afraid I'd burst my zipper any second. Reaching for the waistband of her jeans, I ripped the button open, desperate to reach her.

"Kellan," she whimpered. "We can't.......not here......." But her hands clutched at my hair as she pushed herself more fully into my marauding mouth. I reached a hand impatiently over my shoulder, grasping the black tee and stripping it off to throw heedlessly to the floor. I swear steam rose in the wake of her hands sliding urgently over my naked chest, my skin pebbled and burning hot and I grabbed her waistband, yanking the jeans as low as they could go in this position.

My mouth raced back to hers, tongue plunging hungrily, our kisses greedy and hard as I reached into the open zipper and slid beneath the white fabric of her tiny panties, fingers reaching for the wetness of her swollen pussy and sinking two deep inside with a long hard thrust that caused her to scream a little and press her feet into my ass, arching and shivering. I moaned at the feel of her soft silky juices drenching my skin with liquid fire, the line between man and beast very very fine. Her arched body allowed me to push her jeans down further with my free hand and she let go of my neck for a brief moment to help, as needy as I was for better access. Her slick inner walls clutched my fingers tightly as I began to thrust them, gliding wetly in and out, twisting them and strumming at her clit with the rough pad of my thumb.

"Kellan, oh God, we can't....... do this here," she groaned in a broken voice.

"I know" I rasped in between deep kisses and deeper thrusts.

"It's wrong" she groaned, kissing back, hips circling at each flick of my thumb, her clit a hard bundle of swollen nerves.

"I know," I repeated and swiped my tongue over her lips before biting the lower one.

She trembled.

I trembled.

Jesus, I'd never wanted like this: never this deeply, this viciously, I'm sure of it. At least in living memory.

"I'm still not.......jumping into bed with you," she proclaimed in a low breathy voice. "No matter where we are." Then she threw her head back in ecstasy as I pressed my thumb down hard on her clit, thrusting my fingers faster. Her thighs clenched tighter around my hips and a groaning laugh escaped me, her statement in complete contradiction to her grasping, willing body.

"Okay," I muttered against her neck. This woman...........

I kissed my way down to her breasts again, pointed tongue swirling around a rosy nipple over and over before sucking her into my mouth and scraping my teeth over the sensitive flesh. She cried out, grasping my nape to hold me tightly against her in sensual demand and I bit down gently. Her deep guttural moan pulsed through my veins, the sound an elemental call to my primal nature as her restless hands slid over my back, my shoulders and chest, short nails scratching over my nipples like a she-cat. Hard, racking shudders ripped through my body as my animal thrilled to the raw feminine need in her.

"This isn't helping to......" she panted. "Ooh yes.......calm you ......God, oh God, more........calm you down ....ahhh."

Throat dry with thirst for a taste of her, I leaned back to watch, my heart thundering; enthralled with the mind-numbingly sexy picture she made sprawled there on the edge of the desk: head thrown back in pleasure, tank top and bra twisted and caught up under her arms, nipples wet from my mouth, tight and sweet and jeans barely clinging to her hips as my hand worked her body.

Slickness coated my thrusting fingers, the hard glide creating a wet noisy friction that ripped at my tortured control, thumb circling in ever smaller loops around her pretty little clit. With cheeks flushed and lips kiss-swollen, her body wound tighter and tighter.

She was magnificent.

Sensing my stare, she opened heavy eyelids, breath trembling through her parted lips and as our gazes locked, that connection punched at my heart with vicious fists, indisputably powerful. "It's helped enough" I grated out roughly and her chest heaved as she took note of my hazel eyes, the gold gone for now; my beast fully content to be tethered in her arms.

"But I need you to come, Charlotte ," I told her with a voice like sandpaper and her eyes flared. Stepping up the pace of my thrusting, I gave her more and more, twisting and curling my fingers inside her so they scraped against her g-spot. Her body writhed and shook, hips tilting and circling, breathing hitching as she climbed higher and higher.

God, yes, that's the way.

"I want you to come hard," I growled, biting down gently on her collar bone before soothing the spot with soft licks, the small pleasure-pain shivering her smooth, fragrant skin.

"With my name on your lips, Charlotte. Gimme all you have," I demanded, desperate for her release. Ready to catch her when she fell, I watched her lush, slim body undulate, trembling as she reached for that pinnacle and with a hard pinch to her clit I pushed her over the edge. She seized up, hips thrusting against my hand as she came hard, my name ripping from her throat in a loud scream, just as I wanted. But she quickly smothered the sound by sinking her teeth into the ball of my shoulder, hard enough to sting but not enough to do damage. I grunted with the wildness of her climax; her body spasmed around my fingers, feminine walls milking them endlessly, wet and silky against my rough skin.

GODDAMM, yes...... Oh fuck yes.

With muscles taut and burning hot, it took every bit of my restraint not to climax too and I needed beast-backup to hold it together, even as piercing pleasure shot up from my balls and exploded in my clenched belly.

Watching her come had to be the most beautiful thing I'd ever seen - elemental and raw as she let go, giving me all of herself as she shook and stretched in bliss. I wanted to roar in triumph, in pure male pride that I could give her this. My blood pounded through my veins, one word echoing in time with its' racing beat: mine. Over and over while she rode through her orgasm.

She opened dazed eyes as I slowly withdrew my wet fingers from her clutching body, locking her gaze to ensure she watched while I raised them to my mouth and sucked the glistening juices off. My beast quaked at the taste of her essence, snarling in aching need and I dropped to my knees, latched my mouth to her still shuddering flesh, growling "mine" against her almost bare kitty and moaning as I lapped at her. She gasped as I plunged my tongue into her wet channel, engorged and still pulsing in the aftermath of release. Her hands fell to my hair, clutching fistfuls as her hips thrust at my face and she whimpered. "Oh, God, oh, oh, ooohhhh,Jesus! Kellan!! Oh fuck!"

Hearing her swear in sexual frenzy cranked up my lust to impossible heights - something about her using foul language was so damn hot I came close to exploding again, sheer force of will the only thing holding me back. That and a desperate hunger to taste her climax flooding through my mouth.Hard flicks, sharp little nips and long glides with the flat of my tongue, I teased her relentlessly, her sweet skin ultra sensitive now. Holding her trembling thighs open with my hands, I thrilled to the sound of her breathless, hitching moans.

"Again," I demanded gutturally, frantic with need. "Again."

Wrapping my teeth around her, I bit down carefully and she exploded with a loud yell, coming hard against my mouth, drenching my tongue with her essence and I lapped it up hungrily, wanting more.

Wanting it all.

God damn, she tasted so good. My beast was delirious, as high as a freaking kite on her body's natural elixir.

And I was not much different - the shock of pleasure that her satisfaction gave me was simply staggering. Soothing her quivering flesh with gentle kisses and soft licks, I helped her come down slowly. Then, when she'd caught her breath, I rose to my feet as I took my lips on a leisurely wander over her shivering body, from thighs to belly to breasts, until I reached her face and there pressed my mouth - still tainted with her essence - against her pouty lips, letting her taste herself.

Leaning back to meet her dazed and slumberous eyes and elated to know I was the cause of that look, I smiled at her before pulling her against my chest and wrapping my arms around her, running one hand over her hair as she sighed. Despite her screwed up clothes, her chest was as naked as mine and our skin slid smoothly against each other, her nipples scoring a burning path as she cuddled against me, arms looped loosely around my waist.

For a minute or two, we simply held each other, regaining our scattered senses. I focused on her thudding heartbeat, listening to it gradually slow and calm, using it as my anchor to do the same. The corner of my mouth quirked in amusement when I realised how loud she'd been earlier. Not that I was exactly silent myself but God, I loved how vocal she became in the throes of passion - chances were good that we'd been overheard.

Not that I gave a fuck.

Then one of her hands slid along the skin just above my waistband, her fingertips trailing from the small of my back and around my side till she reached the front before sending them in a hard rub down over my still throbbing, still aching cock. My heart rate spiked up again, eyes falling closed at the feel of her hand on me, despite the jeans. She scratched along my entire length, squeezing and outlining my thickness with her small hand. Oh God, yes......

Shudders rolled over my spine as she caressed and cupped, the blood rushing to my groin when her fingers nimbly undid the button and grasped the tab.

Oh fuck, oh fuck....

She'd pulled the zipper halfway down before I was able to gather my senses enough to slap a restraining hand on hers and stilling her movements.

"Honey, don't", I muttered through clenched teeth, desperately holding on to my willpower. "If you touch me right now, I'm gonna lose all control and you'll be down on this desk with me buried inside you faster than a blur." I pulled back to meet her eyes, tense desire in every line of my face and body; letting her see just how close to the edge I was.

"I'm so hard for you right now, I could break," I gritted roughly. "So unless you want that too, then........"

"But........." She blinked wide-eyed at me, face flushing rosily. "What about.....?"

"What about me coming?" I finished for her, loving how she still blushed despite what we'd just done in a stranger's office. Sinking my fingers into her long silky hair and cupping the back of her head, I gave her a deep kiss, missing her taste already.

"Charlotte," I said when I came up for air. "Baby, as much as I'd love to have you....ahh......take care of me.......I can survive, no matter how much it hurts. And believe me, it does." With my lips against the delicate shell of her ear, I breathed: "So bad" then carefully sunk my teeth into the lobe and dropped a tiny kiss there.

She shivered and I pulled back to look down at her, torturing myself with the visual beauty of all her glorious naked skin, tousled hair and kiss-swollen lips. My beast snarled in hunger and I tethered him hard, for both our sake's - his and mine. Then, taking the hand that still lay trapped against my jeans, I brought it to my mouth, pressing soft baby kisses to the back of her long fingers and soft palm before holding it against my chest while I spoke.

"I thought the biggest control issue I'd ever have would be holding back the beast, but I was wrong," I said ruefully, "it's definitely holding back with you." As much as I hated to admit it, even to myself, she had us both weak at the knees. But she didn't need to know that. Or how much.

Only........ what if she already did?

A little unnerved at that thought, I quickly brushed it aside and concentrated on her heart rate, beating strong and steady, knowing she could feel mine pounding just as hard against her fingers. The beguiling pulse echoed through my system; starkly simple in its power.

"You said not here, so........not here," I continued. "But it'll be some where. And it'll be soon." I knew it without a doubt.

"You weren't always this sure of yourself, you know," she said with a smartly raised brow, dismissing my confidence as she began to straighten her twisted clothing; snapping her panties back into place and pulling down her bra to cover those gorgeous breasts. My brain short circuited at all the delicious jiggling. Oh man.....

Although I could cry at the loss of her nakedness, I did the gentlemanly thing and helped straighten her grey tank back into place but when she started to hop down from the desk, I refused to move from my place between her thighs, stilling her with hands to her hips. I liked my spot too much to move just yet.

"Yes. You wanna know why? " I asked her with a little smile. She shot me a wary look from under her lashes, uncertain where I was going with this.

"Why?" She asked carefully.

"Because, this connection we have?" I held her gaze, mesmerised as always by their luminous beauty. "This feeling between us? It's too strong and too deep to ignore. I might not remember everything about you or our relationship just yet, but it's coming back to me in bits and pieces." I paused a moment as her eyes lost their wariness. She held so still, seemingly holding her breath as she stared back at me.

Heavy emotion threaded through my voice as I admitted: "Charlotte, even without a full memory of you, my beast knows you - he recognises you on a primal level. An instinctual level. And I might not have realised that at first, even tried to deny it but.....I know it now." Her eyes widened, a tinge of hope flitting across her face

I let go of her hips to cup her face, tilting it up and rubbing my thumb gently across her cheek as I said in a raspy voice: "I recognise you, Charlotte, subconsciously - but that's enough, that's plenty, for right now."

And leaning in, I laid my lips against hers in a sweet kiss of affirmation.

Raising my head just enough to meet her eyes, I found them soft, glittering more gold than green in the fluorescent light, a gentle smile shining within. Her hands still lay against my naked chest, mine still held her face and the moment felt so charged, so full of potential, that a fine tremor slithered over my spine. The growing intensity threatened to overwhelm us but with a wryly amused twist of her lips, she said defiantly: "That doesn't make me yours. I'm my own person."

And with a quick little push against my chest, she dislodged me from between her legs and hopped down from the desk, zipping and buttoning her jeans as she walked over to where my tee shirt had landed earlier. She picked it up, turned and threw it over for me to catch one-handed as she cocked her hip and crossed her arms over her chest. I smirked playfully at her.

"You caught that, did you?" I said with a little chuckle. Looks like she hadn't missed that frenzied declaration of "mine", despite the heated lust of that moment.

"Why wouldn't I catch that?" She frowned.

"Well, I'd think that you'd have been too lost in pleasure to hear that, what with all the moaning and groaning you were doing......"

"Kellan," she said in a withering tone and I laughed. Fuck, she was so much fun to tease.

I quickly pulled my top on and buttoned my fly, liking the way her eyes zeroed in on my hands at my crotch. Walking over to her, she watched me warily, as if worried I might jump her.

Ha.

As much as I'd love to do just that, I'd finally gotten my dick back under control and didn't want to torture him anymore tonight, if I could help it - he'd suffered enough.

"Come on, let's grab your coat and get out of here. I'll walk you home," I said and grabbing my discarded jacket from the floor, shrugged it on.

"No, there's no need to do that. Casual, remember?" Charlotte said, halting me for a moment.

I raised a disbelieving eyebrow at her. "You don't seriously think this is still casual, do you? "

She opened her mouth to answer but no words came out. "Baby, casual went out the window the moment you draped yourself across the pool table and shimmied your ass at me. I'm walking you home, Charlotte. Now, have you got the key?"

For a brief second, she looked as if she was gonna argue but decided against it.

"Fine," she sighed, "you can walk me home. And yes, I have it." She dug the key out of her jeans pocket and passed it over.

Opening the door, I ushered her through and locked it behind me before grabbing her hand and leading her out into the main room, heading straight for the same bartender....Eric??...... who now stood talking with a customer seated at the bar. He looked up at our arrival with curious eyes, giving me a once over before looking at Charlotte.

"Thanks for that, Derek," she said, smiling charmingly at him.

"Sure thing," he said with a nod then flashed another quick look my way. I snickered to myself - yeah, buddy, she's with me. Holding up the keys for him to see, I tossed them over the bar and called out. "Thanks, man", just the tiniest bit smug.

He caught them, nodded again and reached beneath the bar for Charlotte's jacket. Putting it on, she finally covered up that evil grey tank, thanked Derek once again and turned to leave. I caught her hand and this time, threaded my fingers through hers, holding onto her securely as I lead the way through the games room, under the arch into the cafe area, winding through crowded tables and chairs till we were out the door.

The moment we were on the street, I said to her: "I think Derek might have been a bit upset that you were with me, judging by those looks." It was hard not to gloat but I tried valiantly.

The night air was fresh but not too cold in the mid-spring weather, the eternally busy streets of New York a kaleidoscope of moving colour, noise and light.

As we headed west towards her apartment, she glanced at me, startled and big eyes blinking rapidly before a funny little look crossed her face. With a wry twist to her mouth, she said: "Yeah, that's because he's more likely to wish he was me than you."

"Huh?" I was confused - what did that mean?

"He was checking YOU out, not me," she said at the same moment that I caught on.

"Oh," I said sheepishly, suddenly understanding all those looks. She burst out laughing, highly amused.

Rich, husky and contagiously free, she had an amazing laugh. Slightly bemused, I realised I'd never heard it before. Not properly. And even though it was totally at my expense, her twinkling eyes and flashing dimples were damn irresistible.

I grinned at her.

It was a toss up whether I was more freaked out or reassured by how good she made me feel.

Chapter Eleven

We walked in silence for a minute, a new yet strangely familiar sensation settling in my gut as I rubbed my thumb across the back of her hand, enjoying the softness of her skin. I couldn't imagine that we'd strolled the streets like this too often - if ever. That didn't feel familiar at all but no doubt muscle memory recognised the fit and feel of her fingers entwined with mine.

"So, I can't even imagine what it must be like for you," she said after awhile. I raised a brow at her in query, not sure what she was referring to.

"To not know who you are and then start to get flashes of memory." She shook her head in amazement, compassionate yet bewildered too. "It must be incredibly unsettling."

Glancing over at her face, I was damn glad to see no pity there, no bleeding heart sympathy. Just a quiet understanding for the strange circumstance I was in. There was nothing to feel sorry for as far as I was concerned - given all that I was, what I'd done and would still do, sympathy was the last thing I deserved.

"It's confusing." I told her. "It's all out of contex. Some memories come through sharp and clear but then others will be really vague - more like impressions than images."

"And other than myself and Finn, you haven't remembered any other people?"

"No, nobody. And that doesn't seem right, you know?

I mean, I did have parents, didn't I?" Although it was rhetorical and said in a mildly joking tone, the question sat like a lead balloon between us. My gut twinged as it always did whenever I thought of the fact that I couldn't remember them. Where were they? Were they still alive? Even if they'd passed away a long time ago, someone had to have raised me, right? Surely I'd have memories of that person? Sighing in frustration, I looked over at Charlotte and was disconcerted by the pained look in her eye.

"You know, don't you? About my family?" I asked her, my voice betraying the tension that suddenly gripped my being. Shit... Of course she would know. Why didn't that occur to me earlier?

She squeezed my hand in gentle comfort, saying softly; "yeah, I do." The eyes she lifted to me were full of that dreaded, unwanted sympathy. Christ........Did I want to know what happened to them? I took a deep breath, preparing myself for her next words.

"But, Kellan......I don't know if it's better for you to regain those memories on your own or for me to tell you what I know," she explained in genuine concern.

By this time, we'd arrived at her building so I stopped us by the entrance door in the covered vestibule, turning towards her in the shadowy light and keeping her hand in mine. She looked up at me with such uncertainty, cat's eyes glowing more green and gold.

"I'm not sure......You'll have tell me what you can handle," she told me and gratefully, I grabbed at the reprieve.

"Okay," I agreed. "Except I don't think I'm ready to hear about my family just yet, you know? At least.....not tonight." I figured I'd handled enough revelations for one day.

"Yeah, I get that," she said quietly in understanding.

Funny how she was able to draw out the vulnerable side of my feelings so easily, a side I hadn't thought even existed. Weirder still was the fact that it didn't freak me out.

Much.

The moment stretched out a beat as I sunk into the warmth of her gaze and before I lost myself in them yet again, I pulled back. "Come on," I said as I ushered her through the doors and over to the elevator, pressing the call button with my free hand.

"You don't have to walk me all the way up, you know," she said in mild protest but not doing a thing about it.

"A gentleman always walks a lady to her door," I told her with complete conviction. Say what?

Rolling her twinkling eyes at me, she huffed sarcastically. "Yeah, right."

My brows shot up in surprise. "What? Wasn't I a gentleman, before?" That can't be right. It didn't feel right. Yet.......what the hell did I know about being a gentleman? Where did that cockamamie idea come from?

"No, that's not it. I mean, yes, you were a gentleman," she said with a husky laugh at my offended face. "You were. It's just......well, you're different now."

The elevator arrived and once we stepped in, I pressed 8 and leaned on the side wall as she did the same on the other. I stared at her quietly as I absorbed that comment and her laughter died down at my seriousness.

"Different, how?" I asked. This wasn't the first time someone had said I was different - both Charlotte and Finn had mentioned it but I hadn't asked for an explanation in that moment. Now I wanted to know what they meant - how much different could I really have been?

She sighed. "It's hard to describe but......it's almost as if you have a new personality. Before you disappeared you were less confident." That little line appeared between her brows. "More.....ahh.....wary of things and people. Because of the circumstances of your life, of course......you had to hide and now.......you're ...." She blinked pretty eyes at me as she hunted for the right words.

"Now, I'm an asshole?" I supplied for her.

"No!!" She immediately denied that and I was grateful, even if it wasn't entirely accurate. "No! Not at all. Well, maybe you did some asshole things, but....... nothing I can't deal with. I think...." ...." she added in an undertone before continuing with her halting description. "

"Now you're super confident, even arrogant in many ways.......You're not afraid of who and what you are. You're more in control of ....him."

Was I?

Christ. My control of him now seemed tenuous at best...... How bad must it have been before? And yeah, it did sound like I was different ......Apparently I'd lived as a hermit in the past with no idea of how to control myself or my beast. A coward hiding from the world. "Less confident."

I did not like that.

But I didn't like the sound of "arrogant" either. I cringed internally at the thought of how she'd describe me if she knew the details of my mission work. Asshole and arrogant would be nothing compared to the words she'd use then, no doubt. But part of me wondered: would the cop in her understand?

Would the woman?

"And you're more focused," she added. "Very much a soldier, more assertive and disciplined, the way that soldiers are....you know? You weren't like that before." She gave a tentative little smile, watching me carefully.

I nodded but truthfully none of what she'd said clarified anything in my mind. McGregor had said I "came home from the army" so I'd already been a soldier when she knew me - why wouldn't I have behaved like a soldier then? And when the hell had I been a firefighter? I didn't get the fucking timeline here, didn't know what to make of it all. The frustration was endless and I felt myself begin to tense up again.

We arrived at her floor just then and I shoved those questions to the back of my mind to dwell on at some later stage, took her hand again and led her out the door, refusing to let tension slide back into my date with Charlotte - a date that wasn't over just yet. The short walk down the hallway was silent and as we stopped at her door, she sighed heavily, frowning up at me.

"I'm sorry," she said in unnecessary apology. "I'm not explaining this very well, I know. I'm making you sound like you've been transplanted by aliens or something when that's not the case at all."

"My mouth quirked at that. "It'll make sense when you remember more of your old life."

"If I ever do," I replied. Gotta be realistic about that because there were no guarantee of a fully returned memory. Or anything, for that matter.

The possibility didn't sit well with her and I could see she wanted to argue the point. But she let it go.

"Yeah," she agreed quietly, reluctantly. Then, as a loaded pause filled the air, she bit her lip in contemplation, her gaze roaming over my face thoughtfully.

"Kellan, whoever took you obviously took away all your memories, of everyone and everything and we don't know why, other than to keep you focused on whatever these missions are about. But there has to be more to it. You were gone for three months - that's a lot of time and effort spent on you and it can't be........."

I leaned in and kissed her, just because I could see she was getting agitated and I didn't want that to be how our date ended. After a little yelp of surprise, her lips softened and kissed back, their soft sensuality sparking embers anew. I pulled back slowly, reluctantly - Christ, she had the sweetest lips.

"Charlotte, I don't want to talk about that tonight. There's already so much crap to deal with and I.......... just not now. Okay?"

Her eyes searched mine as she considered my words. Eventually she nodded in agreement. "Okay."

"Good. Tonight, I just want to......."

But I trailed off as the hair on the back of my neck stood up suddenly. With my focus entirely on Charlotte, all senses had been muted to the endless white noise of human activity, scents and heartbeats, reducing the constant barrage to a distant hum but now, as if a switch had been flicked, everything sharpened instantly as one heartbeat jumped out loudly from the rest, in a place where there shouldn't be one at all - inside Charlotte's apartment.

Chapter Twelve

She was instantly alert to the sudden change in my bearing despite its subtlety. "What is it?"

"Gimme your key, quick," I said in a low hiss and she scrambled to get it from inside the coin pocket of her jeans, handing it over without question.

"Stay here," I ordered, unlocking the door hurriedly. It would have been faster and simpler to just break through but I didn't think she'd appreciate that. Instead, I blurred through into the pitch-black living area, the only illumination coming from street lights filtering through the sheer curtains that hung over two tall windows along the east wall. Not that I needed any light; beast vision easily spotting the figure that walked from the kitchen on my right - male, dark clothes, dark hair.

He didn't know what hit him as I slammed him against the refrigerator, my hand wrapped around his neck and squeezing. Shock held him immobile for a moment before he started to struggle, gasping for breath. As I'd known she would, Charlotte raced through the door behind me and the room flooded with bright light as she hit the switch. Two things happened simultaneously: my eyes took in the face of the intruder. And Charlotte yelled, "Lucas!!"

I froze instantly.

Ahhhhh, shit.

A pair of green gold eyes, eerily familiar, glared furiously at me from a sharp jawed face; youthful with angular features and unmistakably masculine - a total stranger with Charlotte's eyes and colouring - holy crap! The jolt of recognition punched through my gut and I immediately eased the pressure on his windpipe but just as I was about to let him go completely, he launched into a series of jabs and blocks, trying to dislodge my bracing arm and damn it, now I couldn't do anything except subdue him because, well.....this was her kid brother.

She wouldn't appreciate it.

But I was bigger and brawnier than him - and a beast - so his blows were rendered useless. Charlotte yelled loudly at us to stop it but I didn't know if she meant me or the kid - who, annoyingly, happened to have some genuine fighting skill. However, as good as his moves were, they were ineffectual against my animal strength and it clearly baffled and infuriated him.

He was gonna end up hurting himself more than me, I figured and with that thought in mind, I released his neck, whipped him around to pin his arms behind his back, yanking the wrists up high between his shoulder blades. He cursed up a blue storm at finding himself suddenly restrained and I twisted his arms tighter in punishment for the foul language he shouldn't be using around his sister. Disrespectful little punk.

"Lucas, stop that! Kellan, don't hurt him!" Charlotte called frantically.

"Hurt me? Like hell!" Apparently hugely offended by that, he began struggling anew and I did my best to stay cool and not swat him like a pesky fly.

"Stay calm, Kellan, please..." She begged but she didn't need to - the beast was fully leashed. However.....

"Charlie, tell this punk to quit it before he gets hurt," I said, resisting his attempts to dip and ram a shoulder into my midsection.

"Punk!!"

"Lucas, for Gods sake, cut it out!"

Charlotte demanded angrily but he ignored her and I lost my patience, shoving him face down on the massive timber island bench, one hand on the back of his head making sure he stayed in place and the other holding his forearms twisted against his back. He grunted, thrashing angrily against my hold and I snarled.

Seriously, this was getting out of hand.

"Now, listen up kid," I growled in warning. "Quit your fighting and settle down. I don't care how good your martial arts is, my skill set is faster and deadlier than you'd ever comprehend. Now, do as your sister says."

"Lucas, please, you don't want to mess with him. Stop!" Charlotte demanded in a no-nonsense tone and he finally took heed of her words.

"Alright! Alright! Let me up!" He called grudgingly, his struggles abruptly ceasing and I waited a moment before letting him go and taking a step back. He immediately shot up straight, twisting around to glare at me in absolute fury, practically vibrating and once again I was struck by his likeness to his sister. The three of us stood motionless for a moment, watchful and wary - the kid breathing heavily, Charlotte on edge and myself taking stock of the fact that this guy wasn't actually a kid. Roughly early to mid twenties, he was much taller than I'd initially thought, probably six feet. Young yes, but not that young and not the skinny little brother as I remembered from the one and only picture I'd seen of him when I'd researched Charlotte online - which she didn't know about. No, this dude had a lean, lanky build with some visible definition in the arms and chest beneath his ragged Nirvana tee shirt. Had I not been what I am, he was built strong enough and certainly was skilled enough to be a challenge in a fight. The picture I'd seen had showcased how similar the siblings were but I hadn't been able to tell the colour of his eyes - the fact that they were so similar to Charlottes' kinda freaked me out and I frowned darkly at him.

In the split second it took to take in these details, the punk threw a tight hard fist at my jaw, colliding solidly with the bone and my head swung to the side with the impact. I didn't do anything to stop him although I easily could have - I'd known it was coming, had sensed it but figured he needed to restore his pride a little. I got that. I could let him have that.

But that was all he was gonna get.

"That's for calling me a punk," he sneered.

Charlotte had automatically jumped forward at the assault but as I swung my head back, I caught her eye and winked, letting her knowing that I was cool with it and she halted, huffing in relief. Rolling my jaw to stretch out the injury, I watched as Charlotte stuck her hands on her hips like an exasperated mama and turned back to Lucas who stood flexing his knuckles surreptitiously. I wouldn't be surprised if we both ended up with some bruising - he had a decent punch, unfortunately.

"Dammit, Lucas! What are you doing here?"

"And why were you sneaking around in the dark?" I added and he gave me a dirty look.

"I wasn't sneaking! I was getting a drink," he snapped, looking like he wanted to go another round with me.

"In the dark?" I scoffed.

"Yes, what's wrong with that? Charlie, who is this asshole?" He turned to his sister to ask scathingly.

"Asshole?" I growled at him.

"Lucas!"

"What?!"

And Charlotte glared at him furiously. Damn, I smirked, highly entertained with her bossy big sister act - she was cute when she was mad. Especially when she was mad at someone that wasn't me.

"I'm her partner," I told him, figuring that label was the most suitable given mine and Charlotte's odd relationship status. Plus, kid-brother here needed to get the lay of the land - whatever that was. Hooking my hands in my jeans pockets, I leaned casually back against the island bench, legs splayed, watchful of the siblings reaction to that statement. Charlotte looked surprised and Junior curled his lip mockingly.

"Partner? Yeah, right. You look just like J.C." "Did I say I was a cop?" I raised a brow at him caustically.

I raised a brow at him caustically. He looked askance at the two of us then flicked his disapproving gaze at his sister.

"You telling me this Neanderthal is your boyfriend?"

Neanderthal?   The nerve of him.......

Charlotte rolled her eyes at him, thoroughly irritated. "Never mind that now. What are you doing here?"

I was so distracted by the fact she hadn't denied my "partner" comment, that I almost missed his answer, tuning back in just in time and telling myself I'd revisit that interesting little tidbit later on.

"You sounded really upset the other day so I thought I'd......." He began but Charlotte interrupted him.

"You thought you'd skip school?" I smirked as her hands went on her hips and the kid-bro scrambled to explain.

"I didn't skip," he replied defensively. "Classes were done for the day and I had nothing on till late tomorrow so I hopped a bus to come check on you and....."

Dammit, why'd he go and say a thing like that? Disgruntled, I frowned at him - that was a decent thing for the punk to do.

Charlotte visibly softened at her brother's words even as she admonished him. "You didn't need to do that. You could have just called," she said.

"Instead of breaking into the apartment and sneaking around like a thief," I couldn't help adding on.

"I didn't sneak!" He snapped at me, green eyes glaring daggers. "And I have a key, dickwad."

"Excuse me?" I said in a cold rumble. He was pushing his luck now.

Charlotte stepped in closer, ready to jump in and hold us at bay. Not that she needed to - I wasn't gonna beat up her little brother, no matter how much he might need it.

"Kellan, please....just ignore my idiot brother," she said whilst giving said idiot the hard eye.

"Hey!" He protested and I wanted to laugh.

"Well, what would you call deliberately antagonising someone?" She challenged him with a smartly quirked brow.

Not to be outdone, he raised a brow back in perfect imitation. "The way he's antagonising me with his dumbass accusations?"

"Listen, kid...." I interjected.

"Don't call me kid!"

"Next time you wanna check on your sister, don't turn up unannounced and you won't get hurt."

"Is that some sort of threat?" He turned a cold eye my way, rolling his shoulders back slightly.

"No, just solid advice for you," I told him, letting just a tiny trace of menace sneak into my demeanour as I stared at him and his eyes narrowed as something infinitesimal shifted in the air. He tensed for a moment, unable to define what the change was.

He sneered defensively and Charlotte once again took one step closer between us.

"Look," she said in a pacifying tone. "It was obviously a misunderstanding, okay? Kellan heard an intruder and was being protective."

"Yeah, storming in like some wanna-be. Very impressive," he said condescendingly, mouth twisted in sarcasm. "Sorry if I ruined your plans for the night......Dude."

Tension snapped down my back with those words. In trying to insult me, he was assuming things about his sister that he had no damn right to assume - the disrespectful punk. My beast growled and tugged angrily at his tethers.

"I'd watch what I was saying if I were you," I said in a low snarl, hands curling into fists inside my pockets.

"Don't make the mistake of thinking you scare me," he taunted foolishly, too focused on sparring with me to realise he was pushing too far. But it was Charlotte who snapped.

"Right!! That's enough! Both of you." She yelled so loudly we instantly shut up, startled into silence. I'm pretty sure the neighbours heard her too. She stood there looking frazzled and irate, scowling at us in turn with her mouth pinched in frustration.

After a loaded beat of silence, she sighed, pushing her hair back from her brow tiredly. "Kellan," she said. "Sorry about all of this. I'm sure my brother will apologise to you when he recovers his brain. And to me." She said pointedly, pinning him with a green gold glare. "Won't you Lucas?"

But he wasn't finished goading.

"If you knew my sister at all, you'd know she doesn't need your macho protection," he snarked and was rewarded with a backhanded slap across his bicep from a fed up Charlotte.

"Owww," he protested and I smirked in amusement - served him right. "Alright, alright. Fine. I'm sorry - I should have let you know first, sis," he said.

In the stilted silence that followed, both Charlotte and I realised that was the only apology he was gonna offer. Which sat perfectly okay with me - I didn't need one. But he owed his sister more than that lame ass attempt and I gave him a hard look, hoping he got the message. Whether he did or didn't, I figured Charlotte would give him a hard time of it anyway, once I left - which I really should do now.......

Wishing I could stick around for more fun and games, I turned towards Charlotte, catching her eye and a silent understanding stretched out between us.

"I guess I better leave you to it, then......" I said reluctantly.

A rueful twist to her soft mouth, she agreed; "Yeah."

But no one made a move, our gazes locked and lingering.

Until Lucas crossed his arms and muttered in a low voice. "Yeah, see ya........ asshole." And Charlotte swung a furious glare at him.

"Dammit Lucas! Not another word. Park your butt and don't move!" She pointed to the sofa, looking for all the world as if she would spank him any moment and I almost burst out laughing.

Trying to suppress the grin that wanted to crack my face, I stepped forward to lead her to the front door, my hand on the small of her back. And, damn, she didn't make it any easier by tossing a hard "don't defy me" look over her shoulder even as I ushered her out into the hallway. Once the door was closed firmly behind us, I stood smiling down into her peeved face, highly entertained over the whole incident and wishing I could be a fly on the wall when she lit into him later. It took her a moment to cool off; her temper easing slightly when she caught the laughter in my eyes and settling gradually until the beautiful green gold twinkled back at me, her frown smoothed out and shared amusement flared between us.

"I take it I've never met your charming kid brother before?" I asked, even though it was obvious by that heated "conversation" that we hadn't.

"No. We never got around to that," she replied then tilted her head slightly as something occurred to her. "You knew his name though. How did you realise who he was?" Ahhh, of course - the cop in her would pick up little nuances like that. Scrambling to remember if she had mentioned his name when she'd talked about her brother and failing, I went with the only thing I could think of. Which just happened to be the truth so I wasn't lying to her.

"He has your eyes, Charlotte," I told her in a gruff voice, letting myself sink into them a little more.

Her beautiful, mesmerising cats eyes.

His were more green and definitely didn't hold the power that his sister's did over me.

She gave a small nod, seemingly satisfied with my explanation and I watched as a soft smile curved her lips.

The air thickened around us in awareness, her pulse skipping a beat as my own began a slow thud. Recalling what had been about to happen before the whole Lucas debacle, my mouth watered.

"As I was about to say before all that melodrama..." I took a step closer, invading her personal space until she had to tilt her head back to maintain eye contact. "I just wanna kiss you good night at your door and ......"

"You've already done that," she interrupted with a flirty smile and raised brow. And damn, her dimple winked at me. My beast was a sucker for her dimple.

"That was to stop you talking," I said, smirking playfully at her. "That wasn't a goodnight kiss. This is........"

And I leaned in, taking her mouth in a deep, open-mouthed, leisurely kiss, devouring her slowly and savouring every sensual glide of her lips. Her arms slid around my neck as mine did around her waist, bodies pressing together and stoking that fire again.

Despite my best intentions of keeping the kiss innocent, it wasn't long before it started to escalate out of control, hunger beginning to claw sharply again, her heartbeat thudding erratically along with mine. Hands wandered, squeezed and caressed, tongues duelled and hips flexed, wanting so much more........... Until finally, long heated minutes later, I dragged my mouth away from hers, resting my hands on her hips and groaning with the effort of holding back.

My body ached, senses full of her luscious taste, the feel and scent of her quivering my belly. I made myself step back and let her go, both of us breathless. Her face was flushed, lips swollen, eyes dazed and glittering like jewels.

"That was a goodnight kiss," I told her in a hoarse voice .

"Oh. Well." Flustered, she was all breathy and rosy cheeked. But it didn't prevent her from retorting: "Good thing you showed me because I didn't recognise it."

"What? I never kissed you goodnight?" I frowned at her, convinced lust was addling my brain.

"Oh, you kissed me goodnight plenty. Just not at my front door," she teased, eyes sparkling with humour.

Right. Not at her door.

I couldn't help the lopsided grin, her sass breaking up some of the intensity that pulsed thickly around us.

"So then, I....ahhh....better go......" I said and something about the way the light caressed her features stalled my breath for a moment. Did she even realise her own allure?

"Yes, I suppose so......." And once again neither of us moved.

Sighing in defeat, I leaned in for one more kiss, cupping her jaw gently and pressing my mouth to hers, lips clinging till the very last second. I didn't bother disguising my reluctance to leave - cool and stoic had disappeared hours ago.

I waited until she'd opened the door and stepped through before saying in a scratchy voice: "Goodnight".

"Good night," she replied huskily, our gazes disconnecting only when the timber barrier was shut between us. Sticking both hands in my front pockets, I stood there a moment longer, took a deep breath and let a shudder roll through my back.

Christ.

With gritted teeth I turned and walked away, taking the stairwell instead of the elevator then the street instead of a cab, knowing physical activity right now would help steady the tension that rippled through my body - a tension that wasn't only sexual.

No.... not just that, I admitted with a frown as I stepped out onto the concrete sidewalk and turned westward. The temperature had dropped substantially and the night air slithered down the back of my neck coldly. Flicking my jacket collar up against the chill, hands in pockets, my long strides ate up the blocks as I headed towards the apartment, tuning out all but my own thoughts.

In some ways, a purely sexual hunger would be easier to deal with, even when that hunger was so vivid and deep I could feel it pulsate in every sinew and muscle and I scowled at the thought of the restless night ahead. Thing was........I knew what to do about blue balls - I'd suffered those before, I'm sure. But I didn't know what to do about a hunger that dug far deeper than mere physical need, that stemmed from my most primal self, beast and man alike.

What did I do with that? How did I contain it?

Every incident between us highlighted the instinctive, unbound awareness we had of each other, building an emotional connection bit by bit and inciting an intense craving for more.

It almost felt like........yearning. One shoulder twitched uncomfortably at that idea and I dismissed it as stupid. Firstly - yearning sounded all poetic and shit and I was no goddamn poet. And secondly, I smirked, who yearned these days?

Not me.

But I did crave her - with a rawness that I hadn't known was possible and I couldn't help but wonder if that came from subconscious memories of her or if it was developing anew, irrespective of any previous relationship. Either way, it was unnerving.

By now I'd reached the dark and empty streets of the warehouse district, nothing but the souls of small critters roaming around in tiny crevices. Huge buildings cast long shadows on the ground, so thick and black that armies of creatures could have hidden within its inky darkness. Human or otherwise. But my eyes were impervious to the night light, seeing all with sharp clarity and as I passed by each building, I wondered for the first time why it was that my studio was the only one fully converted - that and the one next door. Two fully equipped studio apartments within the carcass of an aging brick warehouse - the Commander had mentioned it in passing awhile ago, declaring they were the first of a designated set of future safe houses, curtesy of the government. However if that was the case, then I should be seeing some signs of construction going on and I wasn't. Nothing at all and that now struck me as odd. Even locked up for the night, shouldn't there be equipment and stuff laying around? Scaffolding?

My eyes narrowed to pinpoints as I scanned each building, steps slowing a little. Strangely, none of these looked like any work had begun at all, I noticed. Unless it was only interior work so far? But that still wouldn't explain the lack of building debris anywhere, I realised. If they'd begun the conversion at all, then there'd be signs of it but there was nothing. Figuring it could be delayed due to any number of reasons, I brushed the whole matter aside as unimportant - what did I care?

Except, as I pulled out the key to unlock the side door to the studio, the thought niggled at my brain - it seemed to me that I'd been so focused on firstly my job and then the clusterfuck that began when I'd run into Finn and Charlotte, that I hadn't paid attention to anything else around me.

And that just wasn't acceptable.

Locking the door behind me, I switched on the kitchen overhead lights, leaving the living area in shadow as I parked my ass on the sofa with a long sigh. I threw my keys onto coffee table before putting my feet up the blackened timber. No, not acceptable at all. Okay, sure, there'd been a hell of a lot going on but surely I hadn't forgotten basic observational skills?

Sinking back into the leather sofa, I realised that no, I hadn't forgotten them at all. If I had, then I wouldn't have been able to complete the tasks I'd been given. But I was guilty of being so focused on those tasks that I hadn't noticed things like the oddity of the warehouses. Or the quietness of the apartment to the side of this one, come to think of it. In fact, thinking back to the first mission - tracking, locating and eliminating Tanaka - I could see now how deadly concentrated I'd been in not only the execution of said mission but in every aspect of reconnaissance and strategy. Probably more than what being a good soldier warranted.

Deciding that I wasn't gonna end what had been a damn hot night with a fascinating woman by dwelling on mission work, I got up, switched out the lights and headed upstairs. By the time I climbed into bed and settled back with my hands folded behind my head to stare at the high ceiling, I'd replayed our conversation at the bar three times and several things occurred to me: these damn sheets still held the slightest trace of her intoxicating scent; I would have pursued Charlotte without any prior relationship and I needed to start looking at the bigger picture here.

In all the confusion of the last couple days, I hadn't once thought to step back and look at the situation from a wider viewpoint - I'd simply been reacting. Or following orders. And with events happening fast enough to give me whiplash, I hadn't used any perspective or logic to figure this shit out.

And that had to change right now. Or tomorrow morning at the least.

Shifting my ass into a more comfortable position, I tried hard to ignore the tingle in my groin; a direct result of her scent lingering all around my naked skin. Dammit. I should have stripped the bed earlier. My beast was gonna whine about it all night but I couldn't be bothered changing them right now - that meant getting up.

Besides, I scowled to myself, I didn't actually know if there were other sheets anywhere around this place, linen not exactly on top of my priorities list.

I'd just have to tolerate the sweet torture. But God..... It was so good.

Pursued her? Yeah, right. I would have hunted her down with relentless, compulsive intent, like some lusty big bad wolf. A picture of her wearing a red cape with a huge hood covering her glossy dark hair flashed across my mind and my mouth quirked at the vision. She'd be completely naked underneath, of course, and I'd discover that when I slowly pulled on the long red ties that held the coat closed, the silky ribbons loosening ever so slowly, revealing inch by inch the sweet succulent flesh of her and......... Groaning aloud, I reigned in my fantasy with a quick snap before it got out of hand and I needed to take myself in hand - so to speak. As it was, the burn was on a high simmer and damn uncomfortable.

I set a mental reminder to get back to Detective Red Riding Hood another night and shut out the ache.

The thing was, I realised, while the addiction to her perfume was undeniable, there was more to it than that - she was intelligent, sassy and courageous and that was far more compelling than physical attraction alone. Far more seductive. Argumentative, challenging and entertaining, she was nevertheless in tune with me in unexpected ways: our thoughts and actions seeming to sync with natural ease at times. She stimulated my mind as well as my body and that was a definite double whammy.

Didn't matter to me now how long it took to get those memories back, because with or without them - I wanted her.

Simple as that.

What wasn't simple was figuring out not only what had happened to me and who or what was behind it, but what was I going to do about it? With no solid knowledge or proof of anything at this stage, I was a long way from resolving the shitfest that was my existence.

And it was well and truly past time I started making the puzzle pieces fit.

Chapter Thirteen

The force of the blast threw me back ten feet, the power so immense I was lifted and tossed as easily as a rag doll through the air. Landing hard, the side of my head bounced painfully on the concrete ground, one shoulder taking the brunt of the impact as I managed to twist my body defensively and prevent my head from smashing open like a melon.

I jerked up fast to see the old warehouse engulfed in a massive fireball, flames and black acrid smoke spewing high in the sky, debris flying everywhere as explosions thundered and boomed, shaking the ground.

For a moment, shock held me immobile but that quickly turned into a raging fury that whipped my blood into a frenzy; adrenalin thumping wildly through my veins. I jumped nimbly to my feet as my beast escaped his tethers and I transformed instantly, fangs snapping and snarling, roaring madly in reaction to the almost fatal explosion.

Son of a fucking bitch!!

I stood hunched, hands curled into furious fists and claws biting into my palms, drawing blood. Muscles rippled across my body with vicious energy as I growled deep and low in violent outrage - one wrong decision and I would have been in that inferno. One fucking wrong move......

Gold eyes burning with bitter hatred, I stared and seethed.

From my periphery came a small flash and I spotted my phone lying about two feet away, its small light winking green. It'd fallen from my hand during the blast and was somehow unbroken.

Stepping forward, my beast claws reached out and picked it up. Bringing it to my ear, I caught the thick silence hanging darkly on the other end before the click of the line disconnecting sounded.

A deep craving for this prick's blood swept through my gut, twisting and turning with a need to rip him apart, limb by limb. My clawed hand shook so badly, I nearly crushed the phone and as much as I wanted to smash it to pieces, my human brain knew the device could prove useful in tracking him down. It also told me that this was broad daylight and the fire trucks would no doubt be arriving soon.

I needed to get the fuck out of here. A-SAP.

With every bit of restraint I could grab, I transformed back, pushing down the wild fury that engulfed my beast. He was trembling in blind rage, wanting instant and deadly vengeance that I knew he couldn't have right at this moment and the strain of tethering him sent a fine tremor over my skin, leaving trails of icy coldness in its wake.

Pocketing the phone carefully, I wiped at a trickle of sweat running down my temple - but my hand came away smeared in blood.

Okay.

Not sweat then.

Didn't matter. It was just a graze and would heal fast. Dismissing it, I scanned quickly around the empty parking lot even though I already knew there were no witnesses anywhere and then blurred fast to the nearest neighbouring warehouse - well away from the blaze and equally as decrepit and abandoned as the one burning. Intending to pause only a moment to regroup and plan my next move, I was suddenly hit by a massive wave of dizziness that crashed over me like a tidal wave and I had to lean my back against the old brick wall to steady my suddenly churning system.

Shit.

My stomach lurched nauseatingly, like I was on some damn roller coaster ride and my head pounded with the force of a sledgehammer. Leaning over, I lay clammy hands on my knees and gulped down deep breaths.

Fuck, what the hell was this?

There's no way I should be reacting like this to a simple head knock and graze - I'd dealt with far worse and yet I hurt like a truck had rolled over me. With careful fingers I felt around the area on my temple and discovered swelling split skin, roughly two, three inches long. Crap. Definitely more than a graze. With nothing to clean the blood off either my head or my hand, I swiped my arm across the wound gently, letting my jacket sleeve absorb the dark fluid and ignoring the pained throb that resulted.

This was so freaking not normal.

Scowling furiously that I had yet another shitload of problems to deal with - as if I didn't have enough - I forced myself to just move and as I ran to the next warehouse, I could hear the fire sirens. Any minute, they'd be converging on the scene and I needed to be well away from here. But my speed and gait were diminishing with each step, pain shooting through my shoulder where I'd taken the brunt of the fall and I clutched at it reflexively. I made it to the next building before I gave in and found a hidden spot to rest, not only unable to blur but barely managing to run. Nauseas and clammy, I collapsed back against the old steel factory and let myself sink to the ground, gasping harshly.

Holy shit. This wasn't good. This was bad.

Very bad.

The beast was snarling and snapping, supremely agitated by the unfamiliar sensation of pain, desperate to regain control. But I held on to his tethers with shaking fists. The pounding in my head intensified sharply as blood trickled down my temple, the coppery scent so thick and strong I could almost taste it on my tongue. Raising a hand to the wound and reassuring myself that my brains weren't oozing out with every throbbing beat, I lay my head back against the cold steel and closed my eyes.

But the moment I did, the world began spinning at warp speed, shocking thumps slammed into my skull from all sides and a blinding white light flashed behind my lids. I gasped as a vise-like pressure burned around my brain like a branding iron, red-hot and searing and I grabbed my head with clutching hands, moaning.

But my breath was cut off in a choke as visions began crashing through my mind; one after another in rapid succession.

My God......what..........oh Jesus..........

Scenes of a young kid that I knew instantly was me, maybe 12 or 13 years old; all lanky legs and floppy hair, playing football with Finn McGregor - equally floppy haired and wearing ugly-ass glasses, dressed in school sports uniforms and showing off for the cheerleaders practising their routines. Then quick visions of the two of us rough-housing in what I somehow knew was his home and not my own. Racing our bikes down the street, maybe 8 or 9 years old. Walking down school corridors. Fishing at some lake, legs dangling off the pier. Throwing popcorn at the cinema with a bunch of other teenagers. Saying goodbye when I enlisted with the army. Playing Little League baseball together, maybe aged 6 or something. Cramming for college exams together; each scene illuminated as if with a strobe and twisting my heart into a scream.

Oh God.......

Scene after scene of him and I at various stages of life, each one like a punch to the solar plexus - the impact painful and shocking, stealing my breath.

Finn.

The visions kept flipping over and over: my gut clenching hard as bile rose up thickly in my throat. My mind shrieked, overwhelmed as memories flooded through with the force of a tsunami; smashing all in its path and drowning my soul with wild emotion. My body lurched at the unrelenting assault on my senses.

I wasn't dreaming this time - holy shit, I wasn't dreaming.

He wasn't here yet the memories came from nowhere, from everywhere and from deep within my gut.

I didn't have to question if they were real or not. I knew they were. A lifetime of memories suddenly just.......there.........in my head. My conscious.

I wanted to howl, to roar and scream with the bitter anguish that was filling my chest. Howl like a damn wolf baying at the moon but I held tight to the beast, afraid that if I let go right now, I'd lose my mind.

Finn.

Jesus Christ. How the fuck could I have lost every memory of him?

Sick to my stomach, I dragged in deep shaky breaths, shuddering as the scenes in my mind gradually slowed, several long minutes passing before the nausea and head pain eased to a non-dying level, leaving me clammy and cold.

Fuck.

Stunned, shaken; tremors pricked icily over my skin as my mind reeled. How could I have lost every memory of my best friend? The same way I'd lost the memory of Charlotte; of my family, coworkers and friends; of every goddamn thing I'd ever known......it had been ripped from me.

Brutally stolen by something or someone.

My hands trembled as they lay atop my head, elbows resting on drawn up knees as I tried to gather my scattered senses. Everything I thought I knew was once again shattered into a million jagged pieces and I was left floundering in a quagmire of dark suspicion. A swift and violent need for vengeance rose sharply in my veins. Bloody and merciless vengeance - the only kind that would satisfy my beast.

But that had to wait.

For now.

Right now, I had to get my shit together and get moving again so I hauled my ass off the ground and stood on unsteady legs. The usual speed of recovery that beast DNA gave me still hadn't kicked in and grabbing the edge of my tee shirt, I swabbed the still bleeding wound as best as I could - tricky to do when you can't see what you're doing. Damn thing should quit bleeding sometime soon, I told myself and began a steady walk out of the warehouse district, head down and sticking to as many shadows as possible. My head throbbed in synchronisation with each step and I grit my teeth against the annoying pain.

Eventually I made my way back onto the main streets, busy as they always were and noise never-ending. My stomach roiled at the barrage of heavy smells permeating the air - petrol, grease, food, garbage and a thousand others - all merging into one stinking heap. Normally it didn't bother me as I could deaden my senses to it at will but right now, with my system shaken and hypersensitive, I was unable to block it out and the odour was overwhelming. I refused to think about possible reasons I wasn't recovering in my usual way, telling myself it would return when my equilibrium did, focusing my thoughts instead on the resurfaced memories of Finn.

The visions I'd had played through my mind, gaining clarity with each pass-through and prodding at my subconscious for more. Hazy scenes floated on the edge of awareness, vague pictures of a life that I couldn't have imagined an hour ago .... a life that looked somewhat normal. But how "normal" could it have been really? With what I am? It didn't make sense - not yet, at least. I knew, however, there were many more memories to come, just like with Charlotte and every other aspect of my vanished life. Now, thought, I had a big chunk of it back and I was so goddamn relieved.

Ignoring the stares of passersby, who seemed to be even more leery of me than usual, I concentrated on finding a cab, more than ready to get off the harshly discordant streets and since I couldn't blur in this part of town, didn't know if that ability had returned yet and didn't have the energy to find out, let alone jump rooftops, there was no choice.

A couple of blocks later, I flagged one down and gratefully slid into the back seat. I gave the driver the street name and he took off smoothly. Heaving a tired sigh, I leaned my head back against the headrest and tried to ignore the spiced curry scent that seemed to fill every crevice of the car, mixing with residual body odours and colognes from God-knows how many previous passengers. Goddammit - I quickly wound down a window, mighty peeved at the continual assault on my senses.

"You alright, mister?" The driver asked cautiously in a thick Indian accent. Or maybe it was Pakistani? I couldn't tell and I didn't care.

He gave me a wary look through the rear vision mirror, reached for something on his right and then suddenly thrust a thick wad of tissues over the seat, turning briefly to glare ominously at me and demanding "No blood on my seats, you understand? No blood!"

I lowered my head to get a look in the mirror and sure enough, the cut on my head was still seeping, little tracks of blood trailing down along my hairline and temple.

"No trouble!" He added, shoving the tissues insistently at me and driving one handed.

Shit. No wonder people had stared. I grabbed the tissues from him and wiped the bloody streaks; pressing the wad gently against the cut to hopefully staunch the flow. It needed a wash-out and maybe some antiseptic. Unless my beast-genetics decided to kick back in sometime soon and fix it. I didn't get it - I could feel him there, as always.......why wasn't he doing his little magic trick?

"It's just a graze.....no blood on your seat, don't worry," I told him and although he didn't look the slightest bit convinced, he let it go. With both hands back on the wheel, he sped up a little now, keeping one suspicious eye on me as he ducked and weaved through the traffic. He wasn't exactly smooth about it either, seemingly keen to get me out of his cab as quickly as possible.

Can't say that I disagreed with him on that, I thought with a grimace. The open window wasn't dispelling the musky cloying smells fast enough and taking shallow breaths helped only a little but as long as he got me to where I wanted to go, I'd deal with it.

By the time he dropped me off at the front of Finn's place with a pocketful of bloodied tissue, I was jittery - edgy yet pumped, still a bit dizzy and the graze throbbed like a bitch.

I didn't care.

I bolted up the steps to the entrance and pounded my fist against the heavy timber door impatiently. Nervous energy pumped wildly through my veins, a crazy mix of jubilation, fear and relief as I anticipated the look on his face when I told him the news. When he didn't immediately answer, I tried the door handle and finding it unlocked, I raced through, slamming the door in my haste and charging into the cavernous living area.

"Finn!!! " I yelled loudly, scaring the crap outta him.

He jumped out of the chair where he'd been sitting at his desk, knocking stuff everywhere and tripping over his own feet, shocked at my sudden appearance. Mouth agape and stuttering my name, he gawked fearfully.

Seeing his face now, with all the resurfaced memories of him as a little kid, a teenager and trusted friend, wearing not-so-ugly glasses and fully grown, punched a fist straight at my chest; once, twice, more....pounding madly and my heart swelled as all the shared history, camaraderie, love and support washed through my soul, overflowing and choking up my throat.....Christ....... this........this was my brother, in all but blood.

My beast howled in joyful recognition.

I rushed over to him and he backed up in terror, eyes wide, muttering "no, no, no, no" as he stuck one hand out in a useless stop gesture, scared spit-less that I was attacking him. But I snatched him up in a huge bear hug that lifted him off his feet for a moment and he screamed loudly, nearly busting my ear drums.

But it was a manly scream.

"Finn!" I said excitedly. "I remembered you!! Oh man, I remembered you!" I pounded his back a few times before pulling away, keeping ahold of his shoulders and staring into his stunned face. His glasses were knocked askew and he stood there motionless and slack-jawed.

"Not all of you, but mostly. Jesus, Dude, I remembered fishing and.....and ...... school and......." I was rambling like an idiot, all traces of stoic control absent, but I really didn't care - I was about ready to jump out of my skin.

"Riding bikes and.....football......they were just quick flashes but.......I saw us playing Little League......." I think even my beast was grinning now.

"Holy shit!!" He interrupted, his face a picture of complete stupefaction, storm grey eyes as big as an owl's.

"For real?" His voice rose ten octaves. "You remember that? How? How? How did this happen?" He was stuttering in dumbfounded elation, hands trembling so badly he nearly poked himself in the eye as he straightened his glasses. "When did this happen? Dude, you're bleeding! What the hell is going on?!"

I think he would have torn his hair out if he could.

My chest twinged and I wanted to laugh so hard - there he was......my best buddy acting all Finn-like...... his gestures, his quirks, the slightly dorky mannerisms and too-handsome face - and a thousand little memories of him pushing his glasses back up his nose washed through my mind. Swallowing thickly past the lump in my throat, I let go of his shoulders and stepped back.

"Never mind about that," I said, dismissing the injury. "I remembered you, Finn. I mean, mostly........not all of it .... But plenty. It's a start."

We stared at each other in amazement, the air heavy with stunned hope. Disbelief slowly morphed into cautious wonder, his eyes growing glassy as I felt my own get terrifyingly misty. Jesus Christ......if he started crying, I was gonna wallop him.

Taking a deep breath, I cleared my throat twice but still couldn't shake the thick gravel from my voice. "Dude, I'm......." I paused, started again. "I'm so sorry I was an asshole to you the other day. I'm sorry I didn't remember you."

The words didn't seem enough yet I knew he would hear the sincere regret in my words. I knew he'd understand me, with that subliminal language between friends that's honed over decades, unspoken and indelible and suddenly there in my psych, like it had never been gone. He wouldn't need a hundred words and just like that, something shifted inside me and clicked into place, a deep sigh shivering quietly through my system.

Finn shook his head dazedly. "Oh my God....Kellan....." His voice trembled and one hand reached to his forehead to drag his floppy hair back, a gesture that I'd seen a million times, one that warmed a cold spot in my chest and I smiled a little - he was forever in need of a haircut. He stood gaping at me, like a fish outta water.

But then, in a sudden burst of animation, he grabbed me up in his own hug, slapping my back over and over and laughing as he said: "Oh my God, Kellan. My God! Holy shit.....Thank you Jesus, Mary and Joseph!!" Wrapping my arms around him just as tightly, we hugged fiercely for a fast moment and I swear the frog in my throat was trying to choke me.

We pulled back quickly and punched each other's biceps, smiling like loons. I almost didn't recognise what my face was doing - that's how rusty it felt, but as the significance of the moment settled around us with a heavy warmth, our grins faded away.

"Oh, man, you have no idea........." he trailed off, his deep voice cracking at the end, a wealth of unspoken emotion - sorrow, relief, happiness - chasing across his face and darkening his eyes.

But he didn't need to explain.

"I know," I said quietly.

A beat or two of silence as Finn brushed his hair back from his forehead again and I stuck my hands in my front pockets. Then........

"Oh, hey," Finn said, "sorry about the........you know........screaming in your ear."

"It's cool, dude," I replied. "It was a manly scream."

We both nodded, the matter settled.

Right then, like a balloon pricked with a sharp needle, I felt a sudden deflation, as if all the energy was being sucked out of my body and I blinked rapidly against the returning dizziness.

Shit.

"What the hell happened to your head?" Finn demanded. "Geez, maybe you should sit down. Here, sit down ...."

He half pushed me onto his sofa and I went willingly, the adrenaline rush of the last few minutes draining away, leaving behind a keen exhaustion.

"Yeah," I muttered. "I'm gonna need some stuff to clean up this wound, if you got anything......" I sank onto the big leather sofa with a sigh, grateful to feel something soft and cushy around my battered body. Meanwhile Finn was scrambling through some drawers behind the bar, muttering something that sounded like: "If I've got anything?! Ha. Between your training and my OCD, I think I got a couple things....now, where's the.........ahh...there it is......"

I didn't pay him much attention, relishing the way the huge-ass cushions moulded around me. Damn - now this was a sofa. Far superior to my own back at the studio that I couldn't fully stretch out on. Like his spaceship sized desk, Finn's sectional sofa was no dainty regular couch, suitable for regular sized people but a massive, man-sized thing of beauty. Three of me could stretch out on this.

Sighing in pleasure, my shoulders relaxed and I closed my eyes for a minute.

"Hey, hey, Kellan!!" Finn yelled loudly, rushing over and grabbing my shoulder. "Sit up, man. Stay with it. You gotta get this cleaned up."

I blinked groggily up at him, realising now how much I'd slumped down - he probably thought I'd passed out.

"Wasn't sleeping." I told him and sat up straighter. The head pain was mild now, the dizziness receding again, thank God. Rolling the inertia out of my shoulders, I watched as Finn brought over a small silver bowl of warm water, another bowl filled with swabs, and a mirror.

A handheld mirror.

I quirked an eyebrow at him - why the hell did he have one of those? He just shrugged and sat his ass on the coffee table; a huge, rough timber square block that could double as a dining table for small children.

I grabbed the cloth, soaked it in the water and began to clean the wound while he held the mirror for me, all nonchalant like we'd done this many times before.

"You gonna tell me what the hell happened, now?" He asked, pushing his glasses back up his nose again.

Washing away dried blood and gunk from around the cut, I could see that it was healing finally. Not as fast as it should have but I was damn relieved that some sign of beast healing was back. In the cab, it had looked to be two to three inches long but now was closer to one. It also dawned on me that my tolerance to aromas was back in full working order - having kicked in somewhere between paying the cab driver and scaring the crap outta Finn. A breath I hadn't realised I'd been holding escaped in a grateful sigh - thank God for that.

Flicking a quick glance at his expectant face, I grabbed a clean swab, throwing the bloodied one into the empty bowl, remembered the tissues in my pocket and throwing them in as well. And while I cleaned and treated the wound, I told him the basic outline of what happened with the blast - how I'd been injured and how the memories had come flooding in. He listened without saying a word, waiting until I'd finished before he started with the questions - where was I when this happened, what was I doing there? Was this another mission and why was there an explosion? Who caused the explosion? As he fired them off, one after another, I realised he must have spoken with Charlotte - there'd been no discussion of missions between us the last time I'd seen him and the thought that they'd discussed me struck me as quite......... normal. I blinked in surprise.

Huh.

Looking him in the eye, I told him with complete honesty, "I think the Commander set me up."

His eyes bugged out.

"What the hell? The Commander? The guy you work for?"

"Yeah."

"You're sure?" He frowned fiercely, his brows a dark slash across his concerned face.

"Pretty sure," I said. "Can't prove it yet but it's starting to look that way." The bitter rage returned to simmer quietly in my gut like acid; the explosion and all it meant still echoing through my mind. "Looks like I'd served my purpose and it was time to get rid of me."

A solemn look passed between us as the implications of my discovery sat unspoken and even though there was a tonne of stuff still to explain to him, including this morning's events before the blast, there was no question that Finn believed me. He said nothing, just got up and grabbed his cell phone that was sitting on his desk then returning to his spot on the coffee table where he jabbed a long finger at the device a few times before putting it to his ear. I watched curiously, hoping I'd figured correctly who he was calling.

"Charlie, we got a situation here...... " he said and my heart thumped hard.

"We as in Kellan and I.......... yeah, he's here.........just now.........turned up bleeding and..........yes, yes, he's okay, I think.......he said that he had mem........ Charlie? Hello?......... Hello?"

He pulled the phone away from his ear, shrugged slightly, hung up and said; "I'd say she'll be here soon" in a dry tone.

Beastie-boy and I both smiled.

Chapter Fourteen

"No, I don't want a care-bear bandage."

"You sure?"

"Yes"

"Why?"

"Because, man, it's a ....care-bear bandage," I grumbled. Wasn't that explanation enough?

"Ok, ok, fine," Finn said as he went about putting away the first aid paraphernalia and turfing the bloodied swabs into the trash can. I watched as he then meticulously washed his hands and his muttered comment earlier about being OCD suddenly made sense.

Come to think of it, it probably also explained why everything in this room was so clinically neat and tidy. Taking a glance around the huge open living space, I noticed how very simple and clutter free it all was - nothing left laying around, no books or knick-knacks of any kind, the furniture big and bold. You'd think a single guy would have a lot more junk everywhere but no, not this guy. It was designer-perfect yet somehow still masculine and it made me wonder if he'd had a decorator do the place up. And if so, why?

Even his gigantic desk was clutter-free despite the four computer monitors sitting on its gleaming white surface - one keyboard, one mouse and a pen holder. That's it. Not one scrap of paper.

Where the hell did he keep stuff, I wondered curiously but then noticed something on the wall behind it. There was an odd, faint line running from ceiling to floor and as I zoomed my vision in, I realised that it was actually a pair of very well concealed sliding doors and not a wall at all.

Huh.

Very sleek.

I couldn't see any sort of lever or button anywhere nearby, either. My brows rose in surprise, seriously impressed with the futuristic styling. Smart too, I smirked - shove all your crap in there and your place will never be messed up and no one would know. There wasn't even a remote control laying around offending the pristine neatness of it all.

Speaking of which......where the hell was the television? I scanned around quickly but there wasn't one anywhere to be seen. My brow quirked...... Weird. I'm sure there had been a big ass one here the other day - I think. Was that hidden somewhere? Had to be, I decided - there's no way a single guy living alone wouldn't have one.

Or three.

And that thought came to a screeching halt because......he hadn't lived here alone, had he? I'd lived here too, he'd told me a few days back. However, nothing about this living area was remotely familiar to me which didn't surprise me really - my mind seemed to chose randomly what it would recall and what it wouldn't. What was most disconcerting was the knowledge that somewhere in this massive apartment was my bedroom, a space that contained the personal belongings of a man that I don't remember being. I'd need to face that room soon, I knew, but I wondered if it would bring another onslaught of rushing memories or if I'd feel nothing.

And which would be worse.

By this time, Finn had come to sit in the armchair that sat perpendicular to the sectional sofa and I leaned forward, elbows on knees, figuring now would be a good time to get some clarification.

He met my gaze with wry amusement. "You got a hundred questions, don't you?"

Fully appreciating his mind reading abilities and dry tone, I gave a half smile. "Yeah, kinda."

"Shoot."

"So, ahhhh........." Where do I even start? I frowned in thought then went with what I deemed the most innocuous. "Okay, one of the memories I had was studying for college exams but I couldn't tell for what. What was I doing at college? Did I get in?"

It seemed so improbable given what I was. Reckless, dangerous and highly stupid - the party life of college wasn't exactly a safe place for someone like me and I shuddered at all the horrific possibilities. A beast on campus. A killer. Surrounded by girls and alcohol and God knows what else.....

"Yeah, you did but you dropped out four, five months later," Finn said, leaning forward to mirror my pose; elbows on knees, hands clasped and eyes intent on my face.

"Dropped out?" I repeated, surprised. That didn't feel right, somehow. Illogically, I was annoyed at the idea instead of relieved but I knew instinctively I wasn't a quitter. So why would I do exactly that? "

"Why?"

"You made it into the Fire Department and training was starting."

Oh.

Okay.

That was cool. I liked that reason.

"You'd applied just out of high school and it took a bit of time to go through all the application stages - the academic and physical fitness tests and stuff," he explained with a casual shrug. "So you did those around classes and after you'd passed each stage, you had to wait for training to officially start."

So I'd been what, nineteen? Eighteen maybe? The other day Finn had said I'd left the army seven years ago.....

"How old am I?" I asked him.

"You don't know?" His brows shot up above his glasses.

"I do....I think. Just checking."

"You're 34. Same as me."

That's what I'd thought. Weird how I could remember random things like my age or the kinds of music I like but all the important stuff had been wiped out of my brain.

"So, how did I end up in the army?" I asked, instantly tensing up when his heart beat spiked unexpectedly. He swallowed convulsively, looking lost for words and I narrowed my eyes warily.

"You, errr," he began, his deep voice hesitant. "You decided to enlist when........" He stopped abruptly, brushing his hair back from his forehead in agitation. "Shit," he muttered under his breath, staring at the floor.

"When what?" I demanded gruffly and when he looked back up at me, there was such uncertainty on his face.

"I'm not sure how much to.......dammit........" he muttered, visibly uncomfortable. "How much I should tell you. I don't wanna break your brain, dude. Maybe it's better that some things come back to you naturally?"

An alarm began clanging somewhere in my mind at the trepidation in his tone. What didn't he want to tell me? What was so bad that he looked slightly queasy? My gut shivered at his reluctance and instinct began prodding at me with sharp nasty fingers, telling me to back away from this. But I couldn't drop it entirely; not just yet.

"Give me the basics," I said in a tight voice, silence following as he considered his words carefully.

"You had some, uhhhh......some really tough things to deal with at the time, some........family issues and the only way you could deal with it was to enlist," he finished quietly. "So you did."

Staring into his darkly solemn eyes, the weight of all that he left unsaid sat heavily between us.

Those sharp nasty fingers were holding up a "danger" sign now and the beast growled uneasily. Whatever had happened back then was big - big enough to drive me away from a job that I'd apparently worked hard to get. "Family issues" could mean just about anything but the way he'd said it, I knew it didn't bode well. So I took heed of the warning signs and stepped away from that line of questioning as if it was an unpinned grenade: quietly and carefully.

"Okay," I said, steering the conversation into hopefully safer territory. "How long did I serve?"

Finn sighed, relief crossing his features even as he tried to appear impassive. "Two years."

Not that long then.

Nodding slowly, I did some quick math in my head as a timeline started to form. Seemed odd to me, however - why bother enlisting for only a couple years?

"I had a memory, with all the others today," I said, realising I hadn't mentioned it when I'd barged in here earlier. Thinking back to the very brief scene, I told him what little I could remember of it. "We were saying goodbye. Looked like it was at an airport but I'm not entirely sure; it was all kind of blurry, yanno? There were other people around but I don't know if they were with us or just part of a general crowd. And I was in army fatigues."

There was an odd glimmer in his gaze, a brief flash of....something that was gone so quickly I had no time to define it.

"You remembered that too?" Finn said with a half smile. "That's great. That's real good. And yeah, it was at the airport. You were on Leave for a couple days."

It didn't escape my notice that he offered no information about the other people there and when I met his gaze, I could see that we both knew he was holding back. Surprisingly it didn't bother me, I realised. Because along with the memories of him came an instinctual trust that just slid right back into place somewhere inside. From my gut, I knew this guy would have my back, the years of friendship testimony to that.

And whatever he held back, it was more of the "you're not ready" and "don't wanna break your brain, dude" vibe.

However, as always, each new piece of information left more questions in its wake.

"I don't get how I could have gone to college, been a firefighter or........." I suddenly blurted with a shake of my head, unable to make sense of it. Everything Finn had said was the truth, I knew it was. But how the fuck could it be?

"How the hell is that possible when I'm a........ you know........ a beast. Half animal. How is any of it possible?" Renewed tension began creeping through my back and shoulders and unable to sit still, I stood and paced away a few steps before spinning back to face Finn who sat alert and watchful. I was getting worked up but couldn't seem to stop myself; anger and frustration was scratching at my nerves. "I don't get how I could have been that and you and I did normal stuff like Little League and shit and...... and...... didn't I ever beast out on you? I mean...... fuck...... what about school and our parents...... and......."

Unbelievably, I found myself venting with an ease of freedom unrecognisable to me. Words spilled unbidden from my mouth, revealing more than I was used to. Something about Finn - the sympathy and concern I could see clearly in his eyes - broke down the stoic control that was so much a part of me. But damn it! Why the fuck couldn't I remember everything at once so I could just get it over with? This endless jigsaw puzzle in my brain was screwing me over again and again, unsettling me every time I thought I had myself under control.

"Okay, okay! STOP!" Finn exclaimed loudly but I couldn't hear him above the roaring in my ears, the white noise of constant upheaval.

"Jesus, did I ever beast out on my parents?? On your parents?? Oh God, is that why.........did I........?"

My stomach turned over at the thought of myself as an uncontrollable little beastie kid, tension coiling in my belly tighter than a snake and I ran a shaky hand through my hair, unnerved.

Jesus H. Christ. Had I hurt them? Or.....or.....

My heart thundered in my chest, sheer horror snatching the breathe from my lungs as my skin turned ice cold. No...... Please no.

"Dude, it's all right! Kellan, listen......." He jumped up, hurried over and grabbed my shoulders. It wouldn't occur to me until later how easily I adjusted to someone touching me. Barring Charlotte, no one could - not without risking their life. "Listen, you didn't do anything to either of our parents or me growing up. You didn't hurt anyone! Christ, you weren't a beast then, why would you think that? You weren't born one. It's all right," he said insistently, staring into my face, willing me to calm down. "It's all right."

Wasn't born one?

What the fuck?! What did he just say?

I stared at Finn in complete shock, frozen immobile as ice splintered down my spine and heat raced through my veins. My heart stopped for a moment before galloping wildly, the air around me suctioned into nothingness - my beast snarled in self defence.

"Wasn't born......" I began in a faint raspy voice, but trailed off, unable to get the words out. My mind couldn't grasp his meaning, the implications.

Oh God.......what fresh new hell was this??

"No, you weren't born a beast. Or a half beast. Or whatever the fuck you wanna call it. You were human. You still are." He glared angrily at me, his voice hard: "Shit, man, I don't know what the hell they've done to you but I can tell you this - they've brainwashed you. Whatever they've told you is bullshit. Complete bullshit! You got that? Christ, why would they make you think that?!" Red hot fury burned in his eyes.

I stared at him blankly, my breaths shallow as I tried to absorb his words, to comprehend. But....... Goddammit .... I was made? Not born a beast?

My world tilted, spun out of control and collapsed, knocked ruthlessly off its axis. Vaguely I wondered if I looked as sick as I felt - the blood in my veins had congealed into a sticky gluggy mess and I couldn't find my centre of gravity.

In desperate self-protection I shut down, locking steel barriers around my spinning emotions before they ripped apart my sanity and cramming them into the coldest, furtherest reaches of my mind. Finn squeezed my shoulders once before letting go slowly, giving me time but keeping his watchful eyes fixed on my face.

"Here....Sit down. Before you pass out," Finn said gruffly.

I wasn't gonna pass out but the weakness in my knees didn't know that. So, taking two steps, I sat heavily back down on the sofa. Jaw clenched, fingers curling into claws then stretching loose again, every muscle tight. I felt my eyes flare to gold, then tinge with red dangerously and I looked to the floor so Finn wouldn't see how close to the edge I was; concentrating desperately on slowing my heart rate and using every single trick in my repertoire to tether the beast and calm the chaos in my mind.

Finn sat patiently in his chair, not saying anything, just giving me space and I was grateful for his silence as I took in a slow shuddering breath. Then another. Then a dozen more until I felt the world solidify around me.

Two steps forward, one step back? Yeah, I grimaced. More like three forward and fifty seven back.

Jesus. How do I even begin to process this?

"Look," Finn said in a quiet voice. "Why don't you tell me everything that you remembered, in as much detail as you can and we'll take it from there? Maybe that way I can sort out things for you without freaking you out?"

Looking up into his solemn eyes, his entire demeanour was one of calm reassurance, a quiet steady strength that was like a balm to my frayed nerves. He'd always been that way, my mind whispered. Still waters and all that. People always made the mistake of assuming that because he was a brainiac, loaded and brilliantly clever, that they knew what he was - a pretty boy science nerd. But they didn't. They didn't look below the surface, to the latent strength simmering beneath, both physical and mental. They didn't see his generous, vulnerable heart, the strong moral conviction that he lived by or the loyalty. He was also funny as hell, quirky and always had my back.

Funny how little slivers of knowledge slipped quietly into my thoughts, reassuringly just....there, where they would have always been.

Taking a deep breath, I said; "Okay, you're right. Better that way......"

And so I began to tell him of each of the memories in as much detail as I could recall - everything that I could see, hear or smell in each vision and gradually the conversation soothed and relaxed the tension from my body and I found myself sitting back against the cushions, easy for the first time in hours.

Finn smiled nostalgically at some of the descriptions, filling in bits and pieces for me - the fishing trip was something that our families used to do a lot when we were little kids - head up north to Crystal Lake in Sullivan County for camping and fishing.

He laughed when I told him about the popcorn-throwing at the cinemas, saying that we were idiots - that I'd been trying to get the attention of a girl that he had liked and embarrassing the shit out of him. Huh. That made me smile.

Little League had lasted for only a couple years because Finns' glasses were constantly getting broken and once he'd quit I hadn't wanted to continue, apparently.

We'd gone to the same college that he now taught biochem at - Hudson University - until I'd dropped out and he'd gone on to become a genius scientist - according to him.

The memories of playing football were apparently another regular O'Ryan family event - summer barbecues with my cousins, aunts, uncles and the McGregor clan, not just on July 4th but any chance we could get everyone together.

"And we always played football," Finn said with a reminiscent smile and a slight nod.

"Even the oldies. But then Mom got sick and couldn't....."

I stumbled to a halt.

"Yeah." He sighed then registered what I'd said and did a double take.

I sat dead still, shocked at what had come unbidden from my own mouth. The blood drained to my feet as my skin iced over, all the fine hair standing on edge as an eerie dread swept over me. My beast snapped to attention.

What the hell did I just say?

My mom got sick? With what? A wild sense of disorientation sent my senses scrambling. Why did I say that when I couldn't remember her? Or my father? How could I say something like that and still not see their faces in my mind?

Not even for a split second - they were completely blank, the wall in my mind shut to them.

My throat started to squeeze shut, my breathing shallow and constricted as I stared unseeingly at Finn.

"Shit!" he exclaimed loudly. "Oh shit, Kellan!" His eyes suddenly popped wide in shock and he reached over, panic stricken, to grab hold of my shoulder again.

"Oh hell dude, I'm sorry," he groaned. "I'm sorry. I didn't mean to force that memory on you. Crap......" He looked as white as the ghost that trailed icy fingers down my spine.

"My mom got sick?" I croaked, barely able to say the words. "But I..... I can't see her face, Finn. How can I say she got sick when I can't remember her face. Sick with what?" I searched his face for the calmness I'd found there earlier, dread sitting like rancid oil in my belly, slimy and black. But he was far from calm at the moment.

"Cancer," he replied automatically, looking sideswiped as he blinked like a stunned owl.

Shit, cancer?

"Wait a minute," he mumbled under his breath. "You're not remembering your mom? Or your dad? I thought......" But he trailed off in confusion.

"No, I'm not. I don't remember them. So how can I say something like that?"

Jesus..... Maybe I'd finally lost it, my mind splintered under the constant pressure?

Is that why he wasn't calm and steady like before?

"Oh God, I thought you......" His deep voice trembled for a moment before he shook his head, gathered himself and clamped his broad hand on other shoulder, doing his best to keep me centred and seated even as I felt myself ready to implode into a million jagged pieces.

"Kellan, buddy, look at me," he demanded harshly, his voice sounding miles away and waiting till I faced him before continuing. "I promise you that I will tell you everything when you're ready, okay? I PROMISE you." His intensity was laser sharp; his face darkly determined. "But right now, I don't think it's a great idea because you haven't remembered them on your own yet and obviously you're not ready to."

I blinked.

Okay.

Okay.

I latched onto his words like a lifeline.

He was right - of course he was right. I wasn't ready, that was all, I told myself. My subconscious had let slip one small phrase then snapped back in retreat, not willing to let go. That was it, I decided, grasping tightly to the rational explanation, the only one that made any sense to me at the moment and as tension began seeping out of my shoulders, Finn let go and once again gave me space, sitting back with a sigh.

Jesus, how many more hits was I gonna take today?

When was it enough?

A hollow echo seemed to thud hard in my heart, in a corner that seemed empty and pained. Everything inside of me felt kicked and bruised, pounded by a thousand fists until tender and sore. I pressed the thumb and middle finger of one hand against my eyelids, more tired than I could ever remember being.

"I know you wanna know, K." Finn said after a long while and I looked back up at him wearily. "And you will. It's just that.......... There's a lot to tell, okay? But you're not ready yet and we got more urgent things to deal with right now." He pushed back his hair, jabbed at his glasses and leaned forward, elbows on knees. "We gotta figure out what the hell happened to you. And why you think your commander would set you up."

I nodded slowly, grateful to switch gears and focus on the immediate issues. I'd had enough trauma for one fucking day, thank you very much.

"If he has, then he'll try for you again," Finn added, straightforward and logical.

"He will," I agreed. "So I need to find out who this prick is and get to him first."

"Exactly. But we'll need to....... wait. What? What'd you say?" Finns eyes goggled at me again. "Find out who he is? You don't know??"

"No," I said and his mouth fell open in shock.

"Holy crap." He shook his head in confusion. "How'd that happen? Wait......okay, you need to start at the beginning and tell me everything you can about him and how it all began," and he leaned back into his chair expectantly, crossing ankle over knee, settling in as if for a story.

And so I told him how I'd woken up one morning around a week ago in a hotel room down on Ludlow, on the Upper East Side with the remnants of what had looked like a nice little booze fest scattered all over the room - empty scotch bottles and leftover food congealing on plates, all for a party of two - two glasses, two dinner settings, two coffee cups. I'd had the hangover from hell and couldn't remember a single thing from the night before - who had I been drinking with? Eating with? And what was I doing in a hotel? I couldn't even remember my own name until I'd found the note addressed to Kellan, scribbled on hotel stationery and left lying on the dresser. I hadn't been absolutely certain that "Kellan" was my real name at that point. Not until days later when Finn and Charlotte, two total strangers to me at the time, had called it out at the docks.

"Kellan" was to lay low for a day or two and to prepare for his first mission, said the note. The keys for a refurbished warehouse, fully stocked with everything I'd need, sat on top of the writing pad and once he was there, he'd find further instructions. Contact would be made with the Commander via the cell phone left lying next to the keys.

The crumbled up army fatigues lying on the floor next to a pair of combat boots was proof that I was a soldier, the sight of them flooding my mind with visions of warfare and marching and desert heat, so I knew immediately that I'd been stationed somewhere hot and dry.

After showering, I'd packed up what little stuff I could find around the room, recalling now how the clammy sickness of that morning had given way to a controlled detachment with each passing minute. Other than the fatigues and boots, there'd been just a clean set of underwear and clothes - jeans, tee and jacket plus street boots, left in a small dark satchel. The keys, phone and note I'd pocketed while the army gear was stashed into the black bag. I'd found a wallet stuck inside the inner pocket of the leather jacket but all it contained was a stack of money, a dog tag and nothing else. No ID.

I'd discovered that the hotel bill had been taken care of when I'd tried to check out. The receptionist wouldn't tell me by who, only that it was all taken care of. She'd handed me a receipt made out to Kellan O'Ryan, smiling flirtatiously and yammering that she hoped I'd enjoyed my stay and to come back. Anytime.

So I'd made my way to the warehouse and discovered what appeared to be my home; clothes, food, necessary items like bathroom supplies, kitchen fully stocked, furniture, bedding.....it even had gym equipment.

And in one cupboard, a safe containing money, artillery, ammunition and a laptop.

I'd established first contact with my superior, finding his identity hidden from me - no introductions, simply a distorted voice over an encrypted phone line. I hadn't questioned the secrecy, the orders for complete elimination, particularly that first mission. It hadn't bothered me; I'd blindly accepted the status quo and followed orders as a soldier does.

Looking back on it now though, it should have - I should have been bothered by a helluva lot.

I'd lain low as instructed for a couple days - familiarising myself with the weaponry and digital gear, the Intel left on the laptop and getting a lot of exercise in the home gym.

Finally, a couple of days later, the first mission began with a sting operation to trap Tanaka and eliminate him - which McGregor and the luscious lady-cop had interrupted in spectacular fashion. As pissed off as I was at the time, especially for being shot at by a tranquilliser gun, now.........now, I was damned grateful.

Because now I could see that not only had I not known who I was, I hadn't been "right" either.

Something about the way I'd acted, the cold way I'd functioned wasn't normal - a single-minded, lethal compulsion had dictated my focus to the exclusion of all else. I'd operated in a fog of mechanical servitude, I realised uneasily. And it was only now, after the events of the last few days that I could see the stark difference in my behaviour then.

Finn sat silent for a few minutes after I'd finished my story, a simmering anger lurking behind his stillness.

"What?"

"Buddy, you left the army seven years ago. Those weren't your fatigues and you couldn't have been serving an army superior," he said tensely, stating what I already knew. "You happen to be the only beast that we know of and you were taken three months ago. That isn't and couldn't be a coincidence. They had to have known what you were. So who the fuck is this guy?"

That was the million dollar question, wasn't it?

Chapter Fifteen

Seven years.

Where had I been all that time? The timeline that had formed in my head only went so far and when I added in the date of my alleged "death" it screwed up the order. I was fighting fire in that arson memory so that event had to be before enlisting with the army, right? Yet, according to the news reports I'd read, I'd "died" a little more than five years ago.

Something was missing.

I'd assumed that the news article and the returned memory of beasting out in the arson attack were one and the same. But what if they weren't? What if they were two different occasions? Firefighters' dealt with arson all the time so it was more than feasible. In fact, it was probable.

Christ. I sneered angrily at the floor. Given the hits I'd already taken today, I wasn't entirely sure I wanted to know about the last few years.

I asked, anyway.

"Where have I been, if not in the military?" Seven years was a long time and both Finn and Charlotte had stated I'd disappeared three months ago - possibly kidnapped. But that didn't fit - why would I be kidnapped if the world thinks I'm dead?
"The fire department. When you came home, you went straight back to your firehouse for a while," he told me, his voice calm and careful.

O-Kay......That fit.

But what did he mean by "a while"?

Six months? A year?

I pinned him with a narrow stare and he took the hint immediately.

"Okay. Okay," he muttered with another jab at his glasses. "But, man, that's a long story."

He paused, looking as if he was hoping I'd tell him not to bother. But I wasn't going to do that and after a few moments of contemplation he nodded his head in silent decision.

"I guess I'm the only person that can really answer that for you," he said in a somber tone. "Alright, but we need a drink to get through this."

He got up, hunted down a bottle of whisky from a kitchen cupboard, a couple of glasses and brought it all back to the coffee table. Pouring us both three fingers worth of Jameson's Irish, we gave a small salute before taking a drink, the sharp taste gliding smoothly down my dry throat. As a flash of déjà vu skipped across my conscious, I glanced at the bottle's label and knew instantly that this was my favourite brand and we'd sat drinking this way before - no context or memory of it, just a simple knowing.

He sat staring into his glass for a minute, considering how and where to begin. I waited, letting the familiar barley flavour soothe a couple more of my frayed edges. Nothing of this conversation so far had been easy so if we needed alcohol to get through this part, well.......damn..........he could take his time.

And I could quietly bolster myself with more of the best Irish around, I decided.

I'd just taken a mouthful when he suddenly got up and mumbled, "I'll be back in a minute. You know......bathroom....." He lowered his head and took off for the short hallway off the left side of the enormous kitchen. My brow quirked at his retreating back. Whether he needed the facilities or not, the delaying tactic was obvious.

Not that I minded.

In fact, a pent up breath I hadn't been aware I was holding escaped with a sigh. Placing my half empty glass down on the table, I sprawled back against the couch, tired but wired. My mind was one giant quagmire; the overload of information like an anvil swinging sluggishly around in my brain and I really needed it to just stop for an hour.

Just one fucking hour.

Closing my eyes, I let the exhaustion overtake me for a few moments, slumping down more comfortably into the cushions. The whole day had been a freaking crapfest from the time I'd woken up. I'd spent a long restless night thinking firstly about Charlotte and our burgeoning relationship then when I'd exhausted that topic, I'd gone over the events of the last few days; looking at them from different angles, tossing around different possibilities in an effort to explain the dichotomy of what my life is right now and what I was told it was by a woman who I knew wasn't lying.

But no matter which perspective I looked at it from, I couldn't get it to fit - pieces were missing in every scenario. And adding to that frustration was the nagging feeling I was within touching distance of the one vital piece that I needed above all else - that if I just reached out a little further, a little more, I'd have it in my grasp. But each time I tried, it would vanish back into obscurity, like a candle snuffed out, an odd sense of disorientation left in its wake.

Eventually I'd fallen into an exhausted sleep, unfortunately not dreaming of Charlotte at all this time. Instead my dreams were filled with murky images of blackened streets; of looming shadows that breathed with a fetid menace. As if my subconscious was spewing forth every unreleased fear and emotion, I dreamt in blood-red shades of pain and rage: of being hunted like prey, persistent eyes on my back - watching and waiting - overlaid with booming gunfire and searing heat. Of hiding in dark, cold corners.

Of sorrow and loss.

And crippling loneliness.

I'd woken startled and uneasy, sweat breaking out icily over my clammy skin. Not a great way to start the day.

Deeply disturbed, tired and moody as shit, I'd taken a long shower to shake off the black mood and clear my head. But the lingering sense of doom and gloom didn't budge and although I didn't like to admit it, even to myself, the dreams had shaken me this time. Whether they were repressed memories or not, they left a hollow hopelessness in the pit of my belly that I had to fight to ignore. And it only got worse when an encrypted email came from the Commander - meet the beast-target at a disused warehouse up in Inwoods' 207th Street, confirm his identity as Peter Landers, ex-military and eliminate him. Report back.

Simple.

Except it wasn't.

Firstly....why the email rather than verbal communication? And second, just how many freaking beast targets were there? Plus, there'd been no feedback on either the Gallery explosion or the whereabouts of the two targets. So why send me on a new mission when the previous one wasn't finalised?

That didn't feel right. Even if he'd removed me from that mission, there's no way in hell he would have done so without some major screaming down the phone line - he wouldn't have passed up the opportunity to berate and reprimand my ass. No - he would have screeched his mechanical voice till he was blue in the face. So, why the change in M.O.?

Following instinct, I'd jumped online and discovered that there were seven Peter Landers' in New York State, none of which had any reported military background. However, that didn't mean much as he could be from anywhere. Maybe, I was transferred to this target simply for expediency? Had Lewinski and Ridley perished in the gallery explosion the other day and I hadn't been informed?

Annoyed at the useless speculation, I'd keyed in their names and found the day's digital newspapers reporting on the death of Goldberg Capital's CFO Paul Ridley in a car accident the night of the fundraiser. I'd sat staring at the screen in disbelief, the back of my neck tingling wildly as I read through the details. Ridley had wrapped his Lexus around a pole at considerable speed on the thruway in New Rochelle and with only one car involved, the police were investigating, the article said.

No doubt.

Although this could very easily be the reason the commander had a new assignment, everything about the timing of his death felt ......off. Way off. If Ridley been travelling from upstate New York, you could assume he was on his way to the Bellingworth Gallery, where I just happened to be waiting and where a huge explosion ended up killing three and injuring dozens more that night.

Coincidence? A cruel twist of fate?

Maybe.

But my instincts were twitching madly and I'd spent a restless while pacing back and forth across the floorboards. The beast was growling and stalking with me, both of us edgy and not liking where my thoughts were taking me.

Even after researching everything I could find on both the gallery explosion and Ridley's accident - in case I'd missed something - there was nothing there to alleviate the suspicions that were building in my mind. Sure, maybe it could all be explained logically and reasonably but my system was screaming loud and clear, every hackle on my body alert. Something was definitely not right.

But, Goddamn, I hoped I was wrong in my thinking because if I wasn't......... then I was in a deep load of shit.

By the time I'd headed out to meet Landers, I'd been ready to spit nails - furious tension stretching my patience and control and a curious foreboding gnawing under my skin.

Looking back on it now, that foreboding had undoubtedly saved my life.

When I'd arrived at the site, my senses hadn't picked up any traces of beast and in fact, no human ones either. A thorough scan of the entire building had revealed some residual human activity however there was no way of knowing how old it was - could be yesterday or could be months ago. But no fresh scents. Just the usual critters that infiltrated old buildings.

Landers wasn't here. No one was.

By then, I'd been so acutely alert, every whisper of sound was like chalk on a board across my skin. I'd waited impatiently for five minutes then called the commander who'd snidely questioned whether I was at the wrong place. I'd roared at him in full animal voice, highly offended; snarling as something indefinable had kicked in warning, deep in my gut. Acting on furious instinct, I'd picked up a length of rusty steel pipe laying on the concrete ground nearby and hurled it a couple hundred feet at the windows, watching as it shattered through the glass and landed with an tinny echo inside the cavernous old warehouse.

For a loaded minute, everything had been still, like it was holding its breath and then BOOM - the explosion thundered and shook, spewing giant flames into the sky and knocking me off my ass.

Literally and figuratively - because with that detonation, everything had shifted.

The realisation that my suspicions hadn't been off-base ripped apart everything I'd believed and hearing that click on my cell as the commander had hung up only confirmed them.

In a way, I was damn lucky that memories of Finn had chosen that moment to resurface because if they hadn't, I don't know how I would have contained the enormous rage and shock, what destruction I would have caused with nowhere and no-one to vent to. I shuddered now to think of the psychological damage to my sanity had I not had something, no...... some one to turn to and although I knew I could have run to Charlotte, I'm glad I hadn't - I was a fucking mess at that moment and I would have upset her unnecessarily.

Besides, what would I have done - charged bleeding and yelling into her precinct, like I'd done here at Finn's? I smirked to myself - yeah, right, that would have gone down well.

The pinched tension in my body finally started to loosen as I sank further into the sofa cushions with a sigh, letting myself just drift awhile. But then........ my inner beast pricked up his ears, suddenly alert and aware. A heartbeat thudded rhythmically nearby, getting closer - steady and sure like a drumbeat calling to my soul : alluring, mesmerising.

And it wasn't Finn's.

Just like the hypnotic aroma that began invading my senses, slithering over my body with seductive softness was definitely not Finns'. My beast shivered in ecstasy, eyes rolling in pleasure.

SHE was here.

Detective Make-Me-Purr-Baby.

Keeping my eyes closed, I didn't move a muscle; just enjoyed the sensation of her. Her timing couldn't be more perfect - she was exactly what I needed right now.

I heard the front door open and close and with it, her scent invaded the whole room, saturating my pores with her heady fragrance. My beast growled playfully in welcome and it occurred to me that between Charlotte and I, we just strolled in without any regard for Finn's privacy. He really needed to start locking his doors, I snickered to myself, listening to her footsteps enter the main room.

"Finn?" she called out but he was... ummm...... indisposed. Peeking a little through my closed eyelids, I caught the moment she spotted me and rushed over. Then, mmmmm, she was right there in my personal space, just inches away.

Where I wanted her to be - constantly.

She leaned towards me, concern all over her face as she took in the small wound on my temple, one hand half reaching out as if to soothe. But she wasn't close enough for my liking so I quickly snagged my arms around her waist, pulling her off her feet and across my lap as she yelped in surprise. Keeping one hand supporting her neck, I flipped her onto her back on the sofa, her legs across my thighs and before she knew it, I was kissing her. Thoroughly.

Deeply.

Leisurely.

Moaning at the sweet and spicy taste of her soft pliable lips, the silky smoothness of her mouth as my tongue took gentle swipes across her own.

After her initial shock, she was melting in my arms, a little moan of her own escaping as she kissed me back just as deeply, just as thoroughly, completely enthralling my every sense.

My beast purred with pure delight.

Her hands wrapped around my neck tightly as I slid one hand from her hip to her waist to her midriff, rubbing my thumb across the plumb underside of her breast a couple of times before rising to cup her jaw. My muscles liquified as the heat rose between us, my dick hardening and swelling with want; endless want.

Damn, she felt so good.

My tongue tasted every inch of her lips, devouring, hungry - the wet glide sending tingling warmth down my spine.

If we weren't on Finn's couch......

With supreme reluctance, I slowly pulled back from her, leaving a lingering baby kiss before lifting away an inch or two, just enough to look down at her gorgeous face, all smooth flawless skin and dimpled cheeks, her green gold eyes captivating as she blinked them open.

"Hi," I said quietly in a rough voice, giving her a small smile as I propped myself up on one elbow.

"Hi," she returned, looking dazed and confused. Knowing I'd caused that confusion, I couldn't help but smirk with a little masculine pride. Our eyes hooked, the connection between us tangible as desire throbbed low-key but insistently. As usual, my heart did its weird ass thumping, something that I was beginning to think would always happen whenever I was around her.

This woman's eyes.......... They grabbed me hard and didn't let go.

Every. Single. Time.

Leaning down, needing more, my mouth was just centimetres from hers when Finn suddenly yelled. "What the hell is going on NOW??!!"

Charlotte and I both jerked our heads around to see him standing there, stopped dead in his tracks, eyes as big as an owl's behind his glasses and mouth agog as he took in the two of us tangled up nice and close. He looked so shocked that his hair was almost standing on end and I realised that the one and only other time he'd seen us together was when I'd first woken up on this very couch.

At that time, I hadn't even remembered her name and here I was kissing on her - no wonder he was stunned stupid.

"Progress?" I answered his question with a laugh.

Finn's eyebrows shot to the top of his head and Charlotte pushed against my chest. I looked down to find her frowning and blushing with major embarrassment, cheeks all rosy.

And that just made me wanna push her buttons.

"What?" I said, all innocence.

"Let me up," she hissed at me, flustered.

"Why? Where ya going? I need some TLC," I teased her.

She pushed at my chest in earnest as Finn stood there dumbfounded.

"Kellan!" She was getting pissed now.

"It's true. I've been traumatised today. Ask Finn," I said, trying to keep a straight face. Technically all of this was true - I had been traumatised and did need some special care.

Especially from her, if I could swing it.

I tried to cuddle into her but she was having none of it. She pinched the skin at my hips, above the waistband of my jeans, twisting cruelly till I gave in with a burst of laughter and leaned away from her. She swung her legs off my lap and sat up so fast her head must have spun dizzily. Smoothing her hair, she gave me a reproachful frown before turning to Finn, trying to look calm and composed.

I had to work hard to not laugh again, having no doubt she'd probably wallop me if I did.

My mouth twitched in amusement at the idea. And as I sat back up against the leather and lay my arm along the back behind Charlotte, a fragile warmth flared to life in the centre of my chest, in a spot that I hadn't realised was cold and weary - everything about the last five minutes in her presence lightened my mood and soothed the internal bruises this shitfest of a day had heaped upon my sorry ass.

She made things better just by being here, I realised and that warmth flared stronger.

"Progress?" Finn scoffed and my attention snapped back to the room. He was still gaping at us as if we had green heads. "This is beyond progress. A few days ago, you couldn't remember her name. Then you didn't trust her so you kidnapped her and now you're smooching with her on the couch?"

"Hey, I'm right here, you know!" Charlotte objected but we both ignored her.

"You know about the kidnapping?" Hmmmm. Did she tell him everything that happened at my studio that day?

Surely not.

"Of course I know," He said, coming over to sit in his armchair again. "She wasn't too happy about it."

Wasn't she?

That's not how I remembered it, her cries of sexual satisfaction still clear as a bell in my ear. I raised an eyebrow at her in challenge, innuendo turned up high as I purposely misunderstood Finn's meaning and she caught my drift immediately.

"You kidnapped a cop, Kellan. Of course I wasn't happy about it," she said, her words and meaningful glare clearing adding "smart ass" to the end of that sentence.

"I brought you back, didn't I?" I replied, pushing those buttons just a little more for the hell of it; delighted when her eyes flared in temper as they did now. "That's irrelevant," she declared, tipping her chin up obstinately.

"You shouldn't have kidnapped a cop in the first place."

I held back the wide grin that threatened to crack my face. How was it, I wondered, that she managed to bring out a playfulness in me I'd had no idea was there?

Finn, who'd been watching the exchange with interest, butted in with a droll: "And now you two are kissing on my couch."

Well......yeah.

"How'd it go from zero to sixty so fast?"

While Charlotte scrambled for an answer, I simply told him - "We had a date last night."

"A date. You had a date?" Finns' voice was incredulous. "All this crap is going on; missions, kidnappings and explosions and.............and amnesia and you still somehow manage to date the girlfriend you can't actually remember? Within days. What are you, a heat-seeking missile?" He shook his head in complete bafflement. "And I can't even get a woman to notice me," he grumbled, mostly under his breath.

"What woman?" Charlotte and I said, almost in unison, glancing at each other before facing Finn again. Amusingly, we were in sync in our nosiness.

"Umm, no one," He rushed to deny, getting a little twitchy. "No one at all. Just a figure of speech."

Hmmm, interesting....

"Okay, buddy, if you say so." I knew he was lying but I wasn't going to pull him up on it. Not yet. And not in front of Charlotte. I'd find out soon enough.

"Buddy?" Charlotte said in surprise, glancing sharply from one to the other.

"Errr.... yeah," Finn said with an ironic shrug. "There's been some progress there too."

She quirked an eyebrow at us, waiting.

I leaned forward, resting elbows on knees as I looked over at her beside me. "I had some memories of Finn today, stuff from growing up together."

The impact of that statement could be seen in the sudden sheen of moisture in her eyes, the hopeful happiness in her indrawn breath and the way her hand reached out to clasp one of mine tightly.

"Kellan.........oh.....oh, that's so great..." she breathed.

And she smiled so big and bright at me, I thought the sun had snuck into the room.

She beamed at Finn too before turning back to me, her eyes radiantly soft. My heart twisted painfully to see how genuinely happy she was for me.

"Yeah, he stormed in here, bleeding and yelling about remembering me...... " Finn trailed off with a laugh and a shake of his head. "Scared the crap outta me."

I smirked at him - he didn't give a damn if that sounded at all "unmanly".

I liked that about him.

"And why exactly were you bleeding?" Charlotte asked, eyes flicking towards my temple, a slight frown creasing her brows. As I reached up and felt along where the wound had been, there was only smooth, uncut skin - beast DNA finally taking care of it. She didn't look shocked by the rapid healing at all, only mildly curious and I figured that was because she'd witnessed it before.

I glanced at Finn and he waved his hand at me in a rolling gesture, telling me to "take it away".

Charlotte started to withdraw her hand from mine but I wouldn't let go, liking the sensation of holding hands with her - the connectedness, the warmth. Instead, I slid my hand against hers till we were palm to palm, my fingers threading around her small delicate ones and clasping them tight and close. It amazed me that her hands were so small and fragile-looking when I knew she kicked ass with the best of them and her gun probably weighed more than she did.

I watched my thumb slide against her soft skin, our different skin tones a fascinating contrast.

Looking up from our joined hands, our eyes caught and clung before she gave a small smile of encouragement that made her dimple wink and her gaze glint prettily. And so, starting from the beginning I told them both everything that happened from this morning till now - sparing no details, catching Finn up on the events back at the studio. Charlotte softly squeezed my hand as I retold of feeling sick and in pain when the memories came roaring through, the strange way my self-healing hadn't kicked in and making my way here still bleeding. Recounting how I'd woken up in a hotel and that I now suspected a set-up had Charlotte gripping my hand so tightly, her nails dug into my skin. With her eyes wide and intense and her heartbeat skittering, she was upset yet she displayed only an outwardly calm demeanour, coolly assessing the information like the trained cop she was.

I had to admit I liked that about her; recognising her control as a quality we shared. Respecting it. But the grooved dents she was digging into my skin - I liked them even more; the tiny pain a welcome reassurance of her concern for me.

Finn jumped in to explain how he'd confirmed the memories, that he'd been about to explain more when she'd arrived and now........here we were.

Story told, we sat in silence taking it all in - the total catastrofuck I had on my hands. Hearing it all laid out that way brought to mind just exactly how messed up my situation was.

But, although I was no closer to having any answers now than I was ten minutes ago, there was something about the three of us sitting here that gave me a strange sense of familiarity, of rampant déjà vu, of strength and purpose and ....unity, I guess.

Maybe........solidarity?

It was as if something was shifting internally, something significant. Like a lock sliding into place, a lost puzzle piece was found,

My heart thumped heavily in reaction and in a stunning moment of clarity, I realised that my beast was completely content right now. With me and with the three of us.

This was familiar.

This was solidarity.

My beast knew it. And now I did too.

Chapter Sixteen

"It's either here or a safe house. Your choice," Charlotte said, one hip cocked, arms crossed over her chest.

My beast snarled playfully at her while I glared, a mixture of annoyance, frustration at her stubbornness and lust at her sass tumbling around inside of me, warring for dominance. It was a tightly fought contest because while her tough talk was aggravating, her Detective Spitfire self turned me on.

In equal measures.

If Finn wasn't standing there watching us, eyes bouncing back and forth between us like he was at a tennis match, she would have been over my shoulder in a heartbeat and we would be battling it out somewhere private to see who got their way.

We'd spent the last five minutes arguing about where I was gonna stay - both Charlotte and Finn saying they didn't think it was wise I go back to the studio. Too risky, they said. I had to agree - with the Commander most likely assuming I was dead already, chances were that he or some lackey would come strip the place. Eliminate and destroy every and all evidence.

That's how I'd approach it, in his shoes.

Which is why I needed to set up surveillance ASAP, a plan that Charlotte agreed to but not with me surveying - she wanted to bring in her partner and for them to do it while I stayed here at Finn's, out of danger, like a wuss.

No fucking way, baby, I'd told her.

Except without the "fucking" - I don't talk that way to women. Outside of the bedroom, that is.

She'd glared at me, anyway.

We'd agreed on surveillance but not where I was staying. I'd said that I should stay at her place but she'd flat out said no.

Goddammit. I thought that was a brilliant idea myself.

So she'd come up with the safe house idea which I thought was a waste of police resources, even if she could swing it somehow - I mean, how the hell was she gonna explain hiding me? A beast assassin? A BEAST???

She'd said that she could possibly get something organised through her boss at which point Finn had interjected that he didn't like that idea and my own hackles had risen - her boss? That creep?

Oh HELL no.

She didn't like him herself, her animosity obvious, yet she'd approach him to protect me? I loved that she'd risk that for me - that she'd want to - but she's not going anywhere near him if I could help it and I'd told her so.

And she'd glared at me again.

"He's my boss - I can't exactly avoid him," she'd said in exasperation. Which totally pissed me off because she was right. My beast had snarled moodily. "Okay, fine - you don't want me to speak to him......" she began.

"I don't want you to involve him at all. EVER. There's something not right about him, Charlotte," I'd insisted.

She'd glanced at Finn then back at me. "The old Kellan would say something like that. But why do you?" She'd squinted her eyes at me suspiciously. "When have you seen him? What do you know?"

"Nothing," I'd evaded, not completely lying.

I didn't know all that much about him - only what my instincts told me and that was enough. "But I saw him when I called you at the precinct and there's ....."

"You were lurking nearby?" She'd compressed her lips in annoyance.

"........something not right about him," I'd insisted. "And no, I wasn't "lurking." "

I don't lurk. What gave her that idea?

I'd frowned darkly at her and around we went again until finally she'd tossed the ultimatum at me and here we were.

She was still glaring at me.

Fuck, she was cute.

Even when she made me mad.

"Alright, fine. I'll stay here," I said with a low growl, giving in. "But only for a couple of nights." We should have his identity by then, I figured.

She nodded her head in satisfaction then looked at Finn as she asked him: "Do you think you might be able to trace anything from Kellan's phone?"

"Maybe," he answered as he sat himself in his desk chair and began punching the keyboard. "I can try but I don't think we'll get too much off it. Unless there's some weird distinguishing factor about the phone itself, I doubt that........"

I tuned out the tech-talk for a moment and watched them instead - the Best Friend Forever and Detective Beast-Slayer, standing with my hands in my front pockets, thumbs out, frowning in lingering annoyance at Charlotte.

Seriously - she stood there in all her petite glory, leather jacket over a blue flowy shirt, gun and badge hitched on her belt, another pair of skin tight jeans, black this time, moulding her sexy ass figure - exactly how many of these jeans am I gonna have to suffer through? - calmly chatting with Finn about security as if she hadn't just bent me to her will with no regard for my beastly stubbornness.

She was fearlessly obstinate yet willing to go above and beyond to keep me safe while we hunted down the Evil Commander Prick Guy. She was also sassy, seductive and cheekily playful as proven on our pool-playing date. But I'd also seen enormous vulnerability when she'd relayed her emotions over my disappearance.

This woman had so many sides to her - all of them endlessly fascinating.

Before we'd had our little standoff, the three of us had gone over some of the finer details of my story: did I still have the army fatigues, the note? What hotel was it? Did I remember the date of this event? Was I booked in under my own name?

Yes, I had them still. Yes, I remembered the hotel name and date and yes, the receipt was in my name.

Both had concerns over where and when I'd been seen by the public in the time since I'd woken up in the hotel, particularly if there might be incriminating footage of anything I'd done during my missions. The way they had discussed this was surprisingly matter-of-fact - as if missions and beasts were something quite normal.

I'd assured them I wouldn't be visible on any security cameras except for most probably the Bellingworth charity fundraiser but Finn had said he'd already "looked into that."

Which is code for "Finn hacked into the security system and checked," Charlotte had blithely informed me and I'd blinked in surprise. Her calm acceptance of Finn's computer misdeeds showcased a willingness to bend the rules when situations might call for it.

Hmmmm, how........interesting.

Obviously if I'm presumed dead, then appearing on surveillance video isn't good and when I'd asked if I could be clearly identified on that footage, Finn had so casually stated that yeah, I could be but he was already working on it.

I'd looked at them stoically but completely floored. Was this normal? The two of them doing things outside the range of legal to protect my identity? Finn hacking was one thing, but Charlotte - she was a cop, for God's sake.

Exactly how far was she willing to bend those rules? And for who? It couldn't be only for Finn and I. Could it?

My head spun with that thought - why would she......why would they go to these lengths when I was.....what I was?

Finn had somehow picked up on my silent speculation at that point, giving me a steady look. "Look, I know there's lots of loopholes in your brain at the moment but I promise you that if the missing stuff doesn't come back soon, I'll explain everything myself," he'd said, distracting me with another quirky turn of phrase.

Loopholes in my brain?

Huh.

Well, I guess he wasn't wrong.

"Which reminds me," Charlotte had interjected at that point. "I asked Lucas what he knew about amnesia and......"

"How is the punk?" I'd interrupted. I'd been meaning to ask how her talk with him had gone.

"Wait.......you met Lucas? When?" Finn had asked curiously, also interrupting and Charlotte had looked at us in exasperation.

"Last night, when I walked Charlotte to her door," I'd told him, smirking at the recollection of how we'd met. It was kind of funny in retrospect.

"After your date?" Finn had said, quirking a dark eyebrow.

"Yes, after our date."

"Huh," was all he said before turning to Charlotte. "How is the dude? What's he doing in town?"

"He was checking up on me," she'd replied with a slight roll of her eyes. "Only he didn't tell me he was coming to visit."

"Yeah, he just rocks up and invades her space with no warning," I'd added for clarification, my disdain clear.

"Oh." Both eyebrows had risen as he looked between Charlotte and I. "I guess you two didn't hit it off so well then?" He'd asked, ironic amusement crossing his face.

I'd nearly laughed aloud in appreciation of his phrasing there. Hit it off - perfect description.

"Well, you could say that," I'd said with a snigger. "Did the punk bruise up a lot?" I'd asked Charlotte and she'd rolled her eyes again.

"No, he didn't. He's fine. He was just looking out for me. There was no need for any of that to happen." She'd given me a stern school teacher look that made my inner schoolboy drool.

"What happened?" Finn had done the tennis match thing again.

"I......." But it was Charlotte's turn to interrupt.

"Nothing," she'd said impatiently, trying to get us back on topic. "Never mind about that now. Look, I asked him about how to handle someone with amnesia and...."

"Tell you later," I'd muttered in an undertone to Finn and he'd smirked.

Charlotte had then described how her punk-ass brother, the med student, had explained the different ways to treat amnesia, dependent on what form of memory loss the patient had. Generally, most methods could help to varying degrees and that included medication, hypnosis and different psychotherapy treatments such as cognitive-behaviour, meditation and relaxation techniques. Even eye movement desensitization/reprocessing for someone suffering PTSD. Each patients' treatment plan would be individualised, he'd said, but a lot of dissociative conditions could be helped by surrounding the patient with familiar items, places and people - things that could be memory triggers. Talking about the missing past was also advisable but to treat the patient very gently and carefully monitor their responses. To not force memories but gently prompt them.

I'd curled my lip at that, not pleased with how he'd made me sound like a delicate little flower ready to shatter at the first breath of strong wind. Had that smart-ass somehow figured out it was me and was laying it on thick in perverted revenge?

"And no, he doesn't know it's you," Charlotte had said with a pointed look, as if she knew what I'd been thinking.

Damn.

When had I become so readable?

Or did these two just know me that well?

I'd put that thought on a back-burner as I told them there was no freaking way I'd be taking any psyche medication or chanting through some weird yoga type meditation.

They'd looked at me with wide eyes, startled and apparently amused. Charlotte had compressed her lips tightly, fighting a smile and Finn had tried to smother his laugh with a cough. I scowled at them both.

Finn had composed himself, promising there'd be no mantra reciting and Charlotte had lost the battle then, snorting a little laugh and grinning widely at me, her eyes sparkling and I was mollified enough to give her a chagrined smile in return. Okay, fine - I admit.....the thought of chanting and me was funny.

As we argued, *ahem*, discussed, the merits of revealing my "alive-ness" to the Commander and the world in general, a part of me had silently marvelled at the whole situation. If someone had told me even this morning that by late afternoon I'd be discussing tactics and strategies with a cop and a science whiz, I'd never have believed it. But here we were and it felt oddly natural.

They went to great lengths for my protection. Remembering now what each had said about their hunt to locate me, searching relentlessly from the moment I'd disappeared and not giving up till they found me at that pier; the significance of Charlotte being involved with someone like me.... that told me so much about who they were and how much they accepted my beast.

I hadn't fully appreciated any of that till now.

Something in my chest had squeezed tightly at that point, distracting me from the conversation until Charlotte had asked me where in the studio I'd stashed my fatigues and the receipt because she was gonna go get them.

To which I'd said no, she wasn't and that had started our first argument.

I'd won that one.

Charlotte's cell phone beeped loudly now, dragging me out of my thoughts. She looked down at the message on her screen and said : " I have to get back to the precinct. JC can't cover me any longer. Suarez is asking where I am."

She grimaced a little and pocketed the cell. "I better go. Finn, you work on Kellan's phone and getting eyes on the place. I'll see what I can find out about the hotel and its staff."

Meeting my gaze, she said "Kellan, I know you think you'll be okay going back to the studio but promise me you won't go. Not until we have eyes on the place, at least. You just don't......"

"Don't worry," I said softly, seeing the concern in her eyes, the anxiety she tried hard to hide. I didn't like seeing it there but had to admit it did something to my insides to see her so worried for me.

Our eyes locked and held for a long moment, the silent connection broken only when she blinked and I gave her a reassuring little smile. "It'll be fine," I said.

She hesitated for a second then gave me a nod of acceptance. Turning to Finn she said she'll be in touch later on and with a last glance at me, she headed for the door.

"Say hi to J.C.," Finn called out casually to her and that distracted me for a split second so that Charlotte had almost passed me by before I realised she was leaving with no proper goodbye.

That wasn't acceptable.

I reached out and snagged her arm, stopping her in her tracks. "Wait," I said and she turned back to me in surprise, eyes wide.

Holding on to her arm, I leaned down and laid my lips against hers in a slow kiss, her plush lips tantalising and soft, my mouth lingering before reluctantly letting go with one last taste. Lifting my head, I looked into her gleaming exotic eyes, fascinated as always with their unusual colour.

"Okay, now you can go," I told her. She quirked her eyebrow at this statement but only gave me an amused half smile and left.

I stood watching her and her ass - can't help myself - until she'd left and closed the door.

I sighed.

That woman was put on this earth to fill out a pair of jeans. She should have a sticker planted on her butt that read: "Warning - Hazardous to my Heart". Or "Do Not Look - unless you're Kellan".

Ha! I liked that one.

Actually I could think of lots of stickers.......... But nah, I don't think she'd let me........ Pity. I smiled to myself, picturing her naked with half a dozen stickers on her butt........ahhhh man, what a sight. My beast growled a little.

With another sigh, I turned back to Finn and said "So how long have you had a crush on this J.C. person?"

His mouth fell open in shock.

Chapter Seventeen

Much later, Finn and I sat at the wide desk, one at each end. I was scanning data as it rolled across the monitors, searching for information on the studio, for any links that might lead us to the owner while Finn was trying to trace the call history of my cell phone - without much success, judging by his grumbling. We'd been at this for awhile now and I was getting hungry.

Earlier, when I'd confronted him about his crush, he'd tried to deny it, but after reminding him I could tell he was lying, he'd 'fessed up, making me promise to keep that news to myself.

Seems J.C, the tall cop/partner I'd seen with Charlotte at the gallery and precinct had only recently come into Finn's world, both of us having been introduced to her just a handful of weeks before I'd disappeared.

According to Finn, I'd knocked both her and Charlotte out of harms way when an out of control car had almost run them down as they were questioning a cafe owner downtown. Unfortunately I'd partially beasted out to get to them in time and J.C, having seen that brief moment, had totally freaked out. Charlotte had hell trying to explain it all - explain me - to her, my existence a secret kept for a long time but eventually she had calmed down enough to want to meet me. Apparently I hadn't taken offense that it took a week for her to settle down. So Charlotte had brought her here to introduce us all and despite her wariness of me, she'd been an enormous help to them in the search for my missing self.

"So, she's all good with you now," Finn had said. "I think."

Oh..... K.

Man, I had so many questions.......

However, Finn had chosen that moment to ask if I wanted to see my room and with a skipped heartbeat, not only was I thoroughly distracted from those questions but I suddenly had a dry mouth and queasy gut.

Shit......

Was I ready to see this space? A room that I'd lived in, slept in? It had to have all sorts of stuff in there; personal, meaningful stuff, right?

What if it didn't trigger any memories for me?

What if it triggered too many?

Not liking the prospect of either reaction, I'd taken a fortifying breath, looked over at Finn's calm demeanour and nodded. Judging by the look in his eye, he seemed to understand my wariness and with a nod of his own, he'd turned and led the way.

Following him towards a door to the left of the kitchen, my skin had grown cold, belly churning and senses sharpening as defensive instincts kicked in readiness. Through that door was a steel staircase and as our shoes clanged on the metal, my heartbeat had thudded in unison, growing louder with each downward step. The U-shaped stairwell revealed portions of the room slowly and by the time we'd reached the bottom and stood on the concrete floor, every muscle and sinew had been wound tight, tension snapping down my spine as I'd waited for the onslaught of memories to flood through. I'd stuffed my shaking hands into my front pockets, breath shallow and jaw clenched, staring intently around me.

Whatever I'd been expecting, which wasn't much anyway, this.........this wasn't it.

For one thing, it wasn't a "room" - it was the whole damn ground floor - a huge cavernous area the equal size of upstairs. Surprised, I'd taken a couple of steps further in, my heartbeat echoing loudly in my ears as adrenaline rushed like a locomotive through my veins.

Giant sandstone slab walls dominated, whitewashed and raw, over the entire open area, pale sunlight streaming in through high multi-panelled windows to the left and to the north. Steel structural beams ran across the ceiling twenty feet above while low timber benches stretched along the west wall, interspersed with tall piles of books in all shapes and sizes, boxy cabinets sitting on either end.

Thick grey carpet, too large to be called a rug, was laid out over a bare concrete floor, the bed sitting squarely on top, coffee coloured side-tables flanking the timber bed frame of chocolate and tan. A textured charcoal bedspread was smoothly spread across the king-sized mattress while a dark red/brown tallboy pushed up against a partitioned wall running along the east side of the room, sectioning it off and creating an enclosed room, complete with door - these walls were at least twelve feet tall and I wondered what lay behind the closed black door.

Bathroom? Something told me yes.

Oddly, three large picture frames sat propped on the floor against the west wall rather than hanging from it; abstract art framed in simple black wood.

Somehow the whole bedroom area - furniture all held up by stubby timber legs, with its masculine colours and rough surfaces should have looked shabby and old but didn't. Instead, it reeked of a retro style that I hadn't expected and even though I knew nothing of decor and such crap, I knew that I liked this set up. Completely different to upstairs, it somehow felt.....comfortable? Yeah.....Comfortable was the word, I'd decided, an odd sense of ease whispering through my system.

Huh.

It should have felt cold, given the enormous size of the area yet it didn't and I'd wondered briefly what the heating was like during winter.

Slow steps turned me around to face the other side and there stood a massive charcoal sofa, black coffee table and single tan armchair arranged to face a lowline cabinet supporting a flatscreen TV as big and beautiful as the one I'd seen upstairs, tucked partially under the u-shaped stairwell.

The screen's gleaming black surface had to be at least 80 inches and several consoles and remote controls sat strewn across the cabinet top.

But when I raised my eyes beyond the lounge area to the back of the warehouse, my heart knocked erratically at my ribs. Because there - in the back left corner sat a fully loaded home gym and my muscles almost sang in recognition. A state of the art treadmill, power racks, rowing machine, weight plates and bars, dumbbells of all sizes and a multi-gym that had at least 4 stations, all laid out better than any pro gym. Two large boxing bags hung suspended from overhead structural beams, first by long metal rods then chains while black floor padding covered an area spanning at least twenty feet wide.

A shiver ran down my spine. This spoke to me.....spoke of me.

An expensive and comprehensive set up, it was far more than I imagined I would have but undoubtedly something right up my alley. As my eyes skimmed over the weights and bars, overhead lights suddenly flicked on, illuminating the darkened area and glinting off steel and leather. My muscles hummed with a curious energy, eager to take advantage of all the pieces and I almost drooled.

However, my eyes then caught on something that had my breath hitching hard - a silver cover thrown over what looked to be some sort of machine, sitting parked in front of the steel roller door that graced half the rear wall. Nothing was visible beneath the dark plastic yet my heartbeat thundered and raced and an overwhelming need to see what was under it compelled me forward.

But I knew.......Everything within me knew.......

I walked towards it in a fog, drawn inexorably closer, my chest tight and eyes fixed and dilated as anticipation swamped my senses. My heart was hammering by the time I was within range and reaching out with one slightly shaking hand, I grasped the silver cover and drew it off, the cloth sliding away almost in slow motion as my blood pounded through my veins and then......... Yes.......

My heart skipped a beat before rolling over in electrified wonder.

There she was.....

My baby.

My beautiful ride in all her chrome and black glory - a 1960/s style Harley Cruiser....gleaming black saddlebags, fat white spoke-wheels, Hollywood handles and chrome shining so bright, it nearly brought tears to my eyes. Mean and cool, she sat with pure arrogance and pride in her raw power, gorgeous and sexy as hell.

Muscle memory flooded through my system with devastating speed and I instantly felt her beneath me; felt the slide of leather as I straddled her; the vibration that sizzled through my veins when she roared in full throaty voice. I felt the wind against my face, the freedom that surged through my body as I rode. And I felt the deep comforting warmth that settled against my back, clasped around my waist......oh God......this was what I'd dreamt the other night...

Thick emotion swelled in my chest, constricting my breathing like a viper, my throat drying up with the intensity of sensation that flowed across my skin; memories stored in my blood and bone of riding with Charlotte plastered around me...... Christ.... riding together to get away, to spend alone time and just for the sheer pleasure of it.

I swallowed heavily, my heartbeat almost drowning out the sound of Finn's steps as he came up to stand beside me quietly, hands stuffed in his pockets.

She was spotless...polished and beautiful and I couldn't draw my eyes away. Running one hand over the smooth black leather seating, I took a slow walk around and admired her from all angles and as I breathed in the unique smell of her - a clean metallic mix of oil and leather - I desperately wanted to start her up but knew I couldn't. Not yet - I wasn't ready. The day had been one slammer of revelation after another and the emotional haul was too much right now.

My eyes traced over the long chrome pipes, the high gleam of the three headlights, the kickstand; all of her shining with a deep mirror-like gloss and a deep gratitude settled in my belly.

"You took care of her so well....." I said in a thick voice, my throat clogged.

Finn gave a nonchalant shrug, his brow scrunching as a thought occurred to him. "You remember?"

"No, not much ......but I remember riding," I said as a fine tremor shimmered down my back.

"I even dreamt about it but it was so vague I didn't realise what it was."

Silence stretched out for a few minutes as the weight of recognition settled around my shoulders like a forgotten blanket and I stared at my Cruiser gratefully. Nothing else rang any bells in this space except my bike.

At least, so far.

Seems my brain was only willing to release information bit by bit. And most of it while I was either under extreme pressure or comatose. Maybe I had to sleep for three days straight to get all my memories back? Or fight another fire? Or be almost blown up? Christ, if that was what it took, I'd do it in a heartbeat just to get this fuckery over with.

Rolling my shoulders, I took a deep breath, then another and another, aware that my beast sat silently watchful as he held back the roiling emotion that threatened to spill over.

"Thank you," I managed to say in a gravelly voice, meeting Finn's steady gaze and he simply nodded, the moment not needing any more words.

With a quietly muttered "I'll leave you to it," Finn had taken himself back upstairs, knowing exactly what I needed right then. And so I'd spent a while alone, just taking it all in.

I'd mounted the bike and grasped the handles, feeling my body sink comfortably, easily into the leather seat; my fingertips tingling as they curled themselves around the hard rubber grips. My beast purred at the sensory delight, skin prickling and senses humming with pleasure.
Memories of riding into the wind filled my mind, flipping like cards being shuffled - scene after scene of bending to the curve of the open road, rain or shine, day or night. Sometimes alone, sometimes with that distinct and pervasive warmth that told me Charlotte was wrapped around me.

I'd stood amongst the gym equipment, punching the boxing bags a couple of times and picking up random weights, the cold steel emitting a sense of familiarity without any context. I'd wandered over to the lounge and sat facing the television screen. I'd picked up one of the books laying on the bench seat - a glossy pictorial of architecture from around the world - rifling through the pages, reading snippets here and there but none of these had triggered any memories.

I'd opened the wardrobe doors that ran along the east wall separating the bathroom from the rest of the area, discovering loads of jeans, tee shirts and jackets in a wide variety of dark colours and styles. I apparently had a propensity for jackets of all kinds, particularly leather and many specifically for riding. With an approving nod at my style, I'd decided that these definitely felt like something I'd choose - more so than the stuff that hung in the wardrobe at the studio. Knowing as I did now the reasons for that, had me grinding my teeth in dark temper and I'd continued my tour pushing back the need to hit something in frustration.

The bathroom was quite spacious; large open glass shower, classic black and white tiling everywhere; a half wall blocking the toilet from view, there in the top right corner. The basin and taps were an unusual black and silver while black cabinets contained a multitude of thick towels and personal toiletries. Staring at the shaving gear, toothpaste, combs and such, knowing they belonged to me but not having any sense of ownership only strengthened the disconnected sensation that sat in the pit of my belly. Even smelling the cologne I found beneath the sink didn't trigger any memories, despite the deeply powerful olfactory sense of my beast nature.

I'd sat on the edge of the bed, elbows on knees, looking at all the drawers and cupboards I was unwilling to open at this stage. Clothes were one thing but these side tables.......

No, not yet.

I wasn't ready to face what might be in them.

I'd sat and stared at the abstract artwork for a long while, wondering why I had them. The swirls and slashes of deep rich tones, painted with a free and enthusiastic hand, seemed to be an odd choice and didn't really blend in with the rest of the room; the colours clashing and the style completely at odds with everything else. They had to mean something, I figured. Otherwise why have them? But instead of triggering even a vague recollection, the longer I looked at each frame, the tighter my chest became. My heart rate thickened, growing sluggish and heavy as my senses became increasingly aware of an invisible wall that stood between myself and these pictures.

There was something there, I knew, but my mind wouldn't let me unlock it, the wall impenetrable no matter how hard I pushed.

Then, as an icy coldness hurtled through my body, my skin had prickled and shivered and something inside wanted to scream out in rage and pain, my beast's hackles quivering with the unseen threat.

Christ.....

I'd gotten up quickly and turned away, unable to bear it further. With a queasy stomach, I'd flicked off the lights and gone back upstairs.

"You okay?" Finn had asked, his concern evident and even though I'd nodded calmly, I was anything but that.

Sitting here now, staring at the screen blankly, I had to admit, if only to myself, that I was shaken. Despite the lack of full memories, it was clear that I'd lived downstairs. The bike, the gym - that was all me and I knew that when I looked through the drawers and cupboards, I'd find parts of my soul and psyche in shards of jagged edges, broken by whoever or whatever had done this to me; one life stolen to create another.

But surely if the name of the game was to eliminate all traces of beast experiments, there would be easier ways of getting it done? And wouldn't I be the ultimate target?

Of course, I would be.

That had to be the reasoning - use me to eliminate them all and then destroy me too. All of us gone.

It's the only thing that made any sense.

With no regard for the trauma they inflicted, something or someone had ripped my life from me with ruthless calculation; stealing my identity, stealing everything that made me who and what I am, and for that, they must pay. This faceless entity calling himself Commander, him and anyone else involved....... they would all pay, I vowed as seething rage boiled like lava through my blood, hands clenching into fists against the desk.

No matter how long it took, I'd track them down. To the ends of the earth, if I had to.

Because it was also clear - if I had a target on my back, then anyone around me could also be in danger.

And that meant Charlotte and Finn, two people whose importance to me I was only just beginning to fully understand. A shudder coursed down my spine at the thought of either of them getting hurt because of me.

There was no way, no fucking way I'd allow either of them to be collateral damage.

And that was vow number two.

Feeling the pinprick of talons against my palms, I reined it in before I lost control, breathing slow and deep until the red haze bled away from my eyesight. Finn was so engrossed in his task he didn't even look up and that was a good thing right now.

Several minutes later, tethered and calm again, I tried to refocus on the screen but my stomach growled. Loudly.

"Dude, you got anything to eat around here?" I asked.

"Just leftovers," Finn answered distractedly. "But I can't remember from when."

Great.

"I really need to clean out my refrigerator....." he muttered, typing furiously on his keyboard.

"So, there's nothing here at all??" That shocked me - I mean, really? No food? There must be something - even a granola bar.

"Sure, there's stuff - but not enough to make a decent dinner," he said, finally glancing up from his monitor to give me a wry grin. "So I'll order in pizza."

Pizza? Somehow I didn't think that was such a healthy choice.

"You weren't that much of a health-nut that you couldn't eat pizza," he said with a laugh, catching the look on my face. "Believe me, with the way you worked out constantly, the occasional pie didn't bother you in the least."

"What do you mean, constantly?"

"You had nothing else to do during the days so you'd work out a lot." He shrugged.

Well.

What to make of that?

Finn picked up his phone and ordered while I thought about what he'd said - "nothing to do." Why? Wasn't I working for the FD? What puzzle piece was I missing? I couldn't rely on sleep to bring up memories everytime. Or some sort of trauma, physical or otherwise - even my own personal possessions downstairs hadn't triggered a full memory recovery. And there was no real way of knowing how or when more would surface.

Turning back to Finn, I waited till he hung up his call before asking him : "You're gonna explain some things for me, aren't you? Not just wait for memories to surface?"

Because who the hell knew how long that could take?

"Sure," He answered as he went back to his computer. "Right after I hack into the security system around your studio..........." He trailed off distractedly.

"Can you do that?" Surprised but excited with that idea, I leaned over his shoulder a bit and watched him work, trying to follow along but the coding was complete gibberish to me.

"Can I do that, he asks," Finn muttered with a smirk, totally focused on whatever he was doing. "I'll forgive you that comment because you've obviously forgotten how brilliant I am."

I barked out an appreciative laugh.

Right.

Sitting back, I left him to it and with no other task for the moment, I picked up my phone and considered sending a text to Charlotte.

Just ~ Hi ~

But, dammit. It wasn't safe to contact her with this phone - who knew how many ears it had on it? Aggravated, I shoved the cell back into my pocket and drummed my restless fingers against the ankle I'd propped against my knee. I needed a new phone. A-SAP.

I wondered what she was doing, if she was at the precinct or not? Had she had dinner herself yet? Maybe I should ask her to come join us for pizza? Did we used to do that?

I didn't freaking know.

And why was I so concerned with this?

Because I wanted her here with me, I realised with annoyance. I felt better when she was near. I........missed her.

Fuck.

I scowled at no-one, reeling a bit at that admission.

I think I was in trouble here.

"Got it!!" Finn suddenly shouted loudly, causing me to jerk a little. Looking over at him, I saw he was muttering "yes, yes" to himself as his fingers flew over the keyboard and pictures zoomed and flashed across the monitor.

"What? What'd you get?" I asked.

"Ta da!" He threw his arms in the air triumphantly and grinned at me. "We got eyes on the studio!"

"We do?"

"We do!!"

"Way to go, buddy!" And we high-fived. So natural, no awkwardness - as if we'd done it a thousand times before.

My heartbeat skidded and I blinked dazedly, surprised at my unthinking outburst.

I guess we probably had.

The doorbell rang just then and as Finn went to answer it, I sighed as I settled into that idea - that not only did I have "dude" behavioural tendencies but that I was already in deeper with Charlotte than I'd thought.

Truly, it was a toss up which was more disturbing.

Rolling my shoulders and telling myself I'd think about it later, I turned to study the monitor where I could see the studio and its surrounds displayed in grainy black and white. I knew immediately which security camera we were looking through, having noticed it from my first day there, hooked up to one of the lamp posts dotted sporadically along the walkway surrounding the warehouse.

How the fuck did Finn manage to hack it? That took some serious skill and now we could monitor the studio without sitting in a car for endless hours. That alone merited his self-tagged label of brilliant, I conceded with amusement. I was willing to bet, however, that it wouldn't take long before either the Commander himself showed up or he sent someone in to destroy the place - I mean, if I was "dead" as he believed then why wouldn't he eliminate evidence of my existence there?

The overwhelming smell of melting cheese, tomato and pepperoni assaulted my senses suddenly, slamming the brakes on all logical thought processes and jacking up my hunger pangs cruelly.

Thank God. Food.

The next few minutes were filled with the sounds of glassware, plates and and pizza boxes clunking onto the cleared coffee table and the scoffing of at least one slice of Italian goodness. By each of us.

"God, this is good," I moaned in appreciation as I started on my second. My stomach rumbled in joy.

"That's cause it's your favourite," Finn explained, talking with his mouth full. Looking down at my loaded-with-the-works pizza, I could see why.

We ate in silence for awhile, conversation abandoned in the priority of killing off hunger. Eventually, once we'd demolished at least half the pies and ate at a slower pace, I asked him why I had so much time to work out, as he'd said earlier.

In between bites, Finn explained that prior to my disappearance for several reasons I hadn't been working as a firefighter but refused to expand on those reasons, saying it was best if I remembered on my own. Said that I'd probably pushed my memory too much for one day already. I'd protested that I wasn't some fragile little flower, dammit, but he'd simply said we needed to give it time, that he didn't want to overload me with everything.

I knew he was right but it pissed me off anyway.

While I sat there scowling, Finn picked up his cell phone and punched in a few numbers. The sound of ringing could be heard clearly as he put the phone on speaker and then the husky voice of Detective Alistair.

"Finn, hi" she said, her voice instantly calming me. Warming me.

"Charlie, we got eyes on Kellan's studio," he said. "No need for a stake out. At least, not in a car."

"Really? That was quick!" She was impressed by his speed, it appeared. But not his deed. "Great. We'll need to monitor that constantly, though. Someone will always have to be watching."

"Well yeah. Unless I can get it recorded overnight. That way, at least we'd get sleep. Otherwise, you and J.C. might have to bunk here in turns. We could set up a roster or something...."

I could hear his heartbeat spike up at the mention of J.C staying here overnight and my brow quirked. Ha. Poor guy had it bad, it seemed.

But then again, the thought of Charlotte here overnight......well.......my own heart raced a little at that. I wondered if she'd ever slept over in that big bed downstairs......

"Yeah, we'll work that out. I have some hotel staff interviews set up so hopefully that'll give us something. Look, I gotta go. Suarez is watching every move I make. I'll be in touch later. Bye." And she hung up abruptly.

Goddammit! What's that meant to mean? He was watching every move?

"Why the hell is that asshole watching her every damn move?" I spat out, anger rising quick and sharp.

Finn sighed and shook his head slightly. "Because he's an asshole."

Giving him a hard look for that droll sarcasm, I couldn't disagree with him. "Just tell me. She's tense and nervous when he's around and twice she's said that he watches her."

"How do you know she's tense around him?" He raised his eyebrows at me quizzically.

"I watched her for awhile at the precinct to make sure she was safe and as soon as he was near her, she was on edge. Why? What did he do?"

Finn smirked. "Some things never change," he said with a slight shake of his head, amused by something.

"What?"

"Nothing. Just that you used to watch over her before and here you are again doing the same. Memory or not," he said, taking a slug of his beer.

Well, what did I say to that? Given the strength of my instincts, animal and human alike, it didn't surprise me. In fact, it was kind of reassuring, knowing I'd fallen back into at least one familiar pattern of behaviour.

But enough distraction....

"What did he do?" I growled. My beast was highly alert now, prepared to protect her, hackles rising sharply at the back of my neck.

"Crap," Finn muttered, tension creeping through his tone.

"Finn....." My eyes bored into his relentlessly.

He frowned, trepidation clouding his eyes as he hesitated.

What the fuck was he planning to tell me?

Chapter Eighteen

Ten minutes later, I stood trembling in rage, hands curled into tight fists, muscles bunched and twitching as fury coiled through my belly like a snake, hissing and biting, ready to strike. My beast strained against his tethers - livid and snarling with crazed anger.

It took every bit of my control to not lose my shit just then, the strain of holding back sheeting my skin with a fine sweat.

Jesus. H. Christ.

From the moment Suarez had transferred to the 75th, he'd been a pain in the ass to Charlotte. And to me. Constantly making sly innuendos and sleazy come-ons to her - someone his subordinate - and making her extremely uncomfortable. Despite her repeated explanations that she was involved with someone - meaning me - he hadn't backed off.

He hadn't believed her, claiming that she was using a fake boyfriend to keep him at bay since no one at the precinct had ever laid eyes on me or talked to me. With my existence a secret, the situation had caused massive aggravation and several flare ups between Charlotte and I.

Then one night, Suarez had "drunkenly" assaulted Charlotte at some police department function, pushing his unwanted advances on her as he cornered her against a corridor wall. She'd claimed it was only a pass that she'd easily deflected but I'd witnessed the incident from the roof of the building next door and knew he'd been anything but drunk. He'd staged the incident as a way to get his hands on her, to manipulate and intimidate her.

Unable to defend her, I'd had no choice but to stay in the shadows and watch as she'd used her considerable fight skills to free herself of his slimy hands.

Charlotte, being more than capable of taking care of herself, was still managing the situation to this day but he was her boss and for that reason alone, she was on edge around him. And as the hidden boyfriend, Finn said, I was helpless.

Helpless?

I'd nearly burst a blood vessel at that.

"And that's why you hate the asshole," he finished off.

My claws unsheathed and a red haze filled my vision.

"Kellan, buddy, take it easy," I heard Finn saying over and over but he was a million miles away, his voice distorted and warped as my focus spiralled down to the wild fury that churned through my whole system.

All I could see in my mind was Suarez crowding Charlotte against some wall, the pictures in my head brutally clear and vivid as my imagination kicked in.

Or was it memory?

With that, my blood pressure snapped and I savagely yanked on the tethers as the beast roared in full voice. Blurring through the door, I barely managed to rein him back as rage throbbed thick and red with every heartbeat, Finn's voice yelling my name frantically completely lost in the backwash.

Speeding furiously downtown, I jumped and blazed across dozens of rooftops till I reached the spot I'd stood watch before, directly across from the precinct. Eyes flashing gold and talons scratching against the concrete barrier I planted my hands against, I dragged in harsh breaths and focused; shutting down the anger to regroup and hone in on my prey.

I knew exactly where Charlotte was; her heartbeat always clear and distinctive to me no matter how many surrounded her.

She was in a second level interrogation room with her partner and a couple other uniform cops.

Vision, hearing, smell - every predatory instinct I owned sharply attuned itself to the hunt. Coldly. Precisely. Then........

Gotcha.

There he was - I found him in a north west office, alone.

Fucking perfect.

Sneering with deadly intent, I blurred down and out of the building, across the road into the cop shop and up the stairs to his office. Within seconds I was opening his door soundlessly to find him standing near a tall filing cabinet reading a document. Charging at him with full speed, I slammed a massive right hook into his jaw, my fist cracking sharply bone against bone, the force of my blow sending him spinning crazily into the cabinet, the file in his hands flying and scattering papers everywhere before he crashed heavily to the floor.

In complete shock and disbelief at finding himself suddenly dumped on his ass, he grunted loudly in pain, lifting a shaking hand to his jaw. Black eyes blinking madly, terror crawled across his face as he scrambled defensively to his feet, wild eyes searching the room for the unseen assailant.

Goddamn, that felt good.

I could have easily broken his face had I chosen to but it didn't suit my purposes just then. Not enough fun in that.

Disorientated and shaken, it took him a few moments to focus but eventually he found me standing in the open doorway, one shoulder against the jamb, feet and arms crossed as I watched his utter confusion.

He gazed at me uncomprehendingly for a minute, his mind trying to understand what had happened to him but he was at a complete loss. I gave him a cold, slow smirk as I waited patiently for him to gather his scattered senses and speak first, not trying too hard to disguise my disdain.

You could almost read the words scrolling over his swarthy face - "what the fuck just happened?"

He brushed himself off, trying to regain his composure and with black eyes still blinking owlishly, he said with false confidence; "Uhhh, can I.....help you?"

"I doubt it," I sneered.

His eyes narrowed and I stared back at him, biding my time.

"Do you have an appointment with me? How did you get in here?" He injected a tone of authority into his voice that was totally wasted on me. Not that he knew it yet.

"The stairs, then the door," I said calmly.

Not appreciating my sense of humour, his mouth compressed in irritation.

"Listen," he said impatiently. "I don't know who you are...."

"Yeah, but I know who you are," I cut in. "And what you are."

"Excuse me?!" Clearly astounded at my insolence, his wiry body stiffened, shoulders arching back, chin thrust forward.

"You're the kind of sleaze that gets off on intimidating those he sees as weaker than himself," I said, letting the contempt seep through my words. "That has a falsely inflated view of himself and gets off on harassing women."

"I beg your.....!!" Now his eyes goggled and he began to vibrate with an arrogant outrage, his stance subtly shifting into a combative readiness.

"Yeah, you will beg," I sneered, my voice unnaturally guttural as I let the beast's seething menace peek through the surface a little. Enough to mesmerise him as I unfolded myself from the doorway, closed the door behind me and stepped closer, the gold in my eyes deepening with each slow, stalking step.

He stood transfixed, his heart rate climbing erratically as confused fear melted his bravado.

Human instinct told him to be scared but he didn't know of what.

"You'll definitely beg if I ever hear of you even looking sideways at my girlfriend again." Pinned with the malevolent force of my un-human gaze, he couldn't look away, his black eyes revealing the latent cowardice beneath his false bravado. But of course, slime like him always showed themselves to be the piss-weak cowards they were.

"Wh.....what....?"

"My girlfriend." I said, taking a step closer.

"Charlotte." I added, taking another.

"Detective Alistair to you." I stopped three feet away from him, the foul stench of his malignant aura offending my nostrils. My beast salivated and strained, growling deep with animosity.

Suarez, like all scum, revelled in others' fear and discomfort, considering himself mean and tough. But once confronted with someone superior, someone stronger, he quickly reverted to his true nature. As he did now, the snivelling maggot.

"You see, I know exactly what you've been doing," I rasped in a low growl, stepping closer still. "The way you've manipulated and harassed her for months. You didn't think I existed did you, you sonofabitch?"

His face drained of all colour, the revelation of my identity hitting him squarely in his two-slow brain. A clammy grey now, his mouth worked silently as he tried to speak but fear robbed him of his voice.

"I know exactly what you tried to do to her at the cop function." Pure hatred seethed within every cell of my being and Suarez's shocked eyes caught the flash of red that hazed my vision.

"I know exactly what kind of pig you are," I said, my voice getting lower, raspier with each word. "I know the things you get up to that you don't want anyone to know about, especially the law."

I didn't but he didn't know that.

His mouth dropped open and he gaped like a stunned fish.

My temper frayed in disgust at having my suspicions confirmed and with blur speed, I suddenly grabbed him by the neck, slammed him up against the nearest wall and got right into his grill, snarling. "And you're lucky I haven't ripped you to shreds."

He gasped harshly, eyes bulging in sheer terror.

"You've been getting your rocks off like the dirty prick that you are. But you underestimated Charlotte, didn't you? You thought you'd have her trapped by now but she's evaded you at every turn." My body trembled with the savagery that coursed through me, fingers squeezing his throat tighter and cutting off his air just a little. "Do you know why, asshole? Because she's a strong, smart woman."

My talons broke through as I growled into his ashen face. "You make her skin crawl."

Squeezing his throat just a bit tighter, my claws almost pierced him as bloodlust ripped through me. I craved to just tear the bastard's heart out, quick and clean right now, but knew I couldn't - not here in the precinct, surrounded by cops.

Charlotte wouldn't be happy.

Holding back with supreme effort and denying myself the pleasure of his spilled blood, I shoved my face to within an inch of his, sending his fear skyrocketing, his heartbeat pounding madly. I eased my chokehold just the tiniest bit, just enough to let him breath.

"So here's what's going to happen...." I told him, gold eyes burning as simmering fury kept me at knife's edge.

"You have two options. Charlotte can press charges against you and you'll lose not only your career but your privacy and sanity 'cause I'll be on your ass at every turn and you'll never know when my benevolence will run out."

Suarez quivered so violently he was like a fucking piñata hanging from my hand. The pungent smell of his fear saturated the air and the beast revelled in it's stench, snarling in satisfaction.

"Or.....you will leave town immediately. Resign and disappear, never to return.

If you come within a thousand miles of Charlotte , you won't live long enough to regret it. Do. You. Understand?"

Only garbled grunts came from him and I shook him by the neck angrily. The coward had enough air to breathe - he could damn well speak.

"Do you? Charlotte doesn't need my protection cause she can kick your ass on her own. But she's got it anyway. And I'm special Ops. Know what that means?" I asked rhetorically, my voice turning gravel soft. "That means I have skills you can't even imagine. And I'm very, very good at my job."

And I swear someone upstairs in heaven must actually like me because right at that moment two glorious things happened in beautiful synchronicity.

First, the sudden acrid smell of urine rose as Suarez wet himself in fear, the trickle of liquid hitting the floorboards loud in my sensitive ears. And second - Charlotte came racing through the door, slamming it closed behind her as she yelled: "Kellan!! Don't!!"

I turned my head towards her, showing her my normal face with my normal hazel eyes - proof that I was in complete control. But she wasn't looking at me. Her wide eyes were staring in shock at her boss, dangling inches off the floor, held in place by my straightened arm as he pissed himself.

Whatever else she might have planned to say was lost as she took in the scene in front of her, mortified disgust crinkling her nose and I wanted to punch the air in triumphant victory. Or laugh like a madman.

Fuck. Ing. Per. Fect.

I let go of Suarez suddenly and he collapsed in a heap on the floor, trying desperately to right himself but failing as he slid in his own puddle.

Oh God. The icing on the cake.

His humiliation was complete and he knew it.

Looking down at him as his horrified gaze flicked between Charlotte and myself, I growled menacingly.

"Your choice, asshole. Make the right one." I flashed him my golden eyes as an added incentive. Personally I didn't care which choice he made, I was good with either.

He nodded weakly, looking utterly gutted and almost on the verge of tears as he took in Charlotte's face, a mixture of pity and revulsion crossing her beautiful features.

"And apologise for your inappropriate treatment of a female co-worker. You're damn lucky my girlfriend hasn't already brought you up on harassment charges." I added in because she deserved an apology. Ten of them, in fact.

"I'm sorry.... I'm sorry......" He muttered hastily in a broken voice, unmanned and disgraced. There was no coming back from this and he knew it.

"Oh God," Charlotte recovered her voice and pinned me with her amazing green gold eyes - bewilderment swirling tumultuously in their depths.

But there was something else there too.....something that looked a lot like .... lust, I realised with a hitched breath.

Well, well, isn't that interesting?

In a sudden flurry of panic, she reached for me. "We need to leave. Right now."

Grabbing my hand and pulling me behind her, she opened the door, surreptitiously looked up and down the corridor then turned left and quickly ran towards a door further down the right hand side, dragging me willingly with her.

God, yes!!

Good things happened when she dragged me places.

Chapter Nineteen

Hands in my front pockets, thumbs out and legs splayed, I stood watching as Charlotte raced around the interview room shutting the blinds on each of the two windows, a half smile of amused anticipation curling my mouth. She'd already locked the door after rushing us into this tiny room that contained only a small timber table and two chairs.

She was gonna explode any second.

I couldn't wait.

Finished with her task, she whipped around to face me, green gold eyes spitting mad fire, brows lowered as she advanced furiously on me.

Three........two.........one.........

"What the hell are you thinking??!!" She whisper-screeched at me.

Boom. There it is.

"Blurring into the precinct? Are you insane!! I can't believe you risked being seen like that!! Do you realise how many security cameras are in this place?!" She was practically hissing at me now, her cheeks heated with angry disbelief, arms akimbo as she yelled at me with all the force of an exasperated mama berating a bratty child.

And my blood was heating up.

"I know. But you won't see me on there," I said calmly, confidently.

"How can you be so sure?!" She scoffed, eyebrows scrunching together.

"Because I'm fast," I said with just a trace of smugness. "There'll be nothing there except a strange breeze."

"A strange breeze?" She repeated incredulously. "A strange breeze!! And that's not gonna look suspicious? How am I supposed to explain that?" She threw her hands in the air before planting them back on her hips, glaring at me in exasperation.

Seriously cute. My beast growled playfully at her.

"Who says YOU have to explain anything? Why would it have anything to do with you at all?" I said with complete logic.

I could see by the sudden rapid blinking of her pretty eyes that this hadn't occurred to her and it stopped her in her tracks. My mouth twisted - she looked so stumped.

"But......but......if somebody starts to ask questions?"

"I promise you, it's gonna be fine. Now, can we argue about this later and get to some kissing and making out now?" I asked reasonably.

"No!!" She sputtered indignantly. "No. We'll argue about this first then....." And she slammed to a halt as she realised where she was taking that statement.

Ha!

Working fast to suppress my grin, I took a couple of small steps towards her while she stared wide-eyed and wary.

"Admit it, honey," I said huskily.

"Admit what? " she tried for an puzzled look but I'd caught the glint in her eye.

I took a step closer.

"Admit that you liked when Suarez was defeated and falling on his ass" I said, giving her a long, meaningful look and listening to her heart rate skitter and trip.

Another step closer.

She took a tiny step back, involuntarily it seemed - as if she didn't want to concede ground but couldn't help herself.

"Admit that it turned you on......" I insisted in a low voice, knowing I was right. She couldn't lie to me.

"I......I.......no, it doesn't turn me on to see a man humiliated that way........" She was flustered; cheeks turning pink as she tried to deflect my comments.

I took the final step to her, reached out and wrapped my arm around her waist, dragging her against me. Her hands automatically landed against my chest and she looked up with those gorgeous eyes that captivated me the same way my arms caged her.

I slipped my free hand along her jaw, cupping her face and whispering lowly: "No, but it does turn you on that I made him apologise to you finally." She gulped nervously. "You liked that, I know you did - I saw it in your eyes, Charlotte."

Our eyes clung to each other, transfixed - mine determined to get her admission and hers waging an internal battle - wanting to remain in denial but quickly realising the futility of it.

"Okay," she said after a long moment, giving in. "Alright, I admit it! I like that you scared the crap out of him, made him apologise."

I rubbed my thumb across the flawless skin of her cheek - so soft, smooth and delicate - and smiled at her confession.

"I deserved that apology," she continued. "And more! That bastard never once apologised for what he did at that dinner. Claimed he was too drunk to remember but he wasn't. I know he wasn't! And all those snide comments about you!" she exclaimed, highly offended on my behalf. "Kept asking inappropriate questions. Crowding me. Turning up in places when I was off duty. I swear he was spying on me but I couldn't prove it, that miserable weasel. He should have apologised a thousand times, TEN thousand times and........."

"Damn right he should have," I agreed.

She was getting fired up in her righteous indignation; stirring and agitating the beast who growled proudly at her, enthralled with her vehement spunk. That uniquely sexy fragrance of hers was weaving itself over and around all of my senses, sending sparks of heat through my veins and igniting the hunger deep in my belly that never really abated. Her silky skin was distracting me - as much as I wanted to listen to her vent her feelings, that spot just...... there.........along her jaw.........was calling me, tempting me and I gave in, leaning down and laying my lips softly on that sweet spot.

My hand slid through the silky strands of her beautiful thick hair as I kissed along her jaw, inching my way closer to her ear. Her words were petering out, slowing down as she lost her train of thought.

"And...and he deserved to be......terrified....and humiliated....." She said throatily, struggling to keep her rant going.

I ramped up the assault on her skin - nibbling, flicking my tongue out to taste her and licking slowly, pulling her tighter against me till not an inch seperated our bodies. She resisted surrender stubbornly, her desire blatantly obvious to my extra senses. But then as I opened my mouth and bit softly, first into her jawbone then her earlobe, she moaned loudly and shuddered hard, her hands curling into fists against my chest, the battle of wills over. Her heartbeat skyrocketed and she reached up and clutched the back of my head, dragging my mouth to hers demandingly.

As if I needed encouragement.

With a shiver of my own, her curves plastered against me, my tongue swept in and tasted all the delicious flavours of her mouth. Her hands slid around my neck, fingers scraping over my nape sensuously as she held on tight. My blood sizzled and snapped as heat burned through my muscles and I was hard as a rock in a split second.

She knew it too.

Torturing me with slow tilts of her hips into mine, she rubbed up against my straining body, her hands running through my hair and I could have purred aloud in greedy pleasure. My beast stretched and rolled into her touch like an overgrown cat and I kissed her harder, deeper, wanting more.

Craving more.

"No, wait," she suddenly muttered in between kisses. "Kellan......wait......we can't do this here.......no.........." Yet her tongue slid across my bottom lip before sweeping back inside to duel with mine.

More kisses.

Wet, open mouth, devouring kisses.

Christ.

"No, wait.....stop. We gotta stop," she tried again, breathlessly trying to convince me even as she struggled to convince herself. She dragged her mouth away from mine but I followed and she groaned as I bit her bottom lip, rewarding me with a hard kiss before finally managing to pull her mouth away properly and gasping for breath.

Not deterred, I began kissing the smooth column of her neck and she shivered, pushing her hips hard into my cock, sending lightening strikes of lust to every throbbing inch of me.

I knew she was right - this wasn't the best place to take things to a higher level - this was her work place after all and I moaned in protest against her skin: "Don't wanna. I'm not done making out with you."

Nibbling, licking, kissing, I feasted on her skin as her scent invaded my every pore, saturating me in her heady arousal.

I could eat her up, bite by slow bite and never be satisfied.

"Kellan, please......" She moaned, beseeching me to help her stop this before it got out of hand.

Fuck. Dammit to hell.
With a pained sigh, I released her mouth, lifting my head to look at her. Her face was flushed with passion, lips swollen and wet from mine, eyes huge and almost black - the pupils dilated so much there was just a thin sliver of green gold ringing the heated darkness.

Breathing heavily with lust thick and damp in the air, our eyes clung as the connection throbbed between us.

My hand shook as I slid it slowly through her hair, enjoying the satiny glide against my skin as we fought for control.

This woman slayed me so easily and the only redeeming thing about that, was that I got to her just as easily, just as deeply.

As the final strands of her hair slipped through my fingers, I grimaced and said : "You're right, I know. This isn't the place, but Jesus, Charlotte ...." My voice was as raw and basic as the need that clawed low in my belly.

Wrapping my second arm around her and linking hands at the small of her back, I kept her close as I leaned in and placed a kiss on her forehead before meeting her eyes again. "If we were anywhere else........"

She didn't dispute my meaning - as aware as I was that our physical craving was elemental, the knife edge of desire twisting keenly, irrefutably in us both.

I wondered if it had always been like that.

My gut told me yes.

Eventually, after several deep calming breaths, our heart beats slowed and she stepped out of my arms. She turned away for a minute, running her hands over the slight mess I'd made of her hair while I concentrated on banishing my erection. Once she'd gathered herself, she turned back to face me, the vulnerable curve of her bottom lip temptingly sweet, long lashes shading molten eyes.

I stuck my shaky hands into my pockets, fingers curling into fists to stop myself reaching out and snatching her back, My beast was hyper-aware, quivering for her taste and scent and I held his tethers tightly, ignoring his low snarls.

"How did you know about him?" She asked huskily, stopping to clear the thickness from her throat. "Did you remember?"

"Finn told me." My own voice sounded like rusted nails. "You're on edge whenever he's around. Or when his name is mentioned. I wanted to know why."

She nodded and we stood quietly for a moment, the air full of residual heat.

"He told me what Suarez did at some police function......" I said, distracting myself with conversation so I didn't succumb to her heightened scent. But, damn.......The pit of my belly trembled with want.

"The Governor's Department Dinner," she clarified, a shadow crossing her delicate features.

"Yeah." I didn't like that shadow even if it did help dispel the sexual tension. "That I witnessed from a distance."

"No, ummm......you couldn't be there."

"Because I couldn't be around your cop buddies," I said rhetorically and with a small nod, she tucked her hair behind one ear, silence stretching out again with the sensitive topic.

"Look, I get that you would be wary of me being around so many cops, I do," I told her, fumbling to get my thoughts out in a constructive way. I'd gone and blown my secret existence but,. to be fair, it was only with Suarez anyway. No one else in the precinct had seen me and that asshole was meaningless. "And I know you can defend yourself but it's not natural for me to just stand by and watch."

I shifted uncomfortably on my feet, not used to justifying my actions in this way yet inexplicably compelled to.

"I know," she said with a wry half smile. "We used to argue about it a lot."

"Yeah, I bet we did."

No doubt they would've been spectacular arguments too, her stubbornness already well known to me. I just couldn't reconcile myself to the idea that I'd tolerated standing in the shadows for so long watching a woman I cared about deal with that creep.

That was just complete bullshit and offended every male instinct I owned. Plus the animal ones.

Yet.....she was right to keep me away from her colleagues, wasn't she?...

Yeah.....

Agitated now, I swept a hand over my hair in a rare show of annoyance, Charlotte's eyes widening as she followed the move.

"Couldn't you have put a picture of me on your desk or something?" I rumbled moodily.

"What?" Her lashes fluttered a few times, seemingly surprised by what I thought was an entirely reasonable question.

"So that prick could at least see I was real." That wouldn't have been too much to risk, would it?

Her eyes suddenly sparkled, mouth twisting as she tried to hold back a grin. Now what?

"What?" I asked, baffled by her amusement.

"You used to say that exact thing," she said, a reminiscent softness crossing over her face, the overhead light shadowing her features and highlighting her cheekbones. I wondered if I had any pictures of her anywhere in those drawers and cupboards back at Finn's....

Pictures.

"Wait....what were you wearing that night?" I blurted as something occurred to me. What if....?

"A dress. Why?" Her head tilted quizzically.

I could have rolled my eyes at that ingenious reply.

"What colour, I mean? I have this really clear picture in my head of that incident. I thought it was my imagination but now...."

"It was blue velvet," she interrupted with hopeful excitement.

"Not lace?" Dammit.

"Well yes, lace too! Blue velvet with lace inserts and a short skirt....." She stepped closer, rushing to explain.

"And he cornered you in the hallway....." I added as my heartbeat skittered - she described her dress exactly as I'd seen it in my mind.

She gasped and our gazes hooked in shocked realisation. A sizzle raced across my nape, hackles tingling with certainty.

Holy shit.

That hadn't been imagination. That was recall.

"We had a huge fight about it that night," Charlotte whispered. "You were liv..... livid, to say the least."

The hitch in her voice was like an anvil thrown against my chest; painful and unexpected and I knew it must have been a helluva fight. Alarmingly, her eyes welled up with tears and she blinked madly to hold them back, winning the war even as her face melted into pained anger.

"That asshole caused us so much grief," she added, the bitter words at odds with the tremble in her voice and my heart lurched. Without thought, I pulled my hands from my pockets, held my arms up to her and she walked into them wordlessly, sliding her hands around my back as I gathered her in close, then closer still.

With her head resting on my chest, I pressed a kiss against her silky hair. Neither of us said anything, just held tight to the other for long silent minutes and I was glad for the chance to settle. Ostensibly I was comforting her but she did the same for me, her warm body fitting snugly against me, my arms overlapping around her slight figure.

I could stay this way for hours.

That particular memory - witnessing Suarez's sleazy prick manoeuvre - that had returned without any instigating trauma. Without being asleep or unconscious at the time.

That was a good thing, right? It meant that my mind was unlocking with more ease, didn't it?

Shit, I hoped so.

I pulled her closer still, drawing a deep breath of her scent, the aroma somehow fortifying and calming.

Eventually, she raised her head from my chest with a sigh, looking up at me with a soft smile and even softer eyes, one small hand lifting to cup my face, the gesture an acknowledgement of shared emotion.

Something about her hand on my cheek made me tremble and I grabbed her free hand and raised it to my mouth, pressing my lips into her palm, eyes locked on hers.

She curled her fingers around the kiss, as if to hold onto it and my heart tripped.

"You better go before anybody else sees you," she said, breaking the moment and my breath shuddered in relief, glad to let go of the building intensity. "I'll go open up the rear exit and you can get out that way. No point risking blurring through the precinct again." She gave me a disapproving little look.

"Aren't you leaving with me now? " I asked as she turned towards the door.

"No, I can't. Not yet. I'll meet you back at Finn's later on." She opened the door a fraction and poked her head out.

"Bring J.C with you," I said, watching as she scanned the corridor. With her back towards me, I was hard pressed not to ogle her butt.

She pulled herself back in quickly, closed the door and stared wide eyed in surprise at me. "J.C? Why?"

"She knows me, doesn't she?" I said with a shrug. "She's seen me. Finn said she knows all about me and she's your partner so.....unless you don't trust her?"

Her forehead scrunched. "No, it's not that! It just surprised me that you'd ask, that's all. But you're right - the four of us can get a lot more done together."

Her thinking process was obvious but it was leading her in the wrong direction - I was looking out for Finn, not gathering troops.

Charlotte opened the door a fraction and peeked out again. This time I ogled her butt, I admit it.

"Ok. It's safe. Come on," she urged, opening the door wider in readiness for the big escape but I walked over and dropped an unexpected kiss on her cheek, causing her to jerk slightly.

"I'll leave the way I came. See you at Finn's, babe - don't take too long." And with a wink, I took off in a blur for what felt like the fiftieth time today - racing through the corridor, down the stairs and out the front entrance - moving so fast that even I was impressed.

And once again, nothing would be visible on any security camera. Just that strange freaking breeze.

I almost laughed aloud imagining Charlotte's reaction to my disappearing act just now. She'd be annoyed, to put it mildly.

Too bad I'd missed it.

Chapter Twenty

It was when I was halfway back to Finn's that I decided to make a detour. It just made sense to go now, I figured. Now, while the Commander hadn't had enough time to strip the place. He wouldn't do it without the cover of darkness if he was smart, so now was the best chance I had of getting what I needed from the studio.

Charlotte wasn't going to like it but since I hadn't actually promised her I wouldn't go alone, I wasn't breaking my word, was I?

As I'd walked past the camera that Finn had hacked into, I just had to send him a discreet wave, wondering if he'd catch it and how blue his swearing would get. Smirking in amusement, it occurred to me that he'd gone from being "McGregor" to "Finn" in the blink of an eye, the switch in my mind effortless.

Letting myself into the studio, I'd stood in the entrance for a minute, scanning the furniture and layout. It was only a handful of hours since I'd been here last yet the difference in how I felt was light years. Because I was different. Recalling how cold and calculating I'd been when I'd first woken up in that hotel, how robotic and disconnected, I almost didn't recognise myself.

Not that I knew enough now. With so much more to reclaim and rediscover, I was a "Work in Progress" I suppose. Sarcastic humour quirked at my mouth - yeah, stick a hazard sign on my ass and be done with it.

But I did know that I was changed.

Charlotte and my returning memory of her had broken through something darkly layered and unemotional, paving the way for my brain to shake loose my history with Finn and release parts of my personality I wasn't aware I had.

The more I discovered about my past, however, the more precarious my situation became, the danger that my existence brought to others now evident. Yeah, it looked like I was the ultimate target in someone's killer-games but I could look after myself. What I wouldn't tolerate is any risk to Charlotte and Finn, two people I was beginning to care a great deal about.

Beginning?

Yeah, right. Who was I kidding?

Funny that as late as this morning, I would have absolutely denied that admission but now....it slid as naturally into my conscious as knowing I hated sugar in my coffee.

Shaking off the introspection, I got on with the job I'd come to do. First, I collected everything from that night at the hotel - the receipt, the fatigues, the sports bag. Then the laptop and other equipment supplied by Commander Prick; any thing that might help identify him. I scoured over every surface and hidden nook and cranny, using both human and beast senses as I searched for surveillance and/or listening devices, thinking for sure the place would be bugged.

But there was nothing.

Which didn't make a helluva lot of sense. Did he have that much faith in me as a paid assassin that he didn't feel he needed to keep an eye on me? Was I that tractable?

I scowled darkly at that insult and slammed a drawer closed with a little too much force. He'd pay large just for that.

Emptying the safe of all the money he'd supplied me with, I estimated the small pile of notes to be around ten grand, an amount that was certainly excessive for daily mission expenses but not enough to be considered payment for "services rendered."

But of course, he wasn't planning on paying a damn cent, was he?

No doubt, it was planted here just for show and with an enormous amount of spiteful pleasure, I took every damn note from the small safe, stashing it all in the gym bag.

As I'd rifled through drawers and cupboards, it was so damn obvious this place wasn't my home. Other than the kitchen, bathroom and wardrobe, there was nothing in them. Not a thing. If I'd actually looked into them at any point before today, I would have been highly suspicious of the emptiness because no one lives completely devoid of junk.

Where were the bills and unopened mail? The condoms packets? The remote control spare batteries? And all the other crap that indicated a life lived here?

Yet, come to think of it, had the Commander actually said that I did? I paused in my searching to focus on that thought but my memory of that day was now hazed and disjointed despite being not that long ago and when a nasty little twinge stabbed at my temple, I gave up.

These head pains..... I'd had them before. Several of them, in fact, I realised with a grimace. And they had to be related to whatever had been done to me. They weren't random headaches as I'd dismissively thought.

With a clenched gut and a pissed off beast, I grabbed the suit I'd worn to the gallery fundraiser, stuffed that and the loaded gym bag into the suit protector it came in, zipped it all up and slung it over my shoulder.

Leaving without a backwards glance, I'd walked out and locked the door, fingers curled around the clothes-hanger and free hand in pocket, satisfied I had everything that could possibly help identify the mysterious Commander.

By the time the cab dropped me off outside Finn's place, the sun was sinking, the drop in temperature bringing a biting sharpness to the early spring breeze. Oddly, once I'd reached the front door, I hesitated a moment, not really knowing whether I should just walk in or knock. Earlier today, I'd barged in heedlessly and nearly given Finn a heart attack but that was due to the chaos of that moment and I couldn't really use that as an excuse this time. Could I?

Technically, I suppose, this was my home too but I didn't feel that connection yet, so.......

Shit. What to do?

Dammit.

Scowling in annoyance at myself, I knocked loudly and stood there marvelling at my lame ass.

Finn opened the door, his brows jumping into his hairline at the sight of me, grey gaze blinking in confusion.

"What're you doing?" He asked in a flat voice.

"Whaddaya mean?"

"Why you knocking?"

"I didn't wanna scare you," I explained, mouth quirking at the ridiculous conversation. Rolling his eyes, he stepped back to let me pass through, muttering dryly; "Gee, thanks."

Walking back into what was fast becoming a familiar room, I dumped all the stuff on the sofa and glanced over to find Finn eyeing it with interest.

"Suarez alive? And how badly did Charlie ream your ass?" He asked casually and I smirked in appreciation of his droll wit. Apparently that was a rhetorical question because he glanced over, grinned widely and asked what was in the bags.

I drew everything out and laid it on the coffee table. All except the dusty suit - that could stay where it was for now. Finn's analytical eyes gleamed as he scanned the laptop and surveillance gear then the pile of cash, his only comment: "We better check that it's not counterfeit."

Hell yeah, we'd check.

And so we set to work on assessing what we could and couldn't do with the items laid out, the cash zipped back up and bag stuffed under the coffee table while we worked up a rough plan.

An hour later, we sat with coffee in hand, keeping casual eyes on the monitors that overlooked the warehouse studio.

While I'd been gone, he'd accessed a few more municipal security cameras and we now had extra views of the place, granting us three seperate angles - front, back and side.

The army fatigues hadn't really given us much to work with, other than the fact they were barely used - something I hadn't picked up on at the time - I'd simply grabbed them off the floor and stashed them in the gym bag, never thinking of them again. But looking at the tags now, it was obvious how new they were. Seeing how easily I'd been duped with the army gear was infuriating despite knowing there was nothing I could've done or thought differently at the time - I was a soldier following orders. And blindly, at that. Nevertheless Finn thought he'd run a scan on missing army supplies "just in case" and I didn't wanna even think about how he hacked into those systems - seriously, the man was Bill Gates-level nerd genius.

Yet another computer was running a search for the laptop's serial number and while we waited for those to finish, I filled him in on the "Suarez Event" as I was going to refer to it from now on. His eyes goggling in amazement, there was a heavy beat of silence at the end of the story and he'd just looked at me blankly before collapsing; busting a gut in sheer hilarity and clutching his sides as he laughed his ass off.

I couldn't help chuckling myself. That vision of Suarez in his moment of total humiliation was going to provide me months of amusement, I knew.

He wiped away tears as he gasped, "Oh my God, I would pay to have seen that."

We now had a ten buck bet on how long we thought it would take Suarez the Maggot-Slimeball to skip town. I figured it would take him a week whereas Finn figured two. I told him he was too generous.

Finn, in another brilliant move, had figured out how to record the view from the security cameras which meant we wouldn't need to stay up all night and watch, stake-out style. Great news because, damn - who wanted to do that?

And now, as Finn punched away on his keyboard and I sat watching for any activity around the studio, we discussed important stuff. Like sport.

Apparently the Yankees were my favourite baseball team because according to Finn, all the O'Ryan's were big Yankees fans. He was a Mets fan and we'd had a friendly rivalry going for years between our two families. Realising what he'd said, he immediately apologised for the off-hand remark about "all the O'Ryan's", knowing I didn't remember them. But I didn't want him to tiptoe around the topic every time it came up so I shrugged casually and simply said: "It is what it is," steadfastly ignoring the hard twinge that shot through my chest.

A quick glance over revealed his solemn gaze fixed carefully on my face but with neither of us willing to delve deeper into yet more emotional stuff, we quickly returned to discussing sport, keen to get past the awkward moment.

In football, he informed me, we both followed the Giants fanatically and had often gone to games together which then led to a discussion on the weird complexities of my memory. I could recall watching games, of both kinds of ball but I couldn't remember in what context - who I'd been with or where. Frustrating and weird as shit to me but Finn was fascinated, "his biochemical scientist mind intrigued and challenged" - to quote him.

My beast suddenly came to sharp attention and I knew even before her aroma hit my senses that Charlotte must be near. And straight after her heady scent came the sound of her heartbeat - a sound that simultaneously stimulated and calmed me.

But I could also hear another heartbeat and so I casually said: "Charlotte and her partner are here," smirking as Finn's heartbeat shot sky high and he fumbled on the keyboard, glancing over at me before swinging around to face the door with wide eyes.

After a cursory knock, in walked Detective Beautiful-Baby together with a tall slim woman I'd seen only at a distance until now. A woman Finn was doing his best to appear cool and unconcerned in front of, much to my amusement.

I studied Charlotte's face for any lingering anger at my earlier disappearing act but either she'd already forgiven me or she didn't hang onto grievances. I suspected it was a bit of both.

I gave her a slight smile and she did the same, our gazes falling into each other so easily.

As Finn and I stood up, he gave a casual "Hey" and both women greeted him with a smile and a hello before J.C turned to me and met my eyes, hers a silvery sky-blue set in an attractive face dominated by sharp cheekbones, stubborn jawline and no-nonsense gaze, her Eastern European, possibly Scandinavian heritage obvious in the dirty blonde/brown hair and smooth pale skin.

She stared impassively and so did I.

No one said anything for a long moment then she took two steps forward and reached out to give me a very awkward hug, moving slowly and keeping about three feet between us, even patting my back a couple times. At a loss as to what to do with my hands, I briefly did the same, tapping her back gently. Her floral scent was pleasant and unremarkable. As she pulled back and stepped away, I decided with an internal chuckle that Finn would disagree entirely.

"Welcome back," she said, her low voice inflected with the tiniest of accents, audible only to my extra senses. "Sorry I didn't say hello to you at the Gallery the other night.......you know.......work duties.....back up...." She trailed off uncomfortably with a shrug.

Tuning into her heartbeat and senses, I got no malice or lies from her so I relaxed and, taking his cue from me, my beast settled back and returned to ogling Charlotte.

"That's ok. Sorry that I don't remember you yet," I said for lack of anything better. Meeting a new person with no recollection of them, in this setting, was awkward as fuck.

She was certainly attractive, even pretty with a slightly tomboyish demeanour - and Finn's heartbeat was still skittering.

The two were an unlikely pair in many ways but for some reason, I kind of liked the idea of them. I couldn't read her well enough yet to see if there was any interest on her side for my newly recovered friend but I figured I'd know soon enough. Just watch and see.

I glanced at Charlotte and found her watching our interaction with interest and catching my eye, she gave me a little smile of approval. My shoulders twitched back infinitesimally even though I had no idea what she approved of.

Didn't matter - I liked seeing that glint of softness in her expression.

Finn morphed into Mr Smooth-Host and made coffee for the women and we all eventually sat in the "lounge" area - defined by the fact that it had that amazing sofa and two armchairs. But really, the whole enormous room was a lounge, barring the kitchen. Charlotte and I automatically sat on the couch together while J.C and Finn took a chair each.

I swung the computer monitors around to face us so the screens would be visible from where we sat.

Finn looked at me oddly, frowning as if to say "why you doing that?" before he silently accepted my strange behaviour. His trust in me, despite my actions and without a word spoken between us, spoke volumes in my mind.

You'll figure it out soon, dude.

Chapter Twenty One

A half hour later, we'd filled J.C in on the catastrofuckery that was my life right now and we'd discussed the action plan, such as it was - going over what we knew so far and what was needed next.

And now I'd had enough - I needed out of here.

Correction - I needed Charlotte and I out of here. Being so close to her without touching her in even the most casual way was pushing my patience beyond its limitations. I'd waited long enough to make my move and now it was game time.

"Charlotte, I think we should go now," I said in a sudden change of topic, abruptly standing up.

"Go? What?" She exclaimed, startled, Finn and J.C echoing equal surprise. Reaching out, I grabbed Charlotte's hand, pulled her up from her seat and held on.

"Yeah. Finn, you won't mind taking the first shift with J.C, will you?" I said in my most reasonable tone, laying on the b.s so thick it's a wonder my shoes didn't get stuck in it. "My head is starting to thump again. I think it must be from all the blurring I've done today so I'm just gonna go rest for a while, you understand, don't you?" And I led a sputtering, bewildered Charlotte to the front door.

This dragging thing between us was becoming a bit of a habit and I was hard pressed not to grin.

Finn's face was just as confused as everyone else's but as I caught his eye and gave him a meaningful "get with the program" look, he finally got it and the mouth he'd dropped open snapped closed and he blushed.

But it was a manly blush.

"Uhhhh........Yeah, sure ...." He stuttered, trying to play along. "You gonna be okay?"

"I'll be fine, I'm sure of it. I'll be with Charlotte. We'll be in touch later, okay?" I said with cool reassurance. "Bye"

And we were through the door.

I hustled her down the front steps, still clutching her hand, stopping at the bottom to ask her if she'd driven here.

"Yeah, my car's just there," she said with a quick wave of her free hand down the street behind me.

"Wait, Kellan, stop." She said, digging her heels in when I turned and tried to walk us towards her sexy-ass car, the gunmetal grey glinting prettily under the streetlights. Her hand tugged on mine and I turned back to find her looking up at me with concern darkening her beautiful eyes. "Are you ok? You're in pain?"

"No, I'm fine." I smiled at her for her sweet caring.

"But........" Her eyebrows scrunched together in confusion.

"Charlotte, the only reason I made up that story was so we had an excuse to get out of there and leave Finn and JC alone." I waited patiently for what I figured would be an entertaining reaction from her.

"Alone? Why do we need to do that...............Ohhh!!" And as my meaning sunk in, her eyes popped open wide and she gaped at me in sheer astonishment. "What?" It was almost a screech.

I smiled at her - she was too cute. My beast wanted to scoop her up and carry her away somewhere. Speaking of which.......

"Come on, I'll explain everything in the car," I said and once again turned to head towards her Camaro SS. One day I'd get her to let me drive it, I vowed.

Letting go of her hand so she could unlock the car, we both got in and once she'd started driving, she immediately demanded, "What's going on?"

"Finn has a crush on your partner." I told her, sitting back to enjoy watching her digest and process that bit of hot news but getting thoroughly distracted with the way she drove.

Damn...

There was nothing sexier than how she handled that purring beast with such skill and finesse, I decided, feeling an echoing hum beginning to slither through my veins.

Well, not nothing............

"A crush? On J.C.??" She frowned, disbelieving. "You're serious?"

"As a heart attack," I answered, entranced by her hands on the wheel and how her small delicate fingers gripped so firmly around.....

"How can you be so sure?" She asked and I reluctantly pulled my concentration back into the conversation. No easy feat when the close confines of the vehicle intensified her aroma and her hands were.......

Cut it out, I growled under my breath.

Yanking myself back on track, I did everything I could to block out my own thoughts and to not breathe too deeply.

"I'm sure," I told her, confident in the subject matter if not in my own control right then. "Because every time her name came up, his heartbeat flew off the charts. Plus, I asked him outright and I can tell when someone's lying. He's crushing."

"Oh my Lord," she said, her voice completely stunned. "I had no idea. I didn't see it." She was silent for a while and I could almost hear her castigating herself mentally for being so oblivious. I would have reassured her but I was busy concentrating on shallow breaths.

"What about J.C.? Is there anything there on her side?"

"Possibly. I don't have any memories of her so there's no context for me yet. But I can tell right now that she's not lying and there's no bad vibes."

I didn't want to admit that I hadn't really paid much attention to J.C.'s behaviour towards Finn, distracted as I had been by Charlotte's proximity.

She mulled that over in silence, navigating the streets smoothly as the car's throaty engine rumbled quietly through my body, an echo of my own simmering growl.

"I'll be able to tell more the next time I see her, " I added on, looking out to see that we'd reached her block. Her apartment wasn't far from Finn's so it hadn't taken long to drive the short distance which was a relief. Even cracking the window open hadn't helped dispel the intoxication that was her scent and I grimaced in discomfort.

"There's more........" I said, figuring I should be upfront about the whole not-needing-to-watch-the-monitors-all-night thing.

"What more?" She asked warily with a quick glance.

So as we reached her building and she parked underground in her designated spot, I told her how Finn had set up the computers to record overnight and there wasn't a need for a stake out at all. I'd turned those monitors around, pretending we needed to keep an eye on them to give Finn an excuse to be alone with J.C. for as long as possible. He hadn't been in on it, I explained, but now that he had time with her, the ball was in his court.

Engine switched off, I got out in a hurry and gratefully took a deep breath of cool unscented air and she scrambled to follow, the two of us meeting at the back of the car. She looked at me in the low light of the garage as we stood facing each other, a slight frown marring her smooth forehead, head tilted thoughtfully.

"So, to clarify........" She began, the shadows playing across her cheekbones and thick hair catching the pale light.

"This whole ruse with the monitors, pretending he hadn't set it up to record - that was all part of your grand scheme to leave them in charge of a fake stakeout while you faked a headache, just to give Finn some alone time with his crush?"

"Well..... Yeah," I admitted, confident she could see the genius in that plan.

Her eyes held and searched mine intently, a gleam in their pretty depths that I couldn't quite decipher, her face giving nothing away.

"What?" I asked as the silence stretched out, wondering what was going on in her mind.

Her face softened and she smiled so gently, the corner of her mouth lifting with a sweet warmth.

"I was wrong," she said in her husky voice, the tone sliding over my skin in a slow scrape.

Wrong? About what?

"When I said you weren't like the Kellan I knew before," she continued, answering my unspoken question. "I was wrong. You are. There's just.......more layers to you."

And she reached out to lay her palm on my cheek again, heat flooding my whole system with just that touch. I felt the power of her skin against mine and my heart kicked at my ribs hard. Green gold into hazel, the connection pulsed between us; a living, breathing entity.

She gave my cheek a parting caress then turned and walked towards the elevator, leaving me to catch up once I'd shaken off the enthralment she put me under with such ease.

The steel doors closed behind us and I pressed the button for her floor, leaning back against the handrail that ran around the walls. Resting my hands on the cold thin metal on either side of me and with Charlotte a few steps away facing the doors, I steadied myself with a calming breath.

It occurred to me just then that we'd automatically made our way here to her apartment - neither one of us saying or planning it that way, neither of us questioning the other as to the destination. We just.......went.

This, like many other instances, showed yet again the level of synchronicity, of instinctive connection between us.

"You know, despite the good things you've done today, you've still been bad," Charlotte said conversationally.

Distracted by my thoughts, I didn't fully register her words.

"Sorry, what?" I asked, looking over at her. She turned around to face me directly, meeting my eyes with an odd little glint in hers.

"I was saying that despite the good things you've done today, you've still been bad," she said as she began walking towards me slowly, with a hip rolling smoothness that dragged my attention away from her face.

There was a deliberate swing to her hips, I'm sure of it.

I think.

Was there?

She was confusing me............

Did she say bad? Huh?

I blinked stupidly at her - something about her demeanour seemed a little........ predatory?

"Very bad," she continued in a low voice and my eyes flashed to hers. There in the gorgeous depths of her exotic eyes was a look of........heat.

Of confidence.

Of intention.

My beast snapped to attention while my brows rose and mouth fell open in complete shock.

What...........???

I froze.

Stalking closer, her eyes hooked into mine and refused to let go. Not that I would - she had my complete and undivided attention.

Getting right into my personal space until not half an inch separated us, she raised her head slowly to mine, coming in for a kiss but stopping just a breath away. With her lips so temptingly close and her scent wrapping itself around my body, slithering and seducing, I trembled in anticipation.

Our eyes held, her pupils dilating as I knew mine were. My skin was tingling and she had me so mesmerised that I had no clue what was going on until I heard the sudden clink of handcuffs locking into place and I looked down to find my left wrist shockingly manacled to the handrail.

What the hell??

With a wild thump, my heart began racing madly and my gaze flew back to her face. She looked so proud of her little trick, smugly satisfied at having caught me off-guard.

Placing her small hands on my chest she said huskily; "You ignored me and went ahead and blurred out of the precinct a second time. That makes you a bad boy." Leaning up the final inch, she placed a slow kiss on my lips before drawing back and looking me dead in the eye as she said; "And bad boys get punished."

Holy....shit.....

Every sinew and muscle in my body seized up, as if struck by lightning. I lost my breath and my beast shuddered. All the blood in my body rushed south and my cock hardened up so fast I nearly passed out.

Jesus.....

Laying her mouth on mine, she kissed me with every intention of killing me there and then. Groaning deep, I started to wrap my free arm around her but she grabbed it, placed it back on the handrail and gave me a stern look as she ordered:

"Keep your hands there. No touching."

Ah......that's what she meant by punishment.

Fuck.

Her mouth returned and I kissed her hard and long, devouring her, my tongue ruthless in retaliation for her sexy bossiness and for being the only part of me allowed to touch her. Her lips were as hungry as mine; wet, open and giving.

But she pulled away again, allowing us both a moment to drag in shaky breaths.

Desire throbbed through my veins with overwhelming intensity and my beast salivated with need as I watched, captivated, while she reached over to press the red stop button and the elevator lurched to a sudden halt.

I was gonna die.

Eyes glued to her every move, my lip curled in raw snarling need, hands gripping the rail for dear life as lust twisted savagely. I held onto my control with brute strength, determined to let her play her games, despite my suffering. These cuffs were no barrier to me - if I wanted out, they'd break as easily as matchsticks in less than a second.

She knew it.

I knew it.

And the fact that she was trusting me to let her play had to be the hottest goddamn feeling in the world. I wanted to howl in glory.

Placing her hands on my pecs again, she began a slow frisk, running her hands teasingly over my shoulders and arms, down over my chest before trailing them over my clenching stomach till she reached my belt. She'd watched her hands as they slid over me but now she looked up into my eyes, the heated desire in hers sending molten liquid through every muscle and sinew.

Licking her lips slowly, she touched her mouth to mine, pulling back when I tried to kiss her fully, taunting me by coming close again only to withdraw once more. All to drive me nuts as her hands began unbuckling my belt, the slide of leather and clink of metal loud in my ears, the rasp of the zipper as she slid it carefully down destroying my equilibrium. I growled low, clutching the rail tightly as my abs spasmed painfully in anticipation of her touch.

God, yes.

And when she laid her hand low on my belly and slid her fingers through the fine hair there, pushing her hand into my boxer briefs, I threw my head back in a gasp, moaning at the feel of her hot hand sliding against my throbbing shaft, her fingers trailing fire from my base over the burning skin to skim around my tip, spreading the pearl of liquid already gathered there in little circles.

Pressing a soft kiss to my exposed neck, she swiped her tongue over my skin and sent trails of fire and ice chasing to every corner of my body and as her hand wrapped around my erection, she whispered teasingly against my ear; "I knew it. I knew you'd be hiding a loaded weapon."

She did NOT just say that.

She ..... Ha.

A short, moaning laugh burst out helplessly. The cheeky little......

Disbelief and delight warred for the briefest of moments before my mind died a quick death. Her hand squeezed my cock before slowly pumping, her skin against mine blazing hot and destroying any coherent thought from my brain. My beast was snarling and begging.

Or was that me?

"Please," I groaned, my voice guttural. "Oh God......"

She sunk her teeth into my neck gently and I hissed in pleasure.

Her hand released me to slide lower, pushing my jeans further open, further down my hips, giving her better access to cup my balls and rub her palm over them.

I quivered with need, my mouth crashing back down to hers in a hard greedy kiss. Every nerve, every muscle trembled, my blood thick and sluggish as I swelled and swelled with every touch.

"Jesus, Charlotte ...." I moaned, biting her bottom lip then soothing it with my tongue. The throb of my heartbeat was battling with hers, the air heavy with want, lust pulsing in thick waves over our bodies.

She pulled her mouth away, our eyes clashing, chests heaving as we chased stolen breath; her fingers dragging their short nails gently across the tight skin of my scrotum and sending hard shudders down my spine.

"Fuck, oh God, Charlotte ....." I panted, deeply afraid I was gonna rip the damn handrail off the wall any second.

And then, as she began to sink to her knees, I think I had a heart attack. Explosive carnality shattered through my entire being at the picture she made there in front of me, watching me as I watched her. A bomb could have detonated next to me and I wouldn't have looked away, every fibre inside of me devastated by the primal rawness of her actions. My claws scraped against the rail as I turned partially, eyes flashing golden.

"Charlotte," I breathed, desperately holding on to my senses with everything I had. Her eyes held mine, green gold into golden as she leaned forward and ran her pointed pink tongue slowly, tortuously from my base, upwards over the hot pulsing thickness till she reached my tip. Then, opening her lips wide, she strained to take me in as deep as she could, her mouth scorching, wet and silky against my skin.

I threw my head back in a loud guttural snarl, roaring my pleasure at the feel of her mouth wrapped around me. Her hands joined in the play, one sliding through the hair at my groin to tease and tug, the other cupping me, guiding me in and out of her mouth, the sensation pushing me to the limits of pleasure-pain, stretching my tethers so hard I thought they'd snap.

Terrified of just that happening, I pounded my unshackled fist against the wall, two, three times, willing myself to stay in control.

As a man and as a beast.

"Jesus, baby" I moaned, my words disjointed and breathless as I strained to get him under control again, coming back into myself and instantly raising my head off the wall so I could look back down and watch, her sultry eyes flicking teasing little glances upwards and stealing the strength from my knees.

No.

THIS was the hottest goddamn feeling in the world.

The brutal sensuality of watching her pleasure me, of seeing and feeling her tongue swirling around my thickness as she slid my flesh in and out of her lips, of watching as I disappeared into the wet warmth of her velvety mouth - this was beyond my imagination. She was every fantasy, every wish and dirty dream I'd ever had and she had me on the very edge of insanity.

Desperately I tried to hold back, my beast whimpering with hunger as her own arousal filled the air and she pushed me harder, higher, her mouth insistent and tongue relentless, showing no mercy. Cruelly, she ramped up my fever by scraping her nails ever so lightly over the skin of my perineum and sending my heart into thundering, crazed palpitations.

"Oh fuck, oh Jesus......" I gasped, quivering helplessly as she did it again.

"Charlotte ......please...... I'm so close.............." I begged, my belly spasming with need. I didn't know if I was begging her to stop or continue, so lost in the turbulence of frantic hunger.

I wanted to be inside her.

I wanted to push my aching cock into her wet and clinging body.

But I wanted her mouth too.

The need to come was swiftly taking a savage hold, winding me tighter and tighter and not knowing what she liked in this area, I tried to give her warning.

"Oh God......ugh........Christ....... I wanna come......Charlotte, please..........." ...." My voice was almost unintelligible, rasping with raw lust.

Instead of withdrawing, she doubled her efforts - swirling and flicking her tongue along the slit at my crown, digging her nails into the V of my groin and scratching hard as she'd done once before, knowing it drove me wild. And as my heart kicked wildly, she sucked her mouth hard around my length in silent command to let go.

Thrusting myself in as deep as I could go, I froze as everything in my body clenched and spasmed, wave upon wave of sheer ecstasy burning through me, the pleasure so intense it hurt and my back arched as I came in thick, hot pulses endlessly.

She swallowed everything I gave her, her throat convulsing smoothly and I shuddered from the depths of my soul, her earthy womanhood a primal call to my animal; my release a rush so powerful the air stilled.

Oh God, oh God, oh God.........

I swear I saw heaven.

As every nerve and sinew in my body buzzed in searing delight, I panted breathlessly, stunned and amazed at what she'd done.

What she'd given.

How willing she'd been to share this playful, sexually adventurous side of herself.

Her trust in me.

What a revelation.

Her mouth released my still quivering flesh, leaving a sweet little kiss on the top in goodbye and vaguely I felt the elevator start to move. But it was slow to register in my mind, blissed out as I was and drifting hazily in the aftermath with legs like jelly.

It wasn't until the movement stopped and I heard the doors open that my eyes shot open to find Charlotte walking through them. As she stepped into the hallway, she turned to face me with a scorching look, small white teeth biting into her lower lip as a challenging light flashed into her eyes. She smiled smugly, giving a sassy wink as the doors closed between us, leaving me shackled to the handrail, jeans wide open and half hanging off my hips.

What the ....?

The little she-devil.....

As the elevator started its automatic return trip to the garage, I scrambled to right my clothes and get my shocked senses straight. Beastie boy and I were a shuddering mess right now but, holy crap, it wasn't over yet.

Because I'd seen the look in her eyes as the doors closed - I'd seen the taunting glint.

Catch me if you can.

Chapter Twenty Two

Catch me if you can.

The words exploded in my head with force of a grenade, unspoken yet blatantly clear.

The thump of the doors closing galvanised me into action and I jerked my hand off the rail, breaking the handcuff encircling the steel rod as if it was made of paper, the other cuff still wrapped around my wrist.

Scrambling for strength and sanity, as the elevator started to move downwards, I lunged forward to punch numbers repeatedly, frantically trying to make it stop anywhere, all while zipping and buttoning my jeans one handed. I didn't not bother with the belt, just pulled my shirt down over the loose leather.

My blood was boiling with lust, excited for the chase - she wanted me to catch her?

Hell yeah, baby.

I might have just climaxed but I was recovering fast - her aroused scent singed my nose, enflamed my throat and tongue with the need to have her.

NOW.

Right now.

Her unexpected sex-play thrilled and tantalised, the hunt calling to every molecule of my being; every muscle, instinct and breath consumed with her.

She was my sexual equal, my beast's mate and he'd known it from the start.

The depth of my craving so potent that I shook with the effort of containing it, I growled in absolute fury when the fucking elevator continued its downward trek. For Christ's sake!! Desperate to make the stupid fucking thing stop, I jabbed my fingers hard against every single button, willing the damn thing to obey me. And when it finally did on the second floor an eternity later, I shot out of the steel cage and raced for the stairs, madly.

Even blurring to the eighth level tested the limits of my patience and by the time I reached her door, every nerve-ending I owned was sizzling. Grabbing the handle, I found it unlocked and I almost howled.

God, yes.

She'd never leave it unlocked - she was a cop.

But she KNEW. She knew I would never back down from her challenge and she'd just made it easier for me.

Or maybe she didn't want a broken door?

Didn't matter.

I charged through, slammed and locked it behind me.

I'd startled her - she spun around at my sudden and loud entrance, eyes wide as she saw me standing there still as a tiger ready to pounce. She'd been heading towards the apartment corridor but now she took in my stance; the clenched fists at my sides, the splayed legs; my chest heaving with deep breaths as I tried to reign in the wildly surging need. I lowered my head, looking up at her through my lashes as I watched her eyes dilate with excitement, the taunting green gold fire of those incredible eyes like tinder to my already blazing desire.

My lip curled as I gave a deep throated growl.

I trembled, straining to hold back but her arousal - that sweet spicy smell of her, heated and wet in her own desire, swirled around me. Through me. In me.

My beast was starving for her. And I was ravenous.

Despite having come not five minutes ago, I was hard as a rock again, throbbing and swollen, weeping for her. The air pulsed with expectation, the stand-off between us vibrating as we each waited to see who would make the first move.

I waited....

Waited.....

And then, there it was...... Her sweet pink tongue peeked out to lick across her bottom lip, her dilated pupils flashing with primal heat.

Like a flag waved at a car race, that was my signal.

I blurred over, grabbed her and pinned her against the nearest wall, holding her arms above her head, the slight thump as we landed adding to the frantic beat of our hearts.

Mouths open, an inch apart and breathing each other's breath, our eyes locked for a intense moment before we crashed into a kiss devastatingly deep and hard.

Tongues duelling greedily, I pushed my hips into hers, thrusting against her seam as she strained against me with equal fire. I freed her arms to send my hands racing over her body, cupping and kneading and squeezing, her broken moans matching my own.

Lust clawed through every sinew and pore as she kissed and licked and bit my mouth with a hunger as deeply vicious as mine, her small hands diving under my shirt to slide over my pecs, her palms scorching hot against my tight nipples.

Driven insane with the incredible aroma of her, my beast was trembling with his need to claim her and without letting go of her mouth for even one moment, I ripped my jacket off, grabbed the back of my tee and ripped that off too, throwing them both to the ground, forgotten immediately.

With that, Charlotte's hands clutched hotly at my chest and back, cold fire chasing over my skin and I groaned loudly.

Desperate for breath, I left her mouth to feast on the succulent skin of her neck and she threw her head back for better access, moaning when I pushed my hand into the back of her jeans, filling my palm with her smooth ass cheek, her underwear something tiny that didn't cover even half her butt.

Jesus. My cock twitched hard.

One handed, I struggled to take her jacket off and she let go of me long enough to help, the leather quickly joining mine on the floor as I grabbed her waist and spun her around, her back to my front, pushing my hips hard into hers and filling my palms with her breasts.

"Charlotte," I groaned, scraping my teeth against the soft skin below her ear and she shuddered convulsively. "Is this a favourite?"

"What," she moaned breathlessly, confused.

"The shirt? I promise I'll get you a new one" I said and grabbing the silk, I ripped it in two, shredding it from her body in my desperation to get to her skin, the sound of the fabric tearing loud and erotic. With two hands I tore her bra in half and as the lace fell away, cupped my hands full of her sweet hot flesh, her tight nipples piercing my palms. Biting into her neck where it joined with her shoulder, I vowed I'd buy her new lingerie too because I was destroying hers.

"Kellan," she moaned. "Oh God.......yesssss........."

Fuck, I loved it when she called my name.

Raising her arms above her head, she linked them behind my neck and thrust herself into my hands, demanding more and while one hand tweaked and rolled and moulded her soft flesh, I hurriedly unbuttoned her jeans, yanked the zipper down and slid my hand into her panties, down through the small strip of curls and into the liquid fire of her folds, sinking two fingers deep into her core. Her velvet inner muscles clenched down hard at my sudden intrusion, her nails raking across the skin of my nape as she shuddered.

Mine.

The need to mark her, claim her as mine, drummed through my blood in a heavy tribal beat, the craving instinctual, animalistic and raw, wanting to make love to her as much as I wanted to fuck her.

Mine.

The word pounded relentlessly through my system, keeping time with the frantic beat of my heart and I pushed her harder, higher - my thumb strumming over her hard slippery clit, fingers thrusting and swirling inside her. My beast salivated for the hot wetness coating my fingers but I needed her to come first.

I pinched and swirled her tight nipples, mouth sucking on the delicate skin under her jaw and as her body coiled tighter, I thrust harder, flicked faster until with a sudden hard spasm, her pussy clamped around my fingers and she gave a strangled low scream.

Yes!

I held her tightly as the climax ripped through her, keeping my fingers still inside her, knowing how sensitive she'd be right now. Her whole body undulated against me, hands clutching my neck for balance, her nails digging into my nape, the small pain welcome.

Opening my eyes, I looked down over her shoulder to watch her smooth belly ripple with tremors and was shocked to see my left wrist still manacled with the handcuff.

Ha. I'd forgotten all about it.

The erotic sight of my hand cupping her lush flesh, thumb gently pressing on her nipple with the silver cuffs dangling down against her midriff and plumb undersides sent a shiver scraping down my spine.

Goddamn, that looked sexy as hell.

Even so............I needed them gone so I gently slid my fingers from her trembling inner flesh and stuck them in my mouth, finally giving my beast the taste he'd been craving; sucking all her juices from my skin and he growled in ecstatic hunger.

I tore the metal cuff from my wrist and let it fall to the floor uselessly, shoving her jeans and panties down her hips, their momentum carrying them past her knees as my hands quickly slid back around her, one wrapped tightly around her waist while the other pressed just above her mound, supporting the trembling aftershocks rocking through her body.

That was just orgasm number one.

Gently licking along her shoulder, I traced little circles under her earlobe. Carnal bliss was seeping from her body into mine, stoking the blazing fire in my groin, my belly and my heart.

Christ Almighty, I wanted her..... My cock was threatening to break through the denim and my beast was out of his mind.

Watching and feeling her sexual gratification had to be the single most exciting thing I'd ever experienced. I'd been wrong - it wasn't watching her pleasure me that was the hottest goddamn feeling in the world.

It was pleasuring HER.

"Charlotte ," I groaned. "What you do to me. If you knew how badly I want you, the things I wanna do to you, not just me but........oh God........my beast........" I muttered mindlessly in between kisses to her jaw, her cheek, my voice guttural. "Christ, baby, you bring out the animal in me."

Her breath hitched then fluttered out in a shaky exhale and I suddenly realised how much I'd admitted to her; how much I'd revealed. Oh crap...... dammit!

Hoping like hell that I hadn't scared her, I told myself that she wasn't someone who frightened easily. That she was able to calm my beast with just her touch - but in this state? In this sexual frenzy? Fuck, I didn't know how she'd feel - it scared ME how out of control I felt, how much I needed to claim her physically.

Claim her as mine.

But as I held my breath, at a loss for the right words, she moaned and pressed her naked hips back into mine, breathing out huskily: "it wouldn't be the first time."

Shock exploded through every nerve-ending in my body.

It wouldn't be.......

Holy shit. Oh Jesus.

......be the first time..........

In case I misunderstood, she slid her hand from my shoulder to my jaw in that reassuring way that she had, whispering; "Kellan.......it's okay......"

Her words were like a gunshot in my head and I lost it.

In a flash, both arms were wrapped around her waist as I picked her up and swung her around away from the wall to the back of the sofa, bending her over with one hand while the other ripped my jeans open and shoved them down before I grabbed hold of her hips and pulled her ass towards me. She used her arms to support herself on the sofa headrests, opening her legs wider for me as I lined up my cock at her entrance and slammed home inside her wetness, her walls immediately squeezing and contracting at the sudden invasion, triggering another climax. She gasped before screaming loudly; " Yes!!!!! Oh God......"

My eyes turned gold, claws unsheathed and I threw back my head and snarled long and loud in victory.

Goddamn heaven.

Despite the blindingly primitive need, the pure sexual heat that hammered through my body, somehow I knew my claws wouldn't hurt her, instinctively protective of her delicate skin even as I craved to mark it. Holding tight to her hips, I began moving, slowly at first to ride out her orgasm with her, looking down through my beast eyes and seeing the long smooth line of her supple spine, the luscious fullness of her ass cheeks and the insanely erotic sight of watching my thickness disappear into the slick swollen folds of her womanhood. Watching it slide smoothly out only to sink to the hilt again and again.

In that moment, half transformed, my beast and I were as one. And as one, we claimed her as ours: the taking primal, elemental and raw.

The moment her climax receded, I thrust harder, longer, setting up a relentless rhythm that soon had us gasping; the force of my driving hips pushing the sofa along the floor. Charlotte ground her ass back into me, tilting her hips demandingly and arching her spine. The slap of our skin, the loud groans and little screams she gave were driving me insane and I clung ferociously to the fine balance of half-transformation, clung to my sanity.

This was Charlotte taking both of us into her body simultaneously: a she-wolf accepting her mate unequivocally and irrevocably - surrendering in complete willingness to the powerful passion and instinctive carnal need between us. And the sensation ripped through my soul to destroy and renew.

This was more than making love, more than simple fucking - this was a soul connection, a primal union - a statement of surrender in its rawest form.

Something crashed to the floor noisily but neither of us gave a damn, deaf and blind to anything except the grinding need to take each other, again and again. She tossed her head back. "Yes, yes, yes........ Jesus........oh GOD!......Kellan ....please.......please...."

Wanting her to come again more than I wanted my next breath, I swiped her hair carefully to one side and leaned down over her body, my chest to her back. Retracting my claws, one hand grasped her breast and the other slid to her folds as I thrust harder, deeper and she yelled brokenly, "Oh....please.... now.....Kellan.... Honey......NOW!!"

Helpless to resist her demand, my fingers pinched her clit and nipple and with that simultaneous pleasure-pain, her walls clamped down on my cock in a relentless grip, convulsing in long waves and I leaned down and bit the nape of her neck in an instinct as old as time. She groaned, one hand suddenly clutching my nape, holding me to her, holding my bite as I grunted in pure pleasure. Pulsating heat burned and sizzled, her pussy milking my throbbing flesh with sensuous silky greed.

Jesus. Have. Mercy.

For long, long moments our bodies rode through the bliss and I held her tightly to me, eyes still burning gold, tremors racking through me in great big shockwaves.

The pleasure was so immense, my breath strangled in my throat and my heart tripped over itself. The world pulsated vibrantly, a kaleidoscope of colour and sharp stinging sensation exploding to every corner of my being.

When it was over, my knees were like jelly, and Charlotte trembled in my arms. I gathered every bit of strength I had left to kick off my jeans and shoes, pick her up in my arms and carry her to her bedroom.

One handed I dragged the bedcovers back before collapsing together on the cool sheets, lying side by side on our backs, naked, panting and stunned.

Unbelievable.

My world was rocked. Earth had moved.

Seismically.

As I caught my breath, the gold in my eyes gave way to hazel and my beast shuddered in supreme satisfaction, the scent and taste of his woman on his tongue and in his throat.

Divine.

He stretched and preened before receding to lay in lazy contentment, quietly smug.

Chapter Twenty Three

When my heart rate finally began to slow, I reached over and dragged her into my arms and she curled up against my side with a long sigh. With her head resting on my chest, she slid her knee over my thigh and her hand across my belly to hook onto my side. I wrapped both arms around her and pressed my lips against her hair in a quick kiss before laying back against the pillow again.

Bodies cooling and hearts calming, we were quiet for a long while and I was replete and content in a way I'd never been before. At least as far as I remembered. But she'd said it wasn't the first time and that meant that I was one hell of a lucky bastard.

She nuzzled into me, dropping a small kiss just under my nipple and a shiver rolled lazily down my spine and I felt.......amazing. That was the only word that fit - blissed out in carnal satisfaction, yes, but it was more than that. It was this woman beside me, I realised. This incredible woman and how she made me feel when I was with her.

She challenged me; engaged me mentally and physically. Cared about and knew me. Intelligent, gorgeous and brave, she respected and accepted all sides of me - something that, had I thought about it before today, I would have said was impossible. Maybe I'd known it before, in my "previous" life but if I hadn't, I sure as hell did now. She was fiesty, patient and funny - a kickass cop that could fight in high-heels.

I don't know how I knew that but I did and my chest twinged with the knowledge.

In heels?

Have mercy......

The Kellan I don't remember being loved her; my beast adored her and I .... Christ, was I ready to go there?

Probably not but I wasn't gonna fool myself - I was in this emotionally far more than I'd anticipated and although a flutter rolled through my belly at the revelation, it didn't freak me out all that much. Maybe because somewhere in my subconscious I'd already known - had never forgotten.

I sighed and squeezed her a little tighter. She was as lost in thought as I was and as much as I hated to disturb the magic of this moment, I had no choice.

"You thirsty? Want some water?" I asked her quietly, my voice hoarse and dry as the desert and she looked up at me, her face so beautifully relaxed, cat's eyes glinting softly in the dim light of the room.

"Yes, please," she answered and I dropped a baby kiss on her sweet lips before reluctantly untangling myself from her arms. Making my way naked through the room to the door, I'm pretty certain I could feel her eyes on my ass every step of the way. But that's okay - she can look all she wants.

With beast night vision ensuring I didn't trip over any of the scattered clothing littering the floor, I made my way into the kitchen, grabbing a glass from the overhead cupboard and not questioning for the briefest moment how I knew exactly which cabinet the glassware was in. I took bottled water from the refrigerator and poured, a tantalising idea slipping quietly into my mind and I smirked lazily.

Oh yeah. Now you're thinking, dude.

I chugged the rest of the bottle till it was empty then took a second glass and filled it with ice.

Looking around the lounge area I could see our clothes and shoes scattered everywhere; the sofa was pushed out of its place and a bowl of some kind had crashed to the floor along with a couple of picture frames.

There was nothing broken though so I shrugged and left it there. I had better things to do right now than tidy up the mess we'd made but I did wonder briefly what her neighbours had thought of all the screaming and crashing going on. Ha. Let them wonder. They better get used to it - Charlotte was vocal and I loved it.

But...nothing broken?

I'm pretty sure her bra and shirt were broken, I thought with a quiet chuckle, my bare feet sidestepping around all the stuff as I made my way back through the darkened room. Arriving safely back in her bedroom, I found her lying on her side, eyes closed with a sheet lightly covering her.

Uh, uh, uh. No hiding from me - every inch of her sexy little She-Mate self should always be on complete display for me. Only me.

Only half joking, I knew I sounded like a possessive ass, but it was only in my head and she couldn't hear my thoughts anyway.....

She opened heavy lidded eyes to watch as I walked stark-naked to her side of the bed, pupils dilating in appreciation as she skimmed her gaze over my body, taking in every detail and heat instantly flashed in my belly.

I sat on the side of the mattress and she scooted over a little, leaning up on one elbow as I silently handed her the glass of chilled water.

"Thanks," she whispered and I watched her take a long drink, her lips pursed around the rim. Her dark hair was a mess, her cheeks still flushed and despite the sheet covering her chest, I knew that the flush would be covering her breasts too.

Finished, she handed me back the glass and I placed both of them on the side-table before leaning over her on straight arms, locking her in between.

Our eyes hooked into each other's - green gold into hazel, warm and gentle with hidden fire beneath. My mouth curved into a half smile as I took in her whole face, her beauty as always hypnotic and fascinating.

"What?" She asked with a little nervous laugh at my continued silent staring.

"In the past, did I ever tell you that you are incredibly beautiful?" I really wanted to know that answer, hoping I'd been at least a little romantic with her.

Her eyes smiled at my question. "Well.......yes, sometimes you did."

"Just sometimes? Now, that's not good enough. I should have been telling you often how beautiful......"

I leaned over and touched her lips with mine.

"How gorgeous........" Another little kiss, a touch longer.

"How sexy you are..........." And I laid my mouth on hers fully, kissing her softly, slowly, thoroughly, keeping her mouth busy while I dragged the sheet away from her and lay myself down on top of her- skin to naked skin, resting my weight on my elbows so as not to crush her. Once I was settled I looked down at her - hair spread out over the pillow, lips glossy from our kiss and her eyes gleaming with soft pleasure.

Her arms wrapped around my back and she drew her fingertips slowly down my spine, her touch as delicate as a feather.

"And yet, you have these little dimples right here.......and here," I said with a kiss to each dimpled cheek. "So when you smile, you go from smoking hot to cute as hell and back......a damn neat trick if you ask me."

She laughed, eyes sparkling with amusement. "You have them too, you know" she said, leaning up to kiss me the same way, her soft lips pressing against the rough stubble on my face. "Except, you've got more than me."

I'd started nuzzling her neck but raised my head to quirk one eyebrow at her in surprise. More than her?

"Yes," she said with a wide grin. "Did you forget that you have two ass dimples right.......here," and her fingertips stopped caressing my back to press firmly in two spots just above my butt.

Instantly, a sharp frisson shot from that pressure point straight into my groin and down my legs. My hips jerked and my toes curled.

Shit! What was that!

I was so shocked my mouth fell open and I blinked madly while she giggled.

"What?.......what was that?"

She did it again and once more, the sensation flashed through my groin and thighs, startling me with its heated sharpness.

"You did forget," Charlotte said in amazement, eyes wide. "That's crazy that you'd forget something you have on your own body. Especially something as sensitive as these."

She stroked gentle fingers over the two areas and I loved that she knew my body so well, knew how it liked to be touched. And where.

"Well, I haven't looked at my ass lately. I've been too busy looking at yours to care about mine," I admitted and she laughed huskily again.

"Besides," I continued smoothly, "you check out mine plenty enough FOR me. In fact, you check it out all the time. Constantly. You can barely keep your eyes off it," I teased her.

She gasped indignantly and poked a finger into my waist in retaliation. "I do not!!"

"Oh yes, you do. Don't think I couldn't feel your eyes on my butt just now when I went to the kitchen," I wiggled my eyebrows at her, daring her to deny it. She blushed, caught out and highly chagrined.

Fuck, she was cute when she was embarrassed. I leaned back down to lay a smiling kiss on her lips as she protested laughingly. "Well, where else was I meant to look, hmm?"

Kissing her jawline and cheek, I muttered; "You can look anywhere you want, Charlotte. For as long as you want....." Kissing her in earnest now, laughter slowly dying off, I explored her mouth thoroughly, leisurely; tongue and teeth playing gently with her plumb lips, taking my time with long drugging kisses.

Her hands resumed their slow caresses up and down my back, fingertips trailing sensuous fire in their wake. I surreptitiously reached out with my left hand to the side-table, grabbed what I wanted while peppering the flawless skin of her neck and chest with warm kisses and little tongue flicks till I reached her right nipple. She moaned a quiet "mmmmm" while I licked her tightly pebbled bud, her breath hitching when I sucked her hard and her hands slid into my hair, cupping my head against her.

Dragging my mouth to her lonely other nipple, I slipped the ice cube from my hand into my mouth and wrapped my lips around her aureole, the icy coldness shocking against her heated skin. She yelled loudly, shuddered then thrust her breast into my face demandingly and I smiled to myself because...... hell yeah - my Detective Sex Kitten was into a little ice-play.

"Kellan...." She gasped, shivering as I trailed the ice cube over every inch of her sweet curves, her skin pebbling and hands clutching my hair. "Oh...... mmmmm......Yes..."

Flicking my eyes up to her face, I groaned at the picture she made; head thrown back, teeth biting down into her lip and eyes closed as she lifted one leg to wrap around my back.

That's it baby. Take all the pleasure......

I trailed the ice to her other breast, holding myself up on my elbows to watch her squirm in hip-tilting arousal even as she shivered from the freezing cube, her breath increasingly laboured as I drew the small block to her cleavage then down her midriff until I reached her belly button.

"Oh....ooooooh," she moaned huskily and fuck, how I loved to hear her - each groan and gasp like a squeeze on my throbbing groin. Drawing wet circles around her navel, my senses became aware of her stare and I looked up to find her gaze burning down on me, eyes wildly hot and nipples so wet and tight they must have hurt. She leaned on her elbows to watch, legs falling open wider around my shoulders as I slid in between her silky thighs.

My eyes flashed golden for a moment, my beast letting her know he heard her - he heard the visceral call of her flesh, her liquefying body an earthy flame that scorched and engulfed my every sense in violent pleasure. Green-gold eyes glinted back lustfully, her pupils an abyss of black need.

When the dissolving ice was just a sliver, I let it melt on my tongue and reached for a fresh cube from the glass, trailing it down her quivering belly, down through her damp curls; the ice making shocking contact with her hot clit and God, she nearly screamed blue murder, falling back in shuddering pleasure-pain and arching hard.

Clawing my fingers gently down the sensitive skin of her bikini line until I reached her folds, I slipped two fingers deep inside her, the dual invasion sending her body into a frenzy and she cried out loud.

"Oh God, Kellan!!!! Oh, oh, yes............oh holy........."

She thrust against my mouth, pleading, demanding and my fingers pumped harder in answer, pushing her closer to the edge.

Her body twisted in agonised pleasure, her wet flesh melting the ice in my mouth with blazing heat and I held tight to the snarling, straining beast within. He was desperate to be inside her again, my shaft so thick and hard that it pressed up against my abs. But I held back, wanting to hear that scream of release once more.

She was hot as hell, my Detective Beauty, her passion soul-destroying, her need as fiercely elemental as mine. Curling my fingers, I found her g-spot and softly stroked it, wrapping my teeth around her clit and holding the sliver of ice against her pulsating skin.

And there it was...... Orgasm number four. Or was it five? I was losing count but I didn't give a damn.

She screamed so damn loud, hands yanking at my hair hard enough I was certain clumps would fall out. But I didn't give a damn.

As I watched her come on my fingers, on my tongue, her body arching completely off the bed, intense satisfaction swamped my body and mind - that I could make her feel that way, that I could give her that much thrilling pleasure.

Hell, yeah.

She might be frightening the neighbours, but I didn't give a damn.

Before her tremors were over, I swallowed the almost-gone ice cube, slid my fingers gently out of her, only to replace them with my self, my shaft gliding smoothly, effortlessly inside her clenching walls, holding still and letting her body ride out its convulsions on me.

She was so beautiful in her physical release. A goddess to be worshipped and treasured. And as her climax spiralled down, I began moving, gentle and slow. Her eyes opened and found mine, the slumberous bliss in them making me wanna beat my chest Tarzan style.

Yet despite the savage need clawing hungrily through my veins, the moment our eyes met and held - green gold into hazel in that deep connection that spoke without words - the feeling that flooded my chest was so all-encompassing, so huge that my breath hitched, my heart stuttered and skipped and I was speechless.

I couldn't look away.

I made love to her.

Worshipped her slowly.

Showed her with my body what I didn't have the words for. Loving her with soft touches, sweet kisses and slow glides of flesh into aching flesh.

She came again eventually, after what felt like hours of pleasure, no screaming this time - but a deep soul-bonding climax that stole our breaths, our eyes still connected as our bodies let go and released in pure pulsing rapture together.

Goddamn magic.

Chapter Twenty Four

Awareness came in small increments as I woke up from the deepest, most relaxing sleep I'd ever had. Or at least remembered having.

Warmth, comfort and a deep contentment filled every part of my body and I fought off a complete awakening for as long as possible, just so I could wallow in the serenity of knowing I was where I was meant to be.

In Charlotte's arms.

In bed, tangled and naked, her arm and leg slung over me while her head lay on my chest. My arm was wrapped around her back, hand splayed over her hip and other arm tossed above my head. I could feel the early morning rays of pale sunlight streaming through the windows onto my chest, my senses slowly rousing to the decadent scent of our bodies.

Her silky long hair draped over my arm in messy abandonment and I remembered drifting off to sleep in this position. It looked like neither of us had moved an inch all night and I would have smiled smugly at the reason why - if I had the energy. After our "ice-capades" we'd collapsed into a trembling heaving mess of satiation, falling asleep that way only to wake up and turn to each other twice more during the night; the desire to touch, to love, irresistible. A blistering round of hard thrusts, broken cries and demanding friction had belied any sense of earlier sexual fulfilment, our need as insistent as ever. Charlotte had been convinced that she didn't have another orgasm in her for the last bout but I'd proven her wrong and coaxed a couple more from her, gently and lovingly as by then we were both feeling the effects of seriously good loving, our bodies slick with sweat and muscles quivering weakly.

I kind of hoped that we ran into some of her neighbours later on, just so I could see the looks on their faces after all the noise we'd made.

Ha. I would have preened just a little - if I had the energy.

Her breathing changed slightly and I knew she was waking up so I ran my fingertips lightly back and forth over the smooth supple skin of her hip and she sighed gently, her breath drifting over my chest and tightening my nipples.

Too drowsy to move, I simply said, my voice croaky from sleep. "Good morning," and continued drawing circles on her hip.

"Good morning," she whispered in return, cuddling infinitesimally closer and we lay there peacefully for long contented minutes.

God, this felt so amazing. If I never moved again, I'd die a happy man.

"Charlotte?" I said quietly

"Hmm?"

"Do you have to go to work today?"

"Yes," she answered just as quietly.

"Damn." Neither of us had moved during this exchange, except for the fingertips that I still rubbed against her silky skin. I hadn't even opened my eyes, as lazy as a jungle cat sleeping in the summer sun. Had I ever felt this good?

Probably.

A few minutes later.....

"Charlotte?"

"Hmm?"

"Are you too sore to ....?"

"Yes."

"Double damn." Well, there goes that idea. My fingertips switched it up from circles to sliding back and forth. Her skin against mine, fragrant and soft and so warm felt perfect......felt right.

"Charlotte?"

This time she gave a quiet snort of laughter as she played along. "Hmm?"

"I bet I could make it better....."

And with that, she grabbed the skin just above my hip and twisted it sharply, just like she'd done once before and I burst into laughter as I yelled "Owwww," in protest of her attack. We wrestled briefly as she gave me a mock frown, trying not to laugh herself.

I rubbed the injured spot, smiling down at her and pretending offence as I muttered: "Alright, alright......sheesh, I was just trying to take care of your needs, oh insatiable one....."

"Me??" Her eyebrows rose over her beautiful eyes, all sparkly with laughter despite the sleepy-sexy look of her.

Yep, a very happy man.

And I leaned down to kiss her, mouth sliding against the sweet fullness of her lips for a moment before we pulled back and returned to our wallowing. My arms pulled her in closer, hers tightened around my waist, both of us keen to simply enjoy the quiet togetherness and.....be.

No urgency, no rush, no concerns.

Just breathing her in and letting her essence soak into my pores anew, my beast purring in supreme gratification.

We'd nearly dozed off back to sleep when Charlotte sighed heavily and began untangling herself, stating in reluctant tones that she had to get up and despite my protests, she rose from our warm bed to walk naked to the fat blue chair positioned next to her dresser. I sighed in disappointment even as I peered at her smoothly swaying butt for as long as possible before she grabbed a tee shirt and covered up all that lushness.

A tee that was way too big for her. And way too masculine.

Was that mine?

I squinted at it. I didn't know for sure but that top was definitely hanging off her shoulders and almost reached her knees, a sloppy joe style in dark army green.

It had to be.

As she disappeared into the bathroom, I had the energy this time to smile smugly. Couldn't help it. Something about her wearing my clothes screamed ownership to me and I didn't give a damn if that sounded possessive.

Stretching, I folded my arms under my head and stared at the ceiling for a few minutes.

I had a right to be, didn't I?

With no question as to the depth of our relationship, Charlotte was mine in the same way I was hers and my acceptance of that fact was now complete. She knew me - on a level that I couldn't explain - just as I knew her and regardless of having only partial memories of her or of any past emotions, it didn't matter.

New or rediscovered - it was all the same.

Despite the chaos of my mind, the confused existence, a bond had been forged between us, strengthening and refreshing my resolve
to reclaim my life, no matter what it had been. The injustice of what had been done to us, to Charlotte and I - to Finn - weighed heavily within me and I felt the sting of malicious intent, of cruel offense from those behind it.

And the biggest question of all was.....why? Why me? Was I the ultimate kill? Or just part of a bigger plan?

Thinking back to when Charlotte had turned up at the Respite Centre and the gallery fundraiser, I now wondered if the Commander had somehow manipulated us both into being in the same place?

Without knowing who and what he was, I couldn't be certain that he didn't have his dirty claws hooked into the police department. Instinct told me Suarez was not the Commander but it also told me he could be a part of it - an opportunistic asshole like Suarez having his stinking hands in some shady corruption was no stretch of the imagination and could easily be the explanation for Charlotte's unexpected appearances at various scenes. And that meant she could be as much of a target as I was.

So could Finn, for that matter.

The realisation was a sharp gut-kick reminder of just how far I'd been lost in whatever vortex of deception I'd been sucked into. My skin shuddered in cold revulsion at how blind I'd been to it all and I swore that the people responsible for this would pay.

Every single one of them.

In the context of all that I faced, however, finding and eliminating the Commander was only one part of it. And most likely not even the worst of it. I had a life to piece together; a past to deal with and heal from.

A life as a firefighter, a son, a partner....

Memories of colleagues, friends and.....family.......to restore in my conscience...

Flashing neon lights in my head warned that the recollection of these would be far more painful and dangerous to deal with than anything else.

Kill someone? Kill the commander?

Sure... No problem. I could do that easily.

But restore a forgotten life without losing my sanity or risking far more than I was prepared to? Not so fucking easy.

But I would, no matter how long it took, I vowed silently.

A hardness coiled through my belly; fierce resolution and protectiveness for those I cared about settling like concrete in my body.

No one would be collateral damage in whatever sick and twisted game was being played with my life.

Not Charlotte. Not Finn. Not me.

And if it should turn out that I never regained all the pieces of my memory? Well, it didn't matter, I realised as I heard the shower turn on. I had all that I needed right now to make a goddamn amazing life.

And she was right there in the other room, getting hot and steamy.

With a smile that spread warmth and incredible gratitude all through my chest, I got up and went where my heart called.

To Charlotte.

The End.........For Now.......

What happens next

Find out when Kellan and Charlotte's story continues in the third instalment of The Unbreakable Series.

Thanks for reading and please consider leaving a review on Amazon, Goodreads or any place that you purchased this book. For authors, this is so important and helps us refine our craft. Even just a line or two.

I love hearing from my readers so please get in touch with me via:

Website. www.zellyjordan.com

Facebook: www.facebook.com/zelly309

Twitter: www.twitter.com/@zelly309

Goodreads: https://www.goodreads.com/ZellyJordan

Amazon: amazon.com/author/zellyjordan

Email: zellyjordan@gmail.com

About the author

The love of a good story is the reason Zelly Jordan says she had her nose in a book most of the time growing up. Escaping into a world of great love, great adventures and sexy-smexy fun times with drool-worthy heroes and feisty strong women was the highlight of every day.

A lover of good coffee, cats and a good chat, with the occasional glass of wine, she lives in the most livable city in the world, Melbourne, Australia with her almost grown son. Divorced and happily single, Zelly began writing as a form of therapy during a difficult period and inspired by a beloved television show, she decided to give writing a try. Not long afterwards she published her first book Fractured and now, it's sequel, Unveiled.

When she's not writing or researching, she likes to spend time having a laugh with friends, watching good movies or shows and delving into the lovely world of Angels, crystals and healing. All with the added magic of music and a good espresso.

www.ingramcontent.com/pod-product-compliance
Lightning Source LLC
Chambersburg PA
CBHW030638110726
47901CB00002B/485